An Unwelcome Bride to Warm his Mountain Heart

STAND-ALONE NOVEL

A Western Historical Romance Book

by

Nora J. Callaway

D1524546

Disclaimer & Copyright

Table of Contents.

An Unwelcome Bride to Warm his Mountain Heart 1

  Disclaimer & Copyright...2

  Table of Contents 3

  Letter from Nora J. Callaway....................................5

Prologue 6

Chapter One...11

Chapter Two..22

Chapter Three 40

Chapter Four..46

Chapter Five...56

Chapter Six 66

Chapter Seven 76

Chapter Eight...85

Chapter Nine 92

Chapter Ten 104

Chapter Eleven 114

Chapter Twelve 123

Chapter Thirteen 129

Chapter Fourteen 136

Chapter Fifteen..146

Chapter Sixteen...156

Chapter Seventeen...167

Chapter Eighteen...172

Chapter Nineteen...179

Chapter Twenty 184

Chapter Twenty-One 193

Chapter Twenty-Two 208

Chapter Twenty-Three 215

Chapter Twenty-Four 224

Chapter Twenty-Five 230

Chapter Twenty-Six 233

Chapter Twenty-Seven 240

Chapter Twenty-Eight 242

Chapter Twenty-Nine 255

Chapter Thirty 264

Epilogue 285

Also by Nora J. Callaway.. 299

Letter from Nora J. Callaway

"How vain it is to sit down to write when you have not stood up to live."
-Henry David Thoreau

I'm a lover of nature in the mornings and a writing soul at nights. My name is Nora J. Callaway and I come from Nevada, the beautiful Silver State.

I hold a BA in English Literature and an MA in Creative Writing. For years, I've wanted to get my stories out there, my own 'babies' as I like to call them, as inspired by my own experience leaving out West and my research of 19th-century American history.

All my life I have been breeding horses, cows and sheep and I've been tending to the land. It's time to tend now to my inner need to grow my stories, my heart-warming Western romance stories, and share them with the rest of you!

I'm here to learn and connect with others who enjoy a cup of black coffee, a humble sunset and a ride with a horse! Bless your hearts, as my nana used to say! Come on, hope in!

Until next time,

Nora J Callaway

Prologue

Rosewood, Texas June 1880

Mary Margaret Barker stood at the door and took a breath. *It's time*, she thought. She had not dared to step foot in the bedroom since her parents died less than a week ago. Cholera had mercilessly invaded and devastated their bodies, one after the other.

The sting of a first loss, that of her mother, had not even settled in her heart before her father followed right at her mother's heels.

Eliza and Walter Barker were Mary's whole world. She had no siblings, and she alone was the light in their eyes. Now those eyes were closed forever.

Mary knew she had to go in there, go through their things, and clean up the room. She couldn't leave it as it was, but she shuddered every time she had to walk past it. Straightening, she turned the knob and opened the door. The room sat just as her parents had left it.

On the bed, which was centered between two windows, a comforter and sheet lay in a crumpled heap. To the right of the bed was her father's armchair, his suit coat lying across it. To the left of the bed stood her mother's vanity, untouched, as if at any moment her mother would sit down in front of the mirror and brush her hair, just as she used to do every night.

Mary noticed her mother's silver-handled hairbrush lying on the vanity. A few strands of fine, blond hair dangled from it. *I thought I could do this*, she thought as an ache filled her soul. *I thought I could be strong.*

She wanted to turn and leave the room, but something drew her over to the vanity. She picked up the brush and ran her fingers delicately over the fine strands. Looking up, she caught sight of herself in the mirror. Her red-eyed and pain-stricken face peered back at her. She hardly recognized herself.

Mary felt strange, peering into the mirror. She wanted to see her mother there, somewhere, in her own reflection, but she could not. The only trait she'd inherited from her mother was her pale blonde hair.

Her mother had been thin and delicate. She had ice-blue eyes and a sophisticated air. *I may not look like you, mother,* she thought, *but I will try to be more like you. I will. You had so much left to teach me.*

Her father had been all vivacity, charm, and intelligence, her mother grit and sophistication.

An old memory flickered in her mind, then grew stronger and clearer the longer she stood there, looking at herself. *Why am I thinking about this right now?* She wondered. She tried to put it out of her mind, but it only grew stronger. Her father's voice rang in her ears, almost as if he were there in the room.

"You're raising her to be a prude!" he had said. *It was one of her parents' rare arguments.*

"I'm raising her to be educated, to speak properly, to be able to travel abroad and get along well," replied her mother.

"She won't fit in here. She already thinks she's better than everyone. That's what all your book learning has done for her."

"You know as well as I that Mary has a wild side that needs to be tamed. Proper education can bring that to heel and reading good literature should produce a humble mind. She's

7

haughty, I don't disagree with you there. However, I do not think it has as much to do with her book learning so much as being an only child who has never had to want for anything. And you must admit you're as much to blame as I am for that."

It was about the last thing she wanted to remember— Her parents' argument over her arrogance.

Why do I have to think of that now? she wondered. *I won't think of it now.*

Putting it out of her mind, Mary set the brush down softly and turned to walk across the room, running her hand across the bed frame. She stopped before her father's chair, picked up his coat, holding it to her face, and breathed in his familiar smell. She intended to grow into a woman her mother would have been proud of, but she knew she'd always be more like her father. She looked like him, and she'd inherited his zeal and vivacity. And perhaps his pride.

Mary had her father's build, strong and on the stocky side. "Strong as an ox. Built like a brick outhouse," her father used to say. She'd been proud of her strength. Her father's bright green eyes, flecked with bits of gold and full of curiosity, peeked out from under her lashes. The freckles speckled across her nose and cheeks followed the same pattern as her father's had, and his big, contagious smile appeared when she laughed. But more than anything, she'd inherited his capacity to dream. All her life, Mary had known she was beautiful, intelligent, and strong. She had never felt the sting of death or loss.

She held out his jacket, examining it, then put it on.

She had expected the sight of their bedroom, left exactly as it was when they'd died, to be difficult. But she did not expect the wave of grief to hit so hard. She doubled over, catching herself on the doorframe.

"You okay?" Susan Marie Butler's soft voice came from the hall. Mary turned to her with tear-filled eyes. Susan had been an orphan, and Mary's parents had taken her on as a housemaid. Susan's parents had died when she was young, so she knew pain. If there was anyone Mary wanted near her right now, it was Susan.

Mary felt Susan's hand on her shoulder. "I... I'm so sorry, Mary. They were good people. Kind and fair." At the touch of her friend, grieving with her, Mary let go of all she'd been holding in since the undertaker carried her parents' cold bodies down the stairs and out the door forever. She cried, convulsing with sobs, and collapsed into Susan's arms.

Susan cried with her and held her tightly. Their grief was tangible, thick. It hung in the air. They breathed it in like the dust of the Texas air. They clung to each other, neither one wanting to let go.

Rusty, Mary's new bloodhound puppy, came hobbling along down the hall, oblivious to the despair of his owner. Mary, finding comfort in him, sat down on the floor in the hall and gathered him up into her arms, crying into his soft fur as he licked her face. Susan knelt beside them, placing a comforting hand on Mary's shoulder.

"My father couldn't have known how much I would need him when he gave him to me," Mary said, stroking the dog. "And now, he won't be here to help me train him on the hunt."

Walter had faithfully taken Mary out on the hunt with the men of the town the day she turned ten, and Mary had been asking for a bloodhound ever since.

Susan said nothing, but she stayed with Mary, petting Rusty lovingly, and it was enough for Mary to know that someone was with her. With the comfort of Rusty's playful licks and cuddles, the sobbing slowed, the tears dried up, and Susan helped Mary to her feet. Hand in hand, they crossed the threshold into the bedroom.

Mary took a breath, "Well, this stuff isn't going to sort itself. We had best get started."

Together, they went through her parents' belongings, packing, cleaning, telling stories, and alternating between laughing and crying, Rusty always at their feet, tripping over his own ears.

"Mary, do you remember the time Walter was so determined to make Eliza laugh that he danced and played the fiddle…"

"Oh, yes!" Mary interrupted, laughing. "He danced like a fool. The faster he played, the faster he danced."

"And your mother wouldn't crack a smile, so he kicked his legs up higher and higher until he fell to the ground!"

"Not before splitting his trousers! Do you remember *that?* Oh, I'd never seen mother laugh so hard."

When everything was cleaned up and packed away, Mary turned to Susan.

"Susan, thank you."

"I loved them, too. Will you be okay tonight? I'll stay if you need me."

"No, you go, Susan, and thank you. Oh, and Susan…. I know we owe you your wages for the week. I'll go into town tomorrow and talk to the banker."

"We're okay for now, Mary. I thank you. John has been so generous." Susan had become engaged shortly before Mr. and Mrs. Barker fell sick. She was to marry John Hartfield, a kind-hearted ranch owner. Mary had been elated for Susan, but now she could only think of her own loneliness at losing her as a constant presence and source of comfort. Mary nodded, and Susan slipped out of the door into the hot night air.

Chapter One

Rosewood, Texas June, 1880

Mary slept soundly for the first time in over a week.

At first, she dreamed of their moans as they tossed and turned in their beds, overhearing them from the next room. But tonight, she dreamt of her mother's smile and pale blue eyes, her father's full-bodied laughter and dancing eyes. Crying with Susan had exhausted her—body and mind.

When she woke, she had to realize all over again that they really were gone. Her heart sank, the peaceful comfort of last night's tears giving way to the harsh reality that she was alone.

She walked over to her own mirror and peered into it. Her eyes were still red, but no longer swollen. She was beginning to look like herself again, but there was a sadness in her eyes that had not been there before.

She stood to her full height, took a sharp breath in, and tossed her head as if in defiance of all the suffering life had brought her way.

She pulled her hair up into a disheveled style and, slipping on a pale green cotton dress, descended the stairs, wiping tears from her eyes. She was not used to the silence of an empty house. She missed the sound of her parents' voices speaking softly, the smell of coffee as her mother brewed it each morning.

She even missed the sounds she'd never realized she noticed before—the rustling of a newspaper page being turned, footsteps in the hall, the whisper of her mother's cotton dress as it brushed up against the wall. She looked around at the silent, empty house.

She heard a knock at the front door.

Several townspeople had come to call when they first heard news of Walter and Eliza's deaths. They'd brought her meals, cards, and flowers, but after the small funeral at the church, the visitors had slowed, then stopped, and Mary was left with only Susan as a source of comfort. As it was, she was not expecting a sympathetic caller that morning, but welcomed the company.

When she opened the door, a large, well-dressed man stood before her. He was clean-shaven but for a thick, black mustache sitting upon his upper lip. It was Christopher Edwards, whom her father had always called "Kit." Most of the single women in town considered him to be a handsome man, though Mary had never been able to see him that way. To her, he had always been her father's friend. She had sensed that the family relationship to Kit was kept out of regard for the connections it provided. However, he had always seemed amiable enough, and in this moment, Mary found comfort in the presence of anyone who had known her father.

"Mary," he said, stepping into the entryway, taking off his hat, and holding it over his heart. "I'm so very sorry for your loss." He looked at her with big, solemn eyes.

"Thank you, sir," Mary said, tearing up again. Moments before, she had been feeling desperately alone and haunted by the silence that this act of sympathy and concern overwhelmed her, and she could not hold back the tears. "Please, come into the drawing room and sit down. I'll bring tea," Mary said, turning to lead him into the drawing room and wiping her eyes quickly. Once he was seated, she dashed into the kitchen, lit the stove, and put on a kettle of water before heading back to the drawing room, hoping her tears were not evident.

"Tea will be ready in a moment." He looked up at her, and she thought she saw a hint of longing in his eyes. He gestured to the chair beside him, and she sat.

"How are you, Mary?" All efforts to conceal her tears were now in vain, as she could not hold them back. "Is there anything you need? I can help," he said.

"No, sir. Well, perhaps there is one thing, sir," she said haltingly.

"Please, call me Kit."

"Kit... I need to pay my maid. I know my father left his estate to me, but I don't know how to handle that side of things. I could use some help in getting my maid her wages, and maybe some advice on what I should do next."

"Your financial situation isn't quite what you think it is, dear." She bristled a little at his patronizing tone. She was not accustomed to being condescended to.

"What do you mean?" She stammered.

"Your father...he was underwater, Mary. He borrowed a large sum of money from me just to keep the house."

She couldn't understand what she was hearing. It didn't make sense. She'd always had everything she could ever need. How could it be true?

"I don't understand," she said after a long pause. "He never said anything about owing anyone any money." Mary was confounded, thinking over the possibility that she might have nothing. Her father's ranch was profitable, for the most part, until the drought came. But even then, he'd been elected Mayor, and Mary had assumed that paid well enough to support their lifestyle. Anyway, she knew grandfather had left an inheritance. Mary had many worries since the loss of her parents, but financial ruin had never crossed her mind. It didn't seem possible. The Barkers? Broke? They were affluent, sophisticated, and generous. She couldn't wrap her mind around it.

In her prolonged silence, Kit perceived her confusion and continued. "He didn't want your mother to know. He was certain he could pay me off by next summer." Mary's mind was swimming.

"You said he borrowed a large sum from you?" She asked. He nodded his head. "I'm sure...I mean...I can find a way to repay you." Kit looked at her for a long while, until Mary began to feel uncomfortable and became restless in her seat. Something shifted in her appraisal of him as she realized that she owed him her father's debts. His condescending looks of pity now felt feigned, and she wondered how she might politely end this encounter so she could think it all over.

"I thank you for your visit and concern for me, Kit. I am confident I can find a way to repay my father's debt," she said, standing, hoping Kit would catch the hint and stand to leave as well. He did not. He only shook his head solemnly.

"It's more than a woman could make in a decade, maybe a lifetime. I'm sorry, Mary. He swore me to secrecy. He was so sure he could manage it. He mortgaged the house."

Mary felt numb. She didn't understand what this meant for her. Even the house was not hers? She'd planned to stay there, in the home she grew up—in the home her parents had died in—so she could be near them and visit their graves, and maybe one day start her own family there. And now, she had nothing but debt, and no way to pay a mortgage on the home she loved, the only home she ever knew.

"I can.... get a job," she stammered as a look of confusion and terror came over her face.

Kit let out a snort, and it seemed as though he was laughing at her. Confusion and fear quickly morphed into anger at the idea of being laughed at in her misery. She started to toss her head in her defiant way, but stopped herself and repeated firmly, "I will find work."

"Even men are hard-pressed to find work these days. The only place they're hiring women is picking cotton or fruit farther west. You're not made for that kind of work," he said, gently taking her hand in his, turning it over, and running his finger down her palm. It was an act of intimacy wholly unwelcome, and she moved to pull her hand away, but he tightened his grip slightly.

"I'm tougher than you think," she said, trying to mask the panic that was rising in her. Her voice cracked and her throat closed up.

"Your father meant for me to care for you... as my wife," he said. Mary pulled her hand away forcefully, and as she did, thought she recognized a brief flicker of rage in his eyes.

"He never got the chance to tell you, I see," Kit said, trying in vain to hide the contempt in his voice. Mary didn't speak for a long while. Marriage to a wealthy man *did* seem to be an easy option out of her predicament, and here was a wealthy man proposing to her, ready to fix all her problems. And yet, something felt deeply wrong about it. She felt it deep in the pit of her stomach. She couldn't put her finger on it, but she sensed something hostile about Kit. She needed time to think, but Kit sat across from her, eyes fixed on her, obviously expecting an answer. She became more and more restless under his gaze. When she finally spoke, the words came out choked and shaky.

"No. I can't. I can't do that." She said, standing up and backing away. He stood and advanced toward her.

The anger in his eyes flared. It was unmistakable this time, and it frightened Mary. His large body loomed over her. "Your father meant to provide you with a good life, even if he could not. I agreed to marry you, to give you the life he wanted you to have and forgive all his debts in return. You're foolish to pass up an offer like that."

"Foolish?" She asked, her voice shaking, from either anger or fear, she wasn't sure which.

"Yes, foolish. Apparently, you don't understand the predicament your father was in," Kit said.

"I think I understand my father quite well, thank you very much," she replied. She tossed her head and flicked her hair in just the way she used to do when her mother would say, *Don't toss your head, Mary. It's haughty and disrespectful."*

"I don't think you *do* understand your father. He intended to pay off your debts and see you provided for through your marriage to me."

"That's not possible."

"It's not only possible, it's fact."

"I don't believe you," she said, staring hard back at him.

"It doesn't matter whether you believe me or not," he replied through gritted teeth, "It's the truth."

"My father wouldn't promise me to someone without my consent. I know it."

"So, you won't marry me?"

"I cannot."

"And why not? I have everything you could ever hope to have. I have hundreds of acres, a beautiful house, and dozens of servants."

"Those things could never make me happy," she said as she lifted her eyes to look at him. It was in that moment that she noticed his eyes. In them, she saw primal hunger. It chilled her to her core. His eyes seemed to look right past her.

I've never seen eyes so cold, she thought. His look frightened her, and she began to wish, desperately, that he would go.

"I'm flattered, Christopher. But I can never be your wife. So I think it's best if you go now."

To her surprise, he stood in his place.

"I don't think you understand. You don't have a choice," he said.

The tension in Mary's heart grew. She wanted him out of her house immediately. She was growing more fearful in his presence by the moment.

"Of course I have a *choice*," she responded, firmly, "I am asking you to leave. I am telling you I cannot become your wife."

Kit, apparently recognizing that his tactics weren't swaying Mary, changed his tone.

"Don't you want someone to marry you and provide for you? Don't you want a family? I'm offering you all of that."

It was true, she'd dreamt of marriage since she was a little girl, but not like this.

I want love to catch me by surprise, she thought, *the way mother and father fell in love. Not like this. This is all wrong.*

The thing was, if she hadn't seen that cold, emotionless stare in his hungry eyes, she might have been persuaded. As it was, in just a few moments, she had seen a side of him that terrified her.

Again, she said, "Thank you for your visit, and I'm sorry I can't oblige you."

She fully expected him to retreat, but instead, he took a step closer to her. Mary backed up. He stepped closer again. She was beginning to feel hot blood pounding in her face.

She tried to retreat further but found herself up against a wall. Kit grabbed her elbow firmly and pressed himself up against her body. She grimaced and her heart began to race.

"Let go!" She demanded. He held on, and lowered his face toward hers, as though he might force a kiss.

That moment, Susan slipped in through the door. Mary turned and flashed her a look of such fear that Susan screamed, and Kit dropped Mary's arm.

"Go on and get out of here!" Susan yelled, "Or I'll tell everyone what sort of man you are and have you run out of town." Mary felt Kit release his grip on her arm. For a moment, the anger in his eyes turned to fear, before turning back to anger again. He huffed, but put on his hat and backed toward the door.

"I'll go. But I'll get what you owe me, Mary Barker. You just made the biggest mistake of your life, but there's still time to change your mind." With that, he walked out the front door and slammed it behind him.

Mary gasped, suddenly realizing she had been holding her breath, and reached for the edge of the sofa for support. She tried to stammer something to Susan, but the words caught in her throat.

"I know, dear. I'll pour us some tea," Susan said, "you just sit down and relax."

While Susan prepared the tea, Mary, with a dazed look on her face, gave her the particulars of what Kit had said.

"What am I supposed to do, Susan? I have no one," Mary said, collapsing into a chair and burying her head in her hands. When she finally looked up, she said, "And now, I have nothing. Not even this house." She looked around at the mahogany wood floors her mother had loved so much, the sheer, beige curtains hanging to floor length, the mantle and fireplace where she'd so often sat on her mother's lap and listened to stories or her father playing the fiddle.

"I can't believe this isn't my home to own. I can't afford the mortgage or your wages. Susan, I don't even know how I'll feed myself. I never could have imagined this. Maybe he's lying."

Susan sat silently for a while, thinking. Susan had found her own way out of poverty, and Mary could see her mind working behind her intelligent eyes.

Finally, Susan said, "you're a lovely young woman, with manners and good breeding. Any man should consider himself lucky to provide for you, debts and all. Perhaps you should find someone else to marry."

This statement caught Mary off guard. After all, she'd only just rejected Kit moments ago.

"You think I should marry?" she asked, pulling away from Susan, her voice full of astounded indignation.

"Hear me out, Mary. Kit will come after you. If the gossip is true, he's loaned large sums of money to over half the farmers and ranch owners around here. I'm sorry to say it, but I don't think he's lying. They say when the drought hit, everyone needed money, and he had it on hand and lent it out with high interest rates. Half the town owes him, and I'd bet my horse no man who owes his livelihood is gonna come up against the man he owes it to."

"I don't understand."

"I mean, I think you should marry, but not here in Rosewood. Men everywhere need wives. You could answer one of those ads they always put in the paper, get out of town, have the protection of a husband." Susan grabbed the day's newspaper from the table and started opening the page.

"So, what you're saying, Susan, is that to escape being married, I should get married? You know that I..."

"So as far as I see it, your options are to marry Kit, or marry someone you don't know. I'd take a chance on a stranger before I'd marry Kit. I get a real bad feeling around him."

Mary pondered this for a moment. She'd had a bad feeling, too, even before he nearly attacked her. Maybe Susan was right. In some ways, she wanted to escape, to run from this place with all its haunting memories. And yet, a love for this dry, Texas land coursed through her veins, just as it ran through her father's, and she could hardly imagine giving it up.

It seemed she only had two options. Stay, and marry an unscrupulous man who'd cheated his neighbors and thought he was entitled to her...or leave everything behind and start again with a man of whom she knew nothing. She thought of the land her father loved, the townspeople he served, and almost succumbed to the idea of marriage to Kit.

Then, the memory of his rage-filled eyes flashed before her, and she knew she could not. Perhaps she'd end up married to another man like Kit if she responded to an ad...but there was still a chance she could land a kind husband. If she married Kit, she'd have security but no chance at happiness. If she married a stranger, she'd have security and at least a chance at happiness. She had always been prone to risk-taking like her father. Anyway, it bothered her that Kit had come to her with full expectation of her acceptance.

The arrogance is intolerable, she thought.

No land, no security or protection could tempt her to give in and give herself to Kit in marriage when he had made it so clear that he felt entitled to her—that he was doing her a favor, even. An ad was at least requesting a marriage. Kit was demanding it. The rage she saw in his eyes when she denied him was enough to make her shudder. She knew she could not marry him, no matter the cost. She would have to leave this beloved land and home behind and take a chance on an unknown man.

As Mary had mulled over these things in her head, Susan had been perusing the ads section of the paper.

"Listen to this," Susan said, and then began reading aloud. "Jefferson St. Just. Kind-hearted, wealthy widower seeks a hard-working wife and mother figure to his three children."

"I'm not ready to be a wife, let alone a mother!" Mary exclaimed. But it was no use talking herself out of it. She had already resolved to answer this ad the moment she heard "kind-hearted" in the description. It was her only way out, and her best chance at safety and happiness.

"Strange name, Jefferson St. Just," Susan said, breaking into Mary's thoughts.

"Strange, indeed," said Mary.

Chapter Two

Rosewood, Texas 1880

Several weeks passed, and Mary had almost given up hope of receiving a response to her letter. Kit had visited more than once. Mary, perceptive as she was, had realized that, in order to keep him civil, she must give him the idea that he had a chance to gain the object he so desperately desired—her affection.

Though it made her stomach turn, she'd played along to keep herself safe, to keep Kit playing the game. If he thought he could win, he would pursue her in more gentle ways.

If he were to be blatantly refused, she perceived that he would grow violent, and then she might truly be in danger. And so, though it curdled her blood to do it, she looked away from him demurely when he spoke to her.

She allowed him to believe that the only reason she turned down his offer of marriage in the first place was that it was so very improper for one of her sex to accept a marriage proposal on the first offer. Her mother was, after all, of gentle breeding, and it was expected that a woman of her status and breeding would refuse a man's first proposal, especially when it was offered in so crude a fashion.

Kit bought it, hook, line, and sinker. When he visited from then on, he was of a gentler nature. He was under the impression that he was winning her heart, little by little, and that he would have her one day very soon.

Only Mary and Susan knew that she was only keeping him playing the game until she could figure out what to do. It had been nearly six weeks since the girls had sent out a response to Jefferson St. Just's ad looking for a wife, and both had all but given up hope that there *would* be a response at all.

Mary went into town on several occasions and attempted to work through her father's disastrous financial state with the banker, Mr. Whalen. He was a kindly old gentleman, with wispy gray hair that stuck straight up and small spectacles. He was honest, with little respect for men like Kit.

Whalen was one of the only men in town who did not owe money to Kit. He, in fact, had refused to loan money to people at interest during the drought, for he had a mind made for numbers and was quite convinced that most people would never be able to dig themselves out of that debt once they were in. He alone remained out from under the thumb of the wealthy, powerful Christopher Edwards. Mary could see his disdain for Kit when he spoke with her about all of her father's loans and debts.

"A sixteen percent interest rate is nothing short of criminal, if you ask me," Mr. Whalen said, in his kind but gruff voice. He leaned forward in his high-backed chair, his beady eyes peering through spectacles at a mound of documents, shuffling through one file at a time. His mahogany desk was littered with papers documenting her father's debts.

Rusty squirmed in Mary's arms, and she dropped him gently to the floor where he bit at her shoelaces and licked her ankles. "I don't usually allow dogs in here..." Mr. Whalen said. Mary ignored his latter statement and answered his first.

"I agree it is. Far too high an interest rate to be feasibly repaid in a timely manner," said Mary. "I can't see any way to ever get out from under this debt. And I can't imagine how on earth Daddy ever got into it in the first place. Seems he had a good enough head on his shoulders to know what he was getting himself into," she said, incredulously.

"Well, that's what wanting does to a man, you know. Wanting and pride. I reckon he couldn't bring himself to take you all down a notch alongside himself. He loved his home and his land, you know."

"Oh yes, even more than I do," she said, her face falling.

"I'm sure he had no doubt in his mind that he would settle those debts and make it all right again."

"I know," Mary said. She'd always known her father to have a kind heart. However, she thought he could have used her mother's practical mind in matters of money, and felt indignant that her mother—the very one who probably could have helped—had been kept in the dark about all of this. Now Mary was left to pick up all the pieces.

"I was thinking perhaps I could find work teaching or as a governess."

Mr. Whalen looked at her with sympathetic eyes.

"I've no doubt you'd make an excellent teacher. And yet, a teacher's salary could never settle these debts, I'm afraid. And Kit will have his money. If there's one thing I know about him, he will get what he thinks he's owed."

She left the bank that day determined to escape Kit, though she wasn't sure how. If she could get far enough away from him, he might never find her. If he never found her, he couldn't try to collect anything from her. Susan was right. Marriage was the only way. Mary knew she'd have to take the chance, though the idea of escaping to a faraway place she did not know without friends or family or home frightened her.

Susan visited that day, as usual, and they talked it over.

"I've brought several more ads I clipped from papers from town," Susan said, laying them out on the kitchen table. Mary looked through them, picking them up and reading them one by one.

None of them stuck out to her the way Jefferson's had. He'd been described as "kind-hearted" and that was just the type of person she needed right now. If she was going to be forced into marriage by circumstances, she at least wanted to find herself with someone kind and understanding enough to be patient with her.

"I don't know, Susan. Maybe there's another way. It does seem silly to escape marriage by getting married."

"We've been over this, Mary. Anyone would be better than Kit, and you can't go out into the world alone." Although Mary had all the benefits of classical education, Susan was by far the more practical, and Mary trusted her judgment.

Still, Mary was a romantic at heart. Her mother's sister had sent her every Jane Austen book from London, and Mary had read each one of them several times. None of Austen's young women had ever responded to an ad in the paper. Something in Mary balked at the idea. It seemed so horribly unromantic to her. And yet, this was real life, not one of Jane Austen's novels. While Mary lived with her nose buried in a novel, Susan lived in the here and now. She was utterly practical, and Mary knew that it was time to follow Susan's practical advice and stop living in a fairy tale.

"I know you're right, Susan, but suppose no one responds. Then what?"

"Someone will respond, Mary. Men outnumber women almost five to one out here. I could have married ten times over before John finally won my heart."

"That's true," Mary said, remembering Susan's many suitors, and her own. Her own mother had told her that she was not to worry about marriage—not until she had finished her education. It was something unique about Eliza. Not many in Rosewood, Texas were very concerned with "book learning," as the locals called it. Her mother had hated that term. She was always careful to say *education* and enunciate every syllable. She had come from London and her family valued education. They were horrified when Eliza ran off with *that uneducated American,* Walter Barker. Eliza did not care. She was in love. Nonetheless, she would ensure that her daughter received a proper education.

Mary was an excellent pupil. She adored literature, and her mind was always in the abstract. Philosophy and theology came easily to her. She paid no attention to suiters. She wanted to marry, one day. But not today. That was how Mary usually thought about marriage.

Mary was pondering all these things as she sat at her kitchen table with Susan, looking through the ads posted by single men in want of a wife and idly feeding Rusty bits of her leftover scrambled eggs and dried breadcrumbs. It reminded her that the pantry was nearly bare and the cellar all but empty.

"I wonder if I am just too old already. Perhaps I've missed my opportunity. Perhaps they all want a younger wife."

"Don't be so silly," said Susan, "You're not old, and you could pass for seventeen anyway. And besides, we never wrote a thing about your age." Still, Mary was beginning to think of other ways to escape Kit and get out of Rosewood.

***

Blessedly, a response arrived by post the very next day. Susan had stopped by the post office on her way to Mary's, just as she did every day, only this time she arrived with a post in her pocket, and a wide smile on her face. She dismounted, and was reading it aloud almost before Mary was within hearing distance. Mary felt her hands begin to shake even before she realized she was nervous.

"Thank you for your response," Susan shouted, reading from the paper she held in her hand. Mary reached her and peered over her shoulder. Susan continued, "I very much look forward to meeting you. If you will kindly travel to Parkville, Georgia, and meet me at Redwood Ranch, we will be married shortly. Someone will meet you at the train station in Parkville on August the 2nd, if you can arrive as early as that." And that was it. It was a short response, void of any feeling or evidence of the "kind-hearted" nature of her soon to be husband which was promised in the original ad. Still, it was her ticket out of Rosewood.

Mary smiled to think of the look on Kit's face when he realized she'd tricked him and skipped town, just when he was thinking he was close to winning her heart. It gave her heart a little leap of joy to think of it. Quickly, however, that joy was overshadowed by the harrowing realization that in a few short days, she would leave her home forever and start over in a land completely unknown to her, with a man she did not know, and people she had never met. She would truly be starting over, and the thought of it chilled her heart.

***

The air was cooler than usual that morning as large gusts of wind came off the Gulf of Mexico. The cool breeze gently tousled Mary's blond hair as she stepped foot over the threshold of what would soon be her former home. She stood on the wooden, wrap-around porch, trying to soak in everything so she would never forget the place.

She stood there, suitcase in hand, chin turned slightly upward, bonnet shading her freckled cheeks. She looked resolute, though her heart was breaking. She looked out over the dry land before her; tufts of prickly grasses and clusters of cactus plants sprinkled the brown plains. The cool breeze brought a welcome relief from the hot, dry air of the day. She breathed in, closed her eyes, and tried to imagine herself someplace different. She could not.

She set her suitcase down and walked around the porch to the swing, where she'd so often sat deep in conversation with her mother or laughed heartily with her father. She ran her hand along the open space next to her, where one or both of them ought to have been. Her face began to soften as she allowed the memories to come sweeping in.

She had promised herself she was not going to cry this morning. Alas, it was a promise she could not keep. The memories were too strong, sitting there looking out across the land that had always been theirs, the land she had fully expected would one day be hers. And now, she was leaving it.

Just like that, leaving behind the graves of the people she'd loved best in all the world, and the only home she had ever known. Grief arose in her breast like a wave, crashing down upon her soul and overpowering her every will to remain composed.

If she remained much longer, she would miss the train. Her tears fell more quickly than she could wipe them away, though she tried. She stood up, retrieved her suitcase, and walked down the porch steps toward the pasture where Susan and her fiancé John Wilson were hitching the horses. John was a tall, lanky man. He rarely spoke, but he smiled often. Mary liked him, and she was thankful that he and Susan would accompany her to the station. From there, she would go on alone.

"We're ready to go when you are," said John, giving her a pitying look. Mary was not accustomed to being pitied by anyone but her mother, and lately, Susan. Her features hardened. She had only just stopped her tears. If people would only stop looking at her like that, perhaps she would be able to keep the tears at bay. She turned her face.

"I took the liberty of taking the portraits off the wall. I've packed them in your suitcase, in between your cotton dresses, to keep them from breaking if they get jostled on the train. I also packed Eliza's journals. I thought you'd want to save those. Walter's pipe and the family Bible are in there, too."

"Thank you, Susan," Mary said, keeping her composure for the time being. That morning, she'd told Susan that she could not bear to decide what to take, and what to leave. She knew that whatever she left, Kit would sell for profit or take as his own.

"Well, we had best be on our way," Mary said. John helped her up into the waiting carriage, and then Susan. He hoisted Mary's suitcase up. She patted the seat next to her, and Rusty clumsily tried to jump up to join them. John gave him a boost up into the seat between Susan and Mary.

***

When they arrived at the train station, Mary hugged John first.

"Thank you, John, for everything. I don't know what I would have done without you and Susan these last few weeks." John was a quiet man. He said very little, but his heart was very big. Mary felt ever indebted to him for all the time and heart he and Susan had poured into her, even when they should have been planning their wedding.

"Oh, you'd have done the same for Susan. No need to thank us," John said, lifting Mary's suitcase out of the carriage.

She scooped up Rusty, who let out a little whimper as John turned to leave. "I know, boy," she said. She turned to Susan. This was the good-bye she was dreading most.

"Oh, Susan. What would I have done without you?" Mary wondered aloud. They embraced and held on for a long while as John unloaded her suitcase.

But she knew it was time to let go of Susan and venture on into her new life.

***

Once she had boarded the Union Pacific, Mary found her seat, stored her suitcase, and finally sat down to think.

Rusty nuzzled into Mary's lap and promptly fell asleep. Mary, exhausted though she was, could not do likewise. Her mind raced with thoughts, with fear, with the unknown.

The train took off with a jolt, and Rusty fell forward, letting out a small whimper.

"It's okay, boy, come here," Mary said, pulling him closer.

"Heavens to Betsy, she brought a dog." Mary looked up to see three young women dressed in the latest French-inspired fashion. Their dresses were gathered, not ruffled like her own outdated dress. They must have come from farther east, perhaps on their way back home. Mary turned her face and looked at the ground, hoping they'd walk right on by. But, as chance would have it, their seats turned out to be directly across from her and Rusty.

Great, thought Mary, *just what I need.*

The girls huffed a little as they took their seats across the way. Thankfully, the train boot was spacious enough that Rusty could stay out of their way, had he not assumed that the three young women sat down there because they wanted to play with him. His tail wagged excitedly, thwapping Mary's legs as it went back and forth. She tried to hold him back, but he was difficult to control once he had set his mind on something.

"Get control of your dog," one of the young women spat.

"Oh Helen, come now," said a sweeter sounding voice. "Look at him. He just wants some attention." Mary turned thankful eyes upon the second young woman, whose bright orange curly hair sprung out from her head in nearly every direction.

Helen huffed, and the third young woman, who had not said a word since they sat down, pulled out some embroidery and sat by quietly.

"I'm Georgia," said the red-headed woman, sticking out a hand to Mary. Mary shook it and thanked her. Georgia quickly moved over to Mary's side of the booth, and Rusty, happy to have gained a new friend, sat satisfied at her feet while she scratched behind his ears. "Well, you will certainly make this trip more enjoyable," she said to Rusty, as he grunted and threw his head back for more ear scratching. "Yes, that's a boy." Then, turning to Mary, "I shall never get over how large Texas is. When I heard we had finally crossed over into Texas on the train ride here, I thought we should arrive within hours. I had seen a map, of course, but it did not convey how truly vast this place is." Mary nodded.

Texas. It was all she had ever known. She had never dreamed she would leave. What reason was there? Everyone was heading west. The farther west, the wilder the terrain, but it was becoming more civilized by the day, and Texans thought of themselves as their own country, anyway. She'd never dreamed of leaving Texas before. It was home... Until Kit drove her away.

"We're sisters," Georgia explained. "Though you'd never guess, would you? We look just as different as we are. They're good sort of people, though. If you knew them, you'd think so." Mary only thought that Georgia was a good sort of person for thinking so.

She was thankful for the company, and by the time they had reached their first stop, they both felt they were kindred spirits, and Georgia had made Mary promise to write and tell everything about her new husband, for she thought it was the most romantic thing she'd ever heard.

Eventually, Georgia grew tired and fell asleep with Rusty still cuddled up at her side.

Mary peered out the window and watched the dry earth as it moved swiftly beneath her. The dry, brown dirt slowly morphed into red, then green, then red again.

The first stop was New Orleans. As the train screeched, Georgia woke up.

"Let's go out for a stroll," Mary said. Georgia nodded sleepily as Mary fastened a leash to Rusty.

They made their way out of the crowded train and into the bright light and bustling city of New Orleans.

For all her twenty years, she'd never gone so far as to see anything but the dry, brown earth of western Texas. This seemed to her like a different world.

"Have you ever seen such a place?" Mary asked.

"Oh, yes. Every time we travel, we stop here. I hear they have delicious eating houses. We have some time before the train moves. Let's find something to eat."

They took Rusty, and left Georgia's sisters in search of food.

When they returned to the train, they had stretched their legs a long while and eaten to their heart's content.

Mary enjoyed New Orleans. She felt it was alive, as alive as herself. Everyone was moving so fast compared to her Texas home, and it seemed like she could find just about anything she needed in one strip of street there.

Tired as she should have been, she couldn't fall asleep even as the sun was going down and the train rumbled beneath her.

It's all so different, she thought. And she wondered what the next stops would look like. She looked at Georgia, who was already sound asleep next to her. Across from her, Georgia's sisters slept, one with her face pressed against the window and the other leaning on her sister's arm.

The train stopped several times to pick up more passengers, and Mary got out to stretch her legs and let Rusty run. Each stop filled her with wonder. She could hardly believe she'd never been outside of Texas before this.

Only yesterday, she'd been devastated to leave Texas. Now, she felt that there was so much of the world to explore, and she was excited to see more.

She breathed in the air, and it smelled different. It even felt different, as if the air was heavier and fuller. She felt she could take a deeper breath than she ever had before. She noticed this around the same time as she noticed the earth turning from brown to red.

***

Finally, the train stopped at Parkville, Georgia. Mary's heart began to beat faster as the train screeched to a stop on the tracks. She waited for nearly every other passenger to exit before she stood, breathed in, and held it for a moment before releasing the air and tucking Rusty under one arm, grabbing her suitcase with the other.

She noticed Rusty's rapidly growing size. She wouldn't be able to tuck him under her arm for much longer. He was growing heavy, and awkward to carry. "Come on, boy. Let's do this together," she said.

Mary readied herself to step off the train and face the man she would spend the rest of her life with.

Well, it isn't going to get any easier, she thought. *I may as well go see him.* She wondered what he looked like and was surprised to realize that she hadn't thought about it before. Would she recognize him right away? Would he seem pleased at the sight of her? She stepped out into the bright, warm, Georgia sun and shielded her eyes.

No one seemed to be looking for her. Her eyes scanned the station. She saw several couples walking together, a family with two small children, a servant girl. That was it. Slowly, the station emptied, and she was left alone. She walked over to the ticket booth.

"Excuse me, but can you tell me where I can find Redwood Ranch?" The man behind the booth cocked an eye at her but grabbed a pen and paper and began jotting down directions, and in a dry, monotone voice said, "Head west for about a mile, then south for another mile. You'll see a white fence running along a gravel road on one side. Miles and miles of sweet corn to your right. The white house way up on top of the hill is what you're looking for." He handed her the paper. She grabbed it, turned to walk away, then stopped.

"Where can I find some water?"

"You're walking that whole distance, ma'am?" She nodded.

"That's over two miles, ma'am," he said, shaking his head. "Wait here." He returned with a canteen full of water. "No need to return it."

"Thank you, sir!" She said. She wondered if, perhaps, there had been a miscommunication about the date she was to arrive. She had been worried that the distance to the ranch might be many miles, which would have been impossible for her to walk alone before dark. Two miles on foot carrying a suitcase would be grueling, but not impossible. She set out in the direction the man had pointed her, hoping her sense of direction would not fail her.

With the fire of her father and the grit of her mother coursing through her veins, Mary pressed onward, suitcase in hand. Her bonnet failed to shade her face from the harsh sun as she walked westward. She could almost feel her freckles darkening on her cheeks. The heat was becoming intolerable. She stopped to tuck her dress up. She was already stiff from having slept on the train, so when she arrived in Parkville, a day and a half after boarding, she was already feeling quite tired and sore.

In the distance, she could see neat rows of corn to one side. She walked on. Shortly, a winding white fence appeared. Hunger gnawed at her stomach. Dirt covered her shoes and the hem of her dress. She began to feel incredulous that no one had met her at the station. *Some way to treat your future wife!* she thought to herself, *and they must have known I'd arrive in the heat of the day, and that it was a two-mile walk. The inhospitality of it! Mother would never have recovered.* She spoke to herself in this way as she trudged on in the heat, for only anger was keeping her from collapsing right there, and that would never do.

Rusty trotted happily at her ankles, as though he'd never been happier in all his life, and when she stopped for a drink of water and poured a little into a cupped hand, he lapped it happily and then trotted onward as if he could go on like that for all his days, always going somewhere, and never getting there.

As for Mary, she was beginning to feel as though this journey might never end. She and Rusty had but a few precious drops of water left. The hills did not look so very far away when she lifted her head, but under the heavy, hot, sun, every step was painstaking and slow. She felt as though she were walking in place at times.

She would have noticed how perfectly beautiful the cornfields were, had she not been so distracted by the heat, her thirst, and her sore feet. She was just rounding a bend in the gravel road when she saw a white house appear, sitting in between two green hills.

She heard the clip-clopping of a pair of horses and the rumbling of carriage wheels. She turned to look, and thank heavens, a carriage was approaching. A tall, blond, spectacled man sat perched atop, gently flicking the reins.

"HO!" he called, pulling the team to a halt as he came upon Mary. "Where are you heading ma'am? I can give you a lift." Mary could scarcely believe her luck, for her strength was weakening, and with every step, she wondered whether she could make it a step farther. She had just been contemplating taking a break.

"Oh, please sir! Redwood Ranch. Thank you!" She said, lifting Rusty up first and then pulling herself up and seating herself beside him. He eyed the dog but said nothing.

"Relative or field hand?" He asked, looking her up and down. Mary realized he was probably confused by dress, for she had arrived at the train station in a dress suitable for meeting her future husband for the first time. But now, it was covered in dirt almost up to her knees, with a slight tear above her right elbow where she had caught it on barbed wire.

It was no wonder he couldn't place her. She did look like an overdressed field hand or a lady who'd been lost in the wilderness for days on end. Now that her feet were finally able to rest, she became embarrassed about her appearance. After all, he was so well-dressed, his white cotton shirt starched and pressed, his thick brown hair combed neatly into place.

"I'm...I'm to be mistress of the ranch," she answered, trying in vain to brush the dirt off her dress.

"Oh, is that so?" He replied in a soft voice, with a look of genuine curiosity coming suddenly over his face.

"Yes, I responded to his last letter, but there must have been some miscommunication, for he was to meet me at the train station this afternoon. Only perhaps I have the date wrong."

"Jefferson, you mean?"

"Yes, Jefferson St. Just."

"How very peculiar. I'd have thought I should have heard of it."

"Oh?" Mary asked, a look of eagerness coming over her.

"I'm to be married to his sister, Violet, soon. My apologies for the lack of introduction. My name is Rupert Blanks. I'm the local doctor."

"Mary Margaret Baker," she replied.

"And this is?" He gestured toward Rusty.

"Rusty."

"A fine hound."

"Thank you. He was a gift from my father."

"You hunt, or your father?"

"Father did," she said.

"He'll make a find bloodhound if trained correctly,"

"Oh, well, he's more of a companion."

"I see...I am heading to Redwood Ranch myself... well, on my way out to see a patient. Violet and I will be married soon, and I should think I'd have heard of this arrangement. But no matter. Jefferson can be a very private man. Perhaps he never told Violet," Rupert said, softly almost to himself.

They rode on in silence, a look of inquisitive bewilderment on his face, and one of eager anticipation on hers. Mary did not know who Violet was. Jefferson had never mentioned her or the doctor. No matter, they had only corresponded a few times, and one could not be expected to tell all in a few short letters. She was certain there was much to learn about Jefferson and his family.

They came to a stop in front of a large, white house. The doctor stepped down and pulled out Mary's suitcase for her, then held out a hand to help her down from the carriage. She took it. He knocked on the door.

A woman with beautiful, long, black hair answered.

"Violet, darling," said the doctor, taking her hand and kissing her on the cheek. "This is Mary Margaret. I wish I could stay, but I'm on my way to a house call. I shall stop by again on my way back if time allows." He kissed the woman he'd called Violet sweetly on the cheek again and nodded at Mary, getting back up into his carriage. As he rode off at a brisk pace, Mary turned to look at Violet. A warm, welcoming smile filled Violet's face.

"Come in," she said, "I'm Violet. Violet Just. And you must be Mary." Violet was a tall woman with fair skin, black hair, and big, brown, doe-like eyes.

"Yes, and this is Rusty," Mary said, as Rusty sniffed at Violet's hand.

Violet smiled at her and reached out her small hands, pulling Mary to herself. She seemed to glow with happiness.

Chapter Three

Parkville, Georgia August 1880

The sun rose, high and hot, scorching the red earth mercilessly. Straight rows of sun-kissed golden corn stretched for miles, cut through with sharp, straight lines of deep red earth, which disappeared where the sky touched them in the distance. Field hands were dispersed throughout the fields, scattered along the red lines in between the golden rows.

They were wet with sweat and growing lethargic under the unrelenting Georgia sun, but on they worked. Across the way, a gravel road wound itself around the golden fields and up towards the setting sun. It disappeared between two green hills, between which was nestled a large white house with red shutters.

Jefferson St. Just stood in the field among the men, towering over everyone else, his broad shoulders bending and lifting repeatedly. The brim of his hat dripped with sweat. He removed it to wipe his brow. His thick, black, hair seemed to attract and soak in the sun within moments. His neatly trimmed beard was as thick and as heavy as his hair, and he could feel sweat building on it and slowly trickling out. A thick, black mustache sat atop his lip, collecting sweat in droplets.

Two piercing blue eyes peered out from underneath a tan, dirt-smeared face. His expression was tired, with a hint of consternation. He wore a serious, concerned look on his face. The crop had to be harvested before the ears were ruined by the scorching sun or pests. For the past three weeks, the sun had been even more unrelenting than it usually was.

Not a cloud in the sky gave relief from its scorching rays. Jefferson stood to his full, towering height, stretching his sore back, and looked out across his fields, praying they would complete the harvest in time. His eyes scanned the neat rows, quickly calculating the rows harvested that day.

My workers are at least as tired as I am, he thought. They can't go on much longer. He silently pleaded with God for some clouds to send relief from the beating sun. Only an infrequent, gentle breeze offered them relief from the intense heat of a Georgia afternoon in August. As he looked out over his fields, he caught sight of his sons, William and Maurice, out of the corner of his eye. They were wrestling at the edge of the field. He sighed and looked at them with sad but loving eyes. He would have left them alone but for the nagging feeling that he wasn't doing right by them.

He set his face like stone and walked briskly toward where the boys were roughhousing. They were supposed to be inside, with their aunt, working on their studies. Rose would have insisted. And by God, he would live to believe that Rose would not have been disappointed in him.

"Boys," he bellowed. "Can you explain to me just what you're doing out here? You're done with your lessons then, I suppose?" The boys jumped apart. Maurice looked up with some trepidation, but William tossed his head defiantly.

Jefferson's heart tightened within him. *I will do right by these boys, whatever it takes.* He told himself firmly.

"Back to the house. You'll not be neglecting your studies. Ma wouldn't have heard of it."

"Ma used to let me come out into the fields with you during harvest time, and you know it," said William defiantly. It took everything in Jefferson not to relent, for he had always felt bonded to William. Everyone said William looked like his father, but Jefferson knew that Rose's very soul lived on in William.

Jefferson's eldest boy was his spitting image, with thick black hair and blue eyes. At twelve, he was tall for his age, and broader than most boys. He could work in the fields as fast as any grown man. He had a sort of quiet intelligence that reflected his mother, but his temper was his father's. Maurice, on the other hand, was cut of the same cloth as his mother. His soft, pensive eyes and inquisitive facial expressions consistently called Rose to mind whenever Jefferson looked at him. He was nine, and the older he became, the more like Rose he became.

"Ma used to make certain you'd completed your lessons first. And you'd never have given her the slip as you did Aunt Violet," said Jefferson, and by his expression, William realized he'd better not push him any farther.

"I like reading, Papa," said Maurice, "but I can't stand those arithmetic books."

"You'll need arithmetic more than stories one day," said Jefferson as he ruffled his younger son's hair. "Now get on."

Maurice ran on ahead and before Jefferson had even made it to the porch, the two were fighting again, rolling around on the ground, all knees and elbows and fists.

Violet, Jefferson's sister, came dashing to the door just as Maurice pushed William, who pushed him back so hard that he toppled right over Anna, his little sister, who'd come toddling out of the house to see what all the commotion was about.

Jefferson felt the anger welling up inside of him. Just how much would it *take* to get these boys to mind the way they'd minded Rose? He didn't know, but feelings of failure came sweeping into his mind, becoming confused with his feelings of determination and responsibility. Above all, he felt a deeply instinctual drive to protect and provide. How could he do that, if they couldn't be bothered to obey him?

I know they've suffered, he thought. *But they will only bring on more suffering if they refuse to be educated and heed authority. I am sorry for them, but no...I must make them mind, or I will fail them. Rose would have known what to do. Oh, Rose, if only you were here now.*

Lost in these thoughts, growing angry at his own inability to control the behavior of his sons, he reached the front yard, scooped up Anna into his arms and patted her lovingly. Then, turning his attention to his sons, said, "William, Maurice, you're supposed to be inside finishing your studies."

"But William said he was going fishing, and I said I'm coming with, and he said no."

"I'm going alone," William said.

"You don't own the pond, William. It's mine as much as yours!" Maurice retorted.

"No one is going. Now back inside," Jefferson ordered. The boys stared at him.

"Go!"

"But...there's a strange woman inside," Maurice said.

"Strange woman?" Jefferson asked, perplexed.

"Auntie Violet knew she was coming," said William, "she came in Doc Blank's carriage just a few minutes ago." Perplexed, Jefferson turned to look at Violet, but she had already slipped back into the house. Jefferson followed.

Having been out in the glaring sun all day, his eyes took a moment to adjust to the dim room. A small figure stood in the corner of the room. In the dim light, he noticed her bright yellow hair first. Then, he noticed green eyes peering out over a freckled face. She was beautiful, though her dress was covered in dirt up well past her ankles, and she wore a tired expression. She looked about ready to collapse, and Jefferson wondered why she did not sit. She held an oversized hound puppy who squirmed and tried licking her face as she stood there quietly.

"Who is *she*?" He said firmly, directing his question to Violet, who rushed to his side. Jefferson noticed that his voice came out louder than he had intended. His anger spilled out on his sister as he rounded on her, demanding to know who this strange woman was who stood in their living room, covered in dirt and holding a pup.

The boys quieted in the presence of their father's commanding voice.

"Don't be angry," Violet spoke softly, casting a quick, apologetic glance at Mary before turning pleading eyes back to her brother.

"Angry?" he said, bewildered.

She looked up at him. Her dark eyes were full of fear and hope. She took a breath and said,

"She's…she is here to become your wife."

Jefferson felt the world spin around him. He knew that his sister had been pressuring him to find a new wife for some time now, but he thought he had made his feelings about that perfectly clear. No one could ever replace Rose, so why try? He remembered the first few difficult years of marriage, adjusting to one another, figuring each other out, learning to love each other more deeply. With Rose, that had all happened within the context of two people deeply in love.

He had no interest in going through that with a woman he did not love—with a woman who was not Rose. And he thought Violet had understood that. So what was going on here? Who was this strange woman in his home, waiting to become his wife?

Chapter Four

At first, Mary did not realize that the towering, seething man before her was Jefferson St. Just. As she listened to Violet pleading with him, she began to realize what was going on.

She looked up at a towering man with broad shoulders and a black beard—lush, but not so thick as to cover the fact that he had a large, sharp jawline. His eyes were blue and fierce, his voice curt and angry.

No, she thought. *This cannot be Jefferson. The ad said he was kind-hearted. This man looks to be anything but kind. No, it can't be.*

But the moment Violet turned pleading eyes on Jefferson and said, "Don't be angry," Mary realized the horrible truth.

God's Nightgown, she thought, using her father's favorite expression, *he hadn't the slightest idea I was coming! He doesn't want me, didn't ask for me. This is all a setup.*

Her stomach seemed to drop. She felt it harden. A lump slowly began to form in her throat, and she knew it would find its way out through tears if she was not careful. *Do not cry*, she commanded herself.

She turned to Violet with stunned eyes and a gaping mouth as she realized that all along, she'd been corresponding with Violet, not Jefferson. Violet's returned gaze seemed to be pleading for Mary's forgiveness.

I've been got, thought Mary. *Jefferson does not even know who I am. I've been writing letters to...to her all along.* She felt disillusioned and dizzy as the reality of the situation hit her. She clung to Rusty, though he tried to squirm out of her arms to greet all the new people.

47

Well, there's nothing to be done right now. I'll think of what to do later. I can't do it now. Years of being taught proper etiquette in social settings took over, and she regained her composure, stepping forward and holding out a slightly trembling hand.

"My name is Mary Margaret Baker."

They stood in silence for a brief moment. Even the children seemed to sense something, and they quieted and stared with big, wondering eyes.

"Why are you here?" He asked, eyes glowering.

"Jefferson, I wanted to tell you, but thought it would be better if you could meet her in person," Violet said.

"Tell me *what?*" he asked, without taking his eyes off Mary. Violet took a step toward him, took a breath, and said, "I put out an ad requesting a wife for you. Mary answered the ad." Jefferson's eyes blazed with anger. It radiated from him, and Mary wondered whether one could feel anger in the air. He took a step closer to Violet, turned his head downward, and said in a harsh, rigid whisper,

"You defied me on this. I explicitly told you no. Just *what* were you *thinking?*"

"Jefferson, please, just consider…"

He cut her off. "Consider? Consider? *You* consider *me. You* are the one who went behind my back and dragged this poor girl here…"

Violet stepped in even closer and slipped a slender white hand into the crook of his arm, looking up at him with big, pleading, brown eyes.

"Brother," she said, in such a sorrowful, repentant, pleading tone that he seemed almost to soften for a moment, and he turned to look at Mary, his eyes scanning her briefly. Her dress was dirty up to her knees, her hair disheveled, and her face smeared with dirt and red from the heat. He sighed loudly but said, "You'll stay for the night until we can figure out what to do with you."

Mary had been standing silent and dumbfounded as this whole conversation took place. Slowly, as she listened, reality sunk in. She was not expected, and not welcome. For a few moments, she simply could not make herself believe that it was true, despite all she heard.

She had come all this way under the pretense that she was wanted as a wife. She felt disillusioned for a long while, but then as reality sunk into her heart, feelings of anger stirred in her. They began to build and fester as Violet and Jefferson talked. Finally, she could bear it no longer.

"I have come *all* this way," she said, her voice trembling with anger, "on the false pretense that I was *wanted* here." She focused her attention then on Violet. "You have done me a great wrong," Mary continued. "I have lost everything. I have left the home I loved. I came all this way, using everything I had to my name and help from friends just to purchase the train ticket to get here, only to find out that you *lied* to me!"

"Please," said Violet, "give me a chance to explain myself. I meant no one any harm."

Mary raised her voice and spoke forcefully. "If you did not mean any harm then you should not have assumed your brother's identity and swindled me into coming here under false pretenses!"

"I agree with..." Jefferson paused, having forgotten her name.

"Mary," Mary and Violet said in unison.

"I agree with Mary," Jefferson said, turning fuming eyes upon his sister. "You have lied and cheated us both." At this, Violet broke down into tears. Mary turned her face away, for another woman's tears nearly always tugged on her heartstrings, and she was in no mood to be compassionate.

"You have misrepresented both your brother's intentions and his character. Now that I am here, I see that even if he did intend to marry me, he is the last man in the world I could imagine being happy with. I'll be leaving," Mary said, but as she began to pick up her suitcase, Jefferson spoke firmly and with a loud voice.

"You will stay!" His tone was so sharp and commanding that she set her suitcase back down immediately.

"William," he called. "Take Miss Mary's suitcase up to Auntie Violet's room, please."

William obeyed, quietly, giving Mary a suspicious, sidelong glance.

"Mary," he continued, "You can wait in the kitchen. I need to talk with my sister in private." Mary nodded as Violet showed her through a doorway into the kitchen.

It was a simple kitchen, but a big one. Mary sat down at a long pinewood dining table in the center of the room. In front of her stood a large wood-burning stove. Across from it was a wide washbasin with a faucet, filled with dirty dishes. A long line of cast iron pots and pans hung on individual hooks above the basin, and above that, a pine shelf held a large variety of spices. Mary was distracting herself by studying them when the children tumbled into the room and stared at her curiously.

"Can we pet your dog?" asked a boy who looked to be about nine or ten. Mary nodded.

The children knelt down and Rusty ran to them clumsily, nearly tripping over his ears, tail wagging excitedly. He began to lick their faces one by one, and their childish giggles brought a smile to Mary's face, despite the exceedingly uncomfortable situation. She could hear low voices rumbling on the other side of the wall. She had just begun to make out what they were saying when the children had come tumbling in.

"But you are lonely," she had heard Violet say. "You need someone to help care for the children when I leave."

"I will be just fine!" He retorted.

"You will *not* be *just fine*! You are not *just fine* now. You must see that, Jefferson. I can't stay here forever."

"No one asked you to," Jefferson scoffed.

"You know as well as I that these children can't be left to fend for themselves while you work in the fields all day," Violet answered in pleading tones.

"We'll find a way," Jefferson said stubbornly.

"And just what other way will you find, Jefferson? You can't afford a governess. And even if you could, it would hardly be proper for one to live here with you, alone."

Ah, so I'm a free governess, too, Mary thought incredulously. She had told herself to be prepared for the unexpected, but she could not have imagined that it would turn out to be such a complete and total disaster. And now, here she was, in a house with a man who never sent for her and did not want her. She had nowhere to go, nowhere to call home, and nothing to her name. It was all so overwhelming she could hardly believe that it was true.

"I have told you time and time again to leave, marry Dr. Blanks, and move on with your life. No one is forcing you to stay here."

Violet's voice softened. "Now be fair, Jefferson. Be fair. You know as well as I what would happen to these children without me. They *need* a mother."

There was a long pause and Mary could not tell whether they had fallen silent or lowered their voices to an inaudible whisper. Finally, she heard Jefferson's deep, rumbling voice carry through the walls.

"You're right. I haven't been fair to you, Violet. You know I want you to be happy, protected and cared for. You know I like Dr. Blanks. You deserve one another. You've been nothing but good to me and my children. Still, my heart is with Rose, as it always will be. I cannot marry. You must be fair to me, too, Violet. You know I cannot." His voice had lost its defensive tone.

"Then there is *her* wellbeing to consider, too."

At this point, their voices lowered to rumblings, which Mary couldn't hear. She turned her attention to Rusty, who was still happily playing with the children.

"Missus?"

"Yes?"

"Why are you here?"

Mary thought for a moment, not knowing what to say. She figured she would be out of here tomorrow, never to see them again, so she may as well speak the truth. It was as good as anything else she could think to say.

"Well, I am here because I was looking for a family. I've lost mine." Then she asked, "and what is your name?"

"Maurice," he answered, then continued, "You've lost them? Don't you think you can find them again? Where did they get lost?" The boy asked.

Mary couldn't help smiling.

"No, dear, I mean they died. My mother and father both died, and I am quite alone."

A look of sadness came over Maurice's face, but William stood and quietly left the room. The small girl with the curly black hair toddled over to Mary and reached chubby little arms up to her. Mary picked her up. "And who is this?" she asked.

"That's Anna," Maurice replied. Anna nestled contentedly into her lap.

"My mother died, too," said Maurice.

His big, brown eyes looking pleadingly up at Mary. She peered down at him and recognized in his eyes that feeling which was embedded so deeply in her heart: a feeling of pain and loss and grief and bewilderment all mixed up together so you can't tell where one ends and the other begins. It's a feeling she had not been able to explain to herself or anyone else. But she saw it, here, in this little boy's eyes. And she thought he seemed to see it and understand it in hers. An unspoken understanding passed between them.

Jefferson and Violet's voices picked up volume again, and Mary could hear Violet.

"She has nowhere to go. See this last letter she sent to me. She explains her situation, briefly, but it appears as though she has no living relatives, no one to care for her either. You could meet one another's needs."

"No one will ever meet my needs again, Violet. I need you to understand that. I'm sorry for her, that much I'll admit. And she did look weary and worn, poor thing. You could have at least..."

"That was a mistake..." Violet interrupted. "I'd meant to..."

"No matter. She'll stay in your room tonight. We'll figure out what to do with her in the morning. But God almighty, if you keep on bringing in more mouths to feed...and that mongrel..."

At this point, their voices trailed off, but soon they both appeared in the kitchen.

"You'll stay for the night," Jefferson said, "and I'll give you the money for the fare for the train home. We'll get you to the station tomorrow. I'm mighty sorry for the misunderstanding, Miss Mary, and that you've come all this way with an expectation that will now be disappointed. I wish I could make it up to you."

Violet looked at Mary with eyes so sorrowful, repentant, and pleading that Mary could not hold on to any anger in her heart toward her. She knew this had all been Violet's doing—Violet had written to her under the pretense of being her brother. She'd deceived her. And yet, Mary still felt a warmth in her presence.

Mary was apt to forgive Violet for the deceit when she saw so clearly that all had been done out of an honest desire to see her brother and niece and nephews cared for. She seemed to Mary to be one of the most kind and beautiful young women she'd ever had the pleasure of knowing, and she had felt within moments that they could have become dear friends under other circumstances.

Mary looked at Violet, hoping that her eyes communicated the forgiveness and understanding her heart felt.

"Thank you, Jefferson. It's as much as I can ask. I apologize for the intrusion."

"You have nothing to apologize for," Violet said quickly. "This has all been my own foolish meddling. I shouldn't have done it. I just thought, if I could get you here... Anyway, I'm sorry. It was wrong of me to interfere."

Mary stepped toward her, taking her hands as if she were an old, familiar friend. "You had the very best of intentions. I'll not hold it against you. In fact, I shall always remember you fondly."

Violet smiled, and tears formed in the corners of her eyes, reflecting off her thick, dark lashes. "Thank you," she mouthed.

Jefferson grunted and left the room.

***

Violet showed Mary into a neat and comfortable room with light blue walls, a single bed, a wooden dresser, and one simple piece of artwork on the wall. It was comfortable, and Mary had the thought that this entire place would have been quite lovely, had it not been for Jefferson. Rusty hadn't followed her up to her room, preferring to stay with the children, who were petting him and sharing dried biscuits with him. Jefferson did not seem pleased with the dog at first but seemed to soften as he watched his children playing with the pup. Mary couldn't quite figure him out, but she did not think that she liked him.

Well, he's certainly not a gentleman, by my standards, she thought. *No common courtesy...no control of his temper. He speaks slowly, and I think he is actually quite dull, and certainly not much of a conversationalist. I think I should have been quite unhappy to have become his wife anyway. It was certainly misleading of Violet to call him kind-hearted, but sisters do seem to always see the best in their brothers.*

A sweet, full scent of lilac swept into the room through an open window, and Mary closed her eyes to soak in the fragrant smell and the cool breeze as it brushed against her skin. She set down her suitcase and walked over to the window. The view nearly took her breath away.

Yes, she thought, *I could stay here forever if it weren't for him. He truly does seem to be the only disagreeable thing about this place.*

Chapter Five

Exhaustion hit Mary like a ton of bricks, and she fell into the bed, hardly able to move. The white metal bed frame creaked beneath her as she glanced around the simple room. There was one wooden dresser, painted white, one simple vanity with a white metal chair which matched the bed frame, and a white-framed mirror against the far wall.

One piece of artwork, a painting of a cascading waterfall, hung on the wall facing the bed. The tidy simplicity of the room stood out to her in stark contrast to the scattered messiness of the rest of the house.

She closed her eyes. Her body was stiff and sore, and she realized that her whole frame was tense. She focused on loosening her jaw, but it was clenched with worry. Her shoulders, too, pressed up against her collar bone in anxiety. Though her whole being cried out for sleep, her jaws and shoulders refused to release their tension, and her mind raced.

She had always had everything she could ever want. She never went without food, and even in times of drought, her father's savings had bought them sugar and flour. There had been no shortage of chicken and venison on her kitchen table, even when others went without.

To Mary, starving was something that happened to other people, the poor dears, not to *her*. Homelessness was something that happened to *other* people, not to her. She knew such states of existence occurred, but she had never done more than cast a sympathetic glance and wonder, existentially, why such suffering existed. Then she'd put it out of her mind and go home for dinner, or ready her dress for a town social gathering.

Occasionally, she'd felt a twinge of guilt, when she was forced to compare her own lifestyle to those suffering around her, but she could usually disregard it fairly quickly. After all, she was only a girl, and it wasn't her fault if her family was more well-to-do than others. Anyway, what exactly could *she* do about it?

But now...now it was *her*. Her home was gone, her inheritance lost, her parents dead. She had no one to turn to, and nowhere to go. Sadness settled into her heart and rested there like a boulder, and nothing could move it. She felt it growing heavier and heavier with each desperate breath.

She remembered the strain on her father's face whenever he'd talked about the war. Mary had only been present for such a moment two times. During one of those times, he'd spoken about marching on bare and bloodied feet, going hungry for days, and finally retreating. This particular memory was crisp in Mary's mind. Try though she did, she could not remember exactly how old she was when she was made privy to his reminiscing. She only remembered the lines in his face, which seemed to become deeper and darker even as he spoke. She remembered feeling so very sad, though she could not really understand why.

As her chest grew heavier, that memory of her father's face grew clearer.

Mary had tried to ask him about the war on other occasions. She had become keenly interested in just what it was that had made her father's face so dark and drawn, his words so grieved and heavy. But when she asked him about the war, he would only say, "Hard days, hard days my girl. Better days are here so let's enjoy them while they last." On several occasions, she'd seen the same dark shadow pass over his face, but he never spoke any more words, so she could only guess what he was thinking.

While they last... Mary repeated in her mind. Perhaps her good days were over. Perhaps it was time for her to suffer, just as her father had.

The memory of hunger pangs on her journey to the ranch was still fresh in her mind, and she was acutely aware that she had no way to even meet her most basic necessities. Anything would be better than that. But suppose he would not let her stay?

For one, dark, wretched moment, she wondered why she had not died along with her parents.

Rusty, seeming to sense her pain, put his front paws on the bed and gently licked her hand. She pet him lazily.

I can't despair. Not now. There must be a reason I'm still here, and it isn't to be turned out to starve. I'll convince them to let me stay. Somehow. At least I have to try. And lying up here in bed is not helping my cause.

She stood, brushed out her crumpled dress, and walked over to the mirror on the vanity. She bent down, wiped the dirt from her face the best she could, and smoothed out her tangled hair.

She stepped out into the hall and walked down to the washroom, where she further cleaned up her dirty, tired-looking face.

She took some deep breaths and tried not to let the panic show on her face, and stepped into the hallway, where she found that a curious crowd had been waiting for her to emerge.

Rusty trotted along after her. The children, immediately seeing Rusty, ran to him with open arms, and Rusty gladly jumped into them, wagging his tail ferociously, and licking their faces with gusto. He loved these children. Mary could see that. And they loved him. She smiled at them and approached.

"Well, he seems to really like you all," she said, smiling.

Rusty bit the edge of Maurice's shirt. He laughed as the dog shook his head back and forth aggressively, ears flopping in every direction. Mary laughed, too, and even William cracked a smile.

"Careful, he'll rip it," said Mary, laughing.

"Aw, that's okay. Hey! I think I have a rope for him!"

Maurice pried his shirt tail out of Rusty's mouth and turned to run down the hall, Rusty bounding after him. He returned with a rope and tried to interest Rusty, who remained interested only in the shirttail.

"Mary?" Maurice said in a questioning voice.

"Yes?" she answered, turning a tired smile on him.

"I helped lift your suitcase upstairs."

"Thank you, Maurice, that was very kind of you."

"How come it's so heavy?"

"Well, that's because I simply couldn't bear to leave my books behind. So there's about fifteen books in that suitcase, and that makes it pretty heavy." His face lit up like a lantern, and a boyish smile crossed it.

"I like books! Can I read some of them? Oh, please! I've read all mine five times already. And the ones in Papa's bookshelf don't make any sense to me. They're all about dead people. I'll be real careful, I promise!" William was glaring at him, but Maurice was whimsically unaware of his brother's disapproval.

Mary laughed, "I happen to have brought along several books just for children. I have Alice in Wonderland and Swiss Family Robinson, and even Tom Sawyer." At the mention of the last title, Maurice jumped, his smile stretching across his freckled face, and his two missing front teeth gaping in between his smile.

"Tom Sawyer? Oh, I've been wanting that one! Have you read it? Don't tell me! Can I read it, please?" Mary was so very pleased to find a child his age so interested in the books she so dearly loved.

"Of course, you can. I'll get it for you now. And you keep it as long as you like!" William, seeing that his scowling looks were going wholly unnoticed by his brother, said,

"Our mother left us plenty of books, thank you."

"But William, I've read them all..."

"We don't need any more than mother has left us," William interrupted with overly enunciated words as he turned glaring eyes upon his brother.

"You're not the boss of what I can read, William!" Maurice shouted. "And if Miss Mary says I can read them, then go ahead and try to stop me." William glared at Mary, turned on his heel, and stormed out of the room.

Well, I'm not off to such a great start Mary thought. Anna, still on her hip, had begun twirling her long strands of golden hair between her fat fingers.

"Let's bring you to supper," Mary said, turning her attention to the round-faced, doe-eyed toddler on her hip. Then, turning to Maurice, she said,

"And you don't worry about the books. I'll ask your auntie to give them to you." Maurice's eyes glistened, and his smile lit up his happy, freckled face.

"Thank you! I'm going to tell William," he said, flouncing off after William and Rusty.

Just then, Violet peeped her head around a corner and called out, "Dinner is ready!" Small feet and paws came bounding through the hallway, down the stairs, and toward the kitchen, and Mary followed.

She was nervous to face Jefferson again. His presence was domineering, though she did not get the same bad feeling in the pit of her stomach that she had around Kit. Jefferson seemed angry, but he did not have an empty stare.

"Daddy, Miss Mary says I can have her *books*!" Maurice announced as soon as they had all entered the kitchen and were finding their seats at the long table. "And," he continued, "She even has Swiss Family Robinson and Tom Sawyer!" And with this last triumphant statement, he turned and stuck out his tongue at William.

Jefferson nodded. "How generous," he said. "Can you pass the rolls, please?"

Mary, trying to be grateful for having a meal set before her, could not help but notice that the rolls were hard as a rock. Her stomach rumbled with hunger after her long journey. She had not eaten since she was on the train. She was grateful in spite of the rock-hard rolls and dry, sticky meat. She accidentally knocked a roll to the floor as she tried cutting it. The meat was hard to swallow without milk. But the green beans were delicious, and she helped herself to three servings.

They ate in relative silence, with Jefferson casting occasional quick glances her way throughout the meal.

Violet, uncomfortable though she seemed, made a consistent attempt at small talk. Jefferson seemed only to be able to grunt in reply, and Mary found that she was too nervous to be much of a conversationalist that night. She badly wanted to make a good impression, to be invited to stay, but the words, whenever she could think of any to say, felt heavy on her tongue.

Anna had quietly slipped out of her seat and reached arms up to Mary again. Mary was quite taken with her. Her thick black curls clustered about her chubby, white cheeks and contrasted with her big, wondering blue eyes. How could she help but love this child at first sight? Mary found her utterly endearing, and when she reached up for Mary to hold her, she could not have refused her.

Maurice was also vying for her attention, in his own way. He smiled at her and would have continually drawn her into a conversation about a great number of books if not for disapproving glances from his father.

William eyed her with an air of skepticism that perfectly reflected that of his father's.

Every few minutes, Violet tried, and failed, to engage them all in a comfortable conversation. Eventually, she gave up, and they finished their meal quietly, silverware clinking on plates.

Mary thought that it could have been quite a pleasant meal but for Jefferson's looming presence and disapproving glances. She remembered the look in his eyes when she'd first encountered him; it was a sort of anger, to be sure, but she could not help contrasting it with the rage she'd seen in Kit's eyes. It was altogether different. Jefferson's was not sinister in nature. She could not put a finger on why, exactly, Jefferson's outburst had seemed so different to her.

Well, if it really came down to it, I suppose I would rather face Jefferson than Kit. And, I suppose, I would rather face starvation than Kit. But, still, I'd rather face Jefferson than starve.

And with that, her mind was made up. She would stay, if ever she could convince him to keep her on, in one capacity or another. Perhaps as a field hand or governess?

After dinner, Mary helped Violet clean up while Jefferson went out to gather more firewood.

The two women washed dishes silently, side by side, for a few moments.

Then, Violet said, "Can you ever forgive me? I know what I did was wrong...deceitful. I'm not that sort of woman, you know. I've never done anything..."

"Don't think of it," Mary interrupted. "I'm no worse off now than I would have been if you had never responded. Anyway, it was a decent thought, if it would have worked out. I will say you might have been a little more forthright about his character."

"His character?" Violet asked, bewildered.

"Why, yes! You said that he was a kind-hearted man."

"Oh, darling, he is! He is!"

"Well, he certainly has not seemed so to me," she lowered her voice to a whisper. "To me, he seems very domineering and demanding."

"Well, yes, I suppose he is. But he is kind. You would see that in time if..."

"If I were allowed to stay?"

"Well, yes."

They finished the dishes silently, and then went into the living room. Mary watched Jefferson as he read the last few sentences of one of Aesop's fables about a snake and a farmer. Anna was already sleeping on his broad chest, and Maurice was nodding off at his feet. Only William was wide awake, listening intently. Violet gently lifted Anna from Jefferson and took her up to bed.

"Off to bed, now," said Jefferson. Mary thought she could hear the kindness in his voice which his sister so generously attributed to him. The two boys rose to go obediently to their rooms, with Rusty following at their heels.

Mary also turned to go, but Jefferson's voice stopped her.

"Mary. Stay."

She turned back to face him.

"Yes?"

"Violet says you have nowhere to go. I will marry you if you like. It will be an agreement. A transaction. I can offer you nothing more in my present state. It will not be as a marriage should be. It will not be what you deserve. But I will if it is what you want."

Mary nodded. She did not say that she did not want to marry him, or that she feared she would be homeless without him. She did not say that she found him overbearing and crude. Instead, she nodded her head and said, "Thank you." And gathered her skirts and nearly ran up the stairs, down the hall, and into her room, where she fell upon the bed.

At first, she felt only relief. She would not be turned out with nowhere to go. She could *stay.* But then, a moment later, she felt horror. She had just agreed to marry a man she did not know, and one whom she had decided she disliked from the moment she laid eyes on him. Then, she thought of Kit and his hungry, raging, unfeeling eyes, and she felt safe. Jefferson, at least, was some protection. He was bigger than Kit, and more fierce.

Still, she felt a little pang. Like so many other little girls, she had always imagined that her proposal would feel different. Instead, it had been a simple, "I'll marry you if you like" and she had said "yes" to a man she did not love. For this, she wept quietly into her pillow until weariness, cloaking her like a heavy blanket, bore her off deep into her subconscious.

Chapter Six

That evening after dinner, Jefferson went up to his room to sit a while. He pulled Rosie's picture off the dresser and ran a finger over it softly. He could hear the muffled voices talking below him.

"I'm the man of this house," he said softly. "I can't hide away up here." He wasn't sure whether he was talking to himself or to Rosie. He wished he could hide in his room and walk away from all of this, but he'd had his head buried in the sand long enough. If he'd been honest with himself, he would have admitted that he knew Violet felt stuck and unable to marry Dr. Blanks. He would have known that he needed to see to a different arrangement for himself and the children.

For so long, he'd chosen not to acknowledge the reality of his situation, but when Mary arrived, he had no choice but to face the facts. His sister, who'd served him so selflessly, was desperate to start her own life. His children, bereft of a mother, needed someone to care for them. He wasn't ready to move on, though. He needed Rosie.

My darling, he thought. *Why did you have to leave us?*

He gathered himself and walked heavily down the staircase, his boots clanking loudly against the wooden stairs. His legs were tired, and his boots felt like dead weights around his feet. By this time, Mary had already gone up to settle into her room, and the children had gone to bed as well. He came into the living room, where the fire was crackling; Violet sat mending one of William's torn shirts.

She looked up at him with some trepidation, but he did not glare or scowl. Instead, he smiled a weak, sad smile, sat down in the chair across from her, and began unlacing his boots.

"I'm so sorry Jefferson. I thought...I just thought—" But he waved his hand to silence her.

"No," he said. "I'm sorry. You're right. I haven't been able to see past my grief to see what sacrifices you've been making. I know I said you were free to leave at any time, but you know as well as I that's not true. You love them, and you could never abandon them. It's not fair to you when you want and deserve to start your own family."

"Oh Jefferson, nothing will ever take their place in my heart," He waved his hand again.

"You've shown that. You've been here for me every step of the way since Rosie died, but you know what I think Rose would say if she were here? She'd say you deserve to marry the love of your life and start your own family. I had that. Rosie and I had that together. We have these three beautiful children. She wouldn't want you to miss out on marrying your love, to miss out on starting a family because you're here filling in her place. Rose would have told you to go, to marry Mr. Blanks, and live your life with him. She would have wanted that for you. In my grief, I've been selfish. I'm sorry, Violet."

Tears had begun to form in Violet's eyes as her brother spoke these words. Jefferson rarely said so much at once.

"But what will you do without me?" Violet asked, tears streaming down her eyes. "I've been a fool to think you could just marry any girl I brought in here when your heart still breaks for *her*." Jefferson rocked back and forth, thoughtfully. He reached for a mahogany pipe from the side table and fumbled around in his pocket for a match. He lit the pipe and drew a long breath on it. He blew out a long, slow, smokey breath and then said,

"I've asked her to marry me." Violet, visibly taken aback, thought she'd misheard him.

"You *what*?"

"I can't love her, not the way I loved Rosie. I don't know her well enough to say whether I'll ever come to feel anything for her at all, but she seems willing to accept that. She's got no place to go, and I can provide protection. Watching her with the children...well...she was so warm and tender. Maurice loves her already, and Anna seemed to take to her. Only William...well, he's old enough to feel as I do, I suppose."

"Yes, yes, that's all true, but has she said yes, then?" Violet asked eagerly, sitting on the edge of her seat.

Jefferson puffed on his pipe again and leaned back in his chair.

"She has," he answered, eying her pensively. "That young woman needs protection, and I need a mother for my children. It is not as it was with Rose. We married for love and built our lives together. This is different. But, yes, I have asked her, and she has agreed."

Jefferson rubbed a finger idly back and forth across his wedding band. Thoughts of Rosie swarmed his mind. He thought of their wedding day and remembered how his heart had beat wildly as she walked toward him down the aisle. He remembered how her smile had lit up her face so brightly that he could see her sheer happiness right through the veil. He remembered the look in her eyes when he lifted the veil, took her into her arms, and kissed her.

I will never forget you, Rosie. Never. He thought as he worked his wedding band off his finger. He stood and moved to sit next to his sister. Taking her hands into his, he pressed the wedding band into her palm.

"Rosie would have wanted someone worthy to wear this. I can't bear to have it sit, untouched. I can't use it again. It will always remind me of Rosie. But on his finger, I'll remember what Rosie would have wanted. For us to *live*. Both of us."

Her name on someone else's lips brought comfort to his soul. He never wanted to forget her. He never wanted anyone to forget her. He wanted to say her name, to hear her name, and to remember her smile.

Violet squeezed her hand around the ring, the tears welling up in her eyes and streaming down her cheeks.

"He will be honored," she said, holding the ring tightly. "Rose would be so proud of you, Jefferson." She wrapped her small arms around her brother's neck and cried. Her small sobs against his chest brought a lump into his throat, which he tried to choke back, but which grew bigger until he let out a soft cry.

He took comfort in crying together with Violet. He often cried alone, in his bed, after everyone else had gone to sleep. Whenever he cried alone, and the tears had all dried up, he was left with a dull, aching, pain in his heart. But here, with Violet, her sobs met with his and they comforted each other, like salve on a wound. Their tears poured like water into each other's dry, parched souls. They held on a little longer and cried until it seemed there were no tears left to cry for the moment.

Exhaustion swept over Jefferson like a wave, and he finally pulled away.

"I have to get to bed; otherwise I'll be no use tomorrow. In the morning we will go to the church and see if we can't be married straightaway. No reason to put it off."

***

Jefferson awoke the next morning with only one thought, *I'm getting married today.* He'd made his decision already. He had asked Mary, and she'd agreed. He had never been a man to go back on his word. Last night, it had all seemed right. Last night, he thought it was what Rose would have wanted. Last night, he cried with Violet, and they had agreed. But this morning, he felt unsure, shaky, and confused. He only knew that he would carry out his promise and marry Mary.

He pulled himself out of bed, sore from a hard day's work yesterday. But today was Sunday, and there would be no work, no matter how badly the crops needed to be harvested. No one harvested on a Sunday. But people did get married on a Sunday, and that is what he would do, provided the clergy was available and able to perform a marriage ceremony that day.

With this in mind, Jefferson showered, dried, put on his best Sunday clothes, and trimmed his beard and mustache. He looked at himself in the bathroom mirror, feeling oddly outside of his own body. Two ocean blue eyes peered back at him, and he felt he did not know the man behind them.

What am I doing? He asked himself.

He had made a promise, and he was a man of his word. Last night, he'd been able to believe that Rose would have wanted this for him. Today, doubt mingled with grief to fill up his mind, confusing him.

My feelings might shift and toss about like the waves of the sea, he thought, *but my situation remains the same. Violet is getting married and moving out. I need a wife. Mary needs a husband. This is in everyone's best interest.*

With this, he set his face like flint, and walked out of the bathroom and headed down the hallway, where he came face to face with Mary. She was wearing one of Violet's sage green dresses. He noticed the way her green eyes danced above her freckled face. Her long, blond hair hung down to her waist in an elaborate braid. He was, in spite of himself, quite struck with her beauty.

"Good morning," he said to her, sheepishly.

"Good morning," she responded, her voice strong, full and vibrant. Rose had always sounded so soft and demure and gentle.

"We'll go to the church today," he said. She nodded.

"It's not much of a wedding dress but…"

"It's perfect."

She seemed a bit startled, but she blushed and thanked him, and he gestured for her to descend the stairway ahead of him.

The carriage ride to the church was silent and awkward. The heavy Georgia air pressed down on them as they drove to the church. Jefferson drove, looking straight ahead, for he could not make sense of his thoughts.

He tried to think about Rose, but his eyes were consistently drawn to Mary, for she truly looked dazzling in that light green dress with her long blond braid blowing in the wind, her bright green eyes peeping out from under her bonnet. He wanted to gaze into her eyes and admire her dazzling figure and return her warm smile.

But Rose, he thought. He kept his eyes trained on the road ahead and answered Mary's questions with only grunts and nods. Memories of his wedding day with Rose filled his mind, and his grief and longing seemed to mix with this new sensation, which confused and terrified him. He *wanted* to look at Mary, to hold her in his arms, and draw her into him, and this sudden and unexpected desire scared him.

It wasn't supposed to be this way. It was supposed to be a business deal—a transaction, an agreement that was to the benefit of all. He was not supposed to feel *this* way. He could not allow those feelings in, for if desire swept over him, he felt that Rose would slip away, and he could not let that happen. He closed his eyes and remembered her face.

Mary saw Rupert arrive in his carriage. She took Anna on her hip and hopped down from the carriage after Violet. The two women ran to greet him, with William, Maurice, and Rusty at their heels. Jefferson followed them absent-mindedly. Again, he looked at Mary as she happily greeted Violet's fiancé. Her smile was so engaging and her eyes so bright he felt he could get lost in them if he let himself.

He noticed how Mary and Violet seemed to fit together, almost as if they'd always been sisters. The two couldn't possibly have looked more different, but somehow Violet's kindness and gentleness blended with Mary's vivacity and warmth. The two were a perfect fit. He was happy for his sister, who would soon be gaining a husband and a best friend.

The marriage ceremony was a simple affair, with Violet standing next to Mary and Rupert next to Jefferson. The children sat in the front pew, watching with interest for a while until they grew bored, at which point they could be found, occasionally poking, teasing, or sticking out a tongue.

At these moments, Jefferson glared at them, and they folded their hands and turned their attention to the ceremony until they were overcome with boredom, and they began fidgeting and fussing again. At one point, Anna scrambled down out of the pew and made her way to the front of the church, where Violet promptly scooped her up.

Jefferson could not deny, even to himself, that his eyes were drawn to Mary's, as they gleamed in her sage green dress. He found himself wondering about her warm smile, which sat between two deep dimples.

She smiles, he thought. *Though she's lost her mother and father, and home. Though she's come to a new place she doesn't know and is vowing to spend her life with me.*

He looked at her with curious eyes, and she returned the gaze, her green eyes equally inquisitive. It seemed to Jefferson almost as if they were trying to figure each other out. He would have gone on, gazing into her bright eyes and getting lost in the warmth of her dimpled smile, but for his looming uneasiness. For some reason, he could not see Rose's face as clearly as he had that morning, and it bothered him.

He tried to picture Rose and their wedding day, but this was so different he couldn't do it. He closed his eyes for a moment and tried to remember Rose's face. But when he opened his eyes again, the image was gone, and Mary stood before him, beautiful, smiling, and glowing in green.

The uneasiness in his soul grew, and he could only allow his mind to go blank and his heart to grow numb. He stared off, above Mary's head, forcing himself to feel aloof and indifferent until the clergy announced them man and wife, and he planted a quick, forced, kiss on her pink lips.

He noticed her smile drop in that moment, but he couldn't think of that now. He took her gently by the hand and walked her down the aisle and out of the church, while Rupert and Violet gathered up the children and followed behind them.

The carriage ride home was silent, save for the clopping of horse's hooves and the consistent clanking of gravel being kicked up against the carriage side. Mary and Jefferson rode home alone, as Rupert and Violet took the doctor's carriage and the children over to the doctor's home.

Jefferson felt betrayed by the clear blue skies and the gentle cool breeze that offered periodic relief from the sun's burning heat. He thought that it ought to have been a dark and stormy day. Instead, the sunny warmth and cool breeze enticed him to smile when he did not want to smile.

He cast a sidelong glance at Mary and found her to be looking at him with the same inquisitive look in her glimmering eyes. He looked away again, without saying a word.

Soon his rows of golden corn came into view, and the gravel road wound its way up and up until the white house could be seen in the distance. He wanted to say something, if only he could think what to say. Instead, the carriage followed the winding gravel road in silence as the white house grew closer and closer.

Once home, Jefferson helped Mary down from the carriage with gentleman-like sincerity and walked with her to the house before unhitching the horses, rubbing them down, and putting them out to pasture.

As he walked back to the house, he tried to put Mary out of his mind and remember Rose.

This is just a practical marriage after all, He reasoned. *She knows I can't love her. I've told her as much. Oh, Rose, what should I do?*

Instead of mounting the steps into the house, he walked around back to the family cemetery, where he knelt next to Rose and Hattie, their little baby girl they'd lost in infancy just two years before Anna was born, healthy and strong.

Rose's face became clear in Jefferson's mind again, but it wasn't her face on her wedding day. It was her face, all twisted with pain and bewilderment when Hattie had been born, took only a few labored breaths, and died in her arms.

"Oh, Rose," he whispered, as memories of his lost wife and daughter flooded his mind. "Oh, Rose, I hope you have her in your arms right now. I wish I had you here now, Rose. You were my rock. You held this family together. Rose, if only you were here. If I could just ask you… if you could just tell me what to do, what I should have done."

With a dull ache in his heart, he stood. He wiped the dust from his best set of trousers and wiped the tears from the corners of his eyes.

He opened the door quietly and slipped into the house. He was alone. Mary must have gone to bed.

He trudged up the stairs as quietly as his lumbering body would allow, walked down the hallway, and opened the door to his room.

He undressed and was about to slip into bed when his eyes fell on the faded picture of their wedding day. Rose's veil and dress flowed down to the floor. He looked stiff, and serious in the photo, though he remembered how his heart leapt for joy.

Rose's brown hair wisped about her face from under the veil, and her soft smile transported him back to her arms. The picture could not do justice to her deep, brown eyes and the way they seemed to gaze into his soul and know him.

Oh Rose, I miss you, he said, lifting the photo from the dresser with gentle hands, as if he might destroy the memory itself if he was not careful. He got into bed, pressed it to his heart, and fell asleep.

Chapter Seven

Mary woke to streams of light coming through her window and warming her face. She must have slept in. The sun was high in the western sky.

I'm married. She thought. She could hardly believe it. Yesterday had gone by in a whirl of confusion. Mary had been saddened by several moments when grief over the loss of her Texas home and family had swept over her. Once, when she breathed in the thick, Georgia air, she missed the thin, dry air of Texas, and wondered whether she would ever get used to even breathing in this new place.

But, for the most part, she decided that she would be happy. After all, she was falling more and more in love with Redwood Ranch. She'd seen few places with such rich, red, beautiful earth, and she marveled at the foamy softness of it when she pressed her hand into it. The ground in Rosewood, Texas had been dry, dusty, and cracked. Here, she loved to sit on the ground and run her hands through the grass.

Yesterday, she'd smiled at Jefferson, feeling truly hopeful about their future together. She knew that he could not marry her for love. She'd happened to overhear Jefferson telling Violet this. But that was okay with Mary. She understood once she'd heard Jefferson pour out his heart to Violet, recalling his love of his late wife.

Mary had grieved that she was not someone's Rose. As a little girl, she'd dreamed of her wedding day, of winning some man's heart, of marital bliss. This was something altogether different, and she had cried for her lost opportunity to become someone's sweetheart, to be the love of someone's life. And yet, when she'd cried all those tears, she looked around her and she felt an overwhelming sense of gratefulness at having been welcomed into this family, this home.

Her father had always told her that she was "made of the right stuff," that she was "resilient and fierce and full of life," and she took this with her now, praying to live up to it, to become the type of person her father thought she was.

Even her mother had once said, "You could stand to calm down some, Mary. You're not invincible, you know," then had smiled on her kindly. But now, Mary *did* want to be invincible, resilient, and fierce. She wanted to see if she was "made of the right stuff." She wanted to make a life here.

So, when she put on Violet's best dress, she had smiled at herself in the mirror, and it was a genuine smile, one full of hope for the future.

She had gone into her wedding ceremony full of hope and warmth and wonder, the fiery passion of her father shining through her eyes, and the resolute steadfastness of her mother settled in her breast. This, then, was how her face shone with warmth and hope even as she walked down the aisle and said her vows to a man she did not know or love.

She remembered standing at the altar, looking curiously into his pale, blue eyes and feeling slightly disappointed to find a sort of dullness there. *I had thought at least we might have some companionship and intelligent conversation. But alas, he looks as though he could not match my wit.* But even amid this disheartening observation, she maintained a spirit of fervor.

It was not in Mary's nature to be dejected. She had discovered that in the weeks following the loss of her parents. Though she grieved with a full heart and did not stifle her cries of despair as she threw herself upon their graves, when

78

the tears dried, and she stood, she found that a flame still flickered in her breast.

She wanted to *live*, not just survive, but *live*. And this little flame, though at times it seemed almost put out, grew in the days and weeks following the deaths, and Mary found that she possessed at least some of the resilience her father had often attributed to her.

This is how she felt as she descended the stairs to the kitchen on her first morning as a married woman. She was relieved that Jefferson had not come to her room the night before. She did not know exactly what to expect in that regard. She knew that they had an agreement and that she would care for and teach the children, and he would protect her and provide her a permanent home.

The deal was satisfactory to her. But it was not until they drove home in silence after the ceremony that she began to wonder whether Jefferson anticipated them to behave as husband and wife in *that* regard. She was greatly relieved to find that he, apparently, did not.

So instead of sharing her wedding bed with Jefferson, Mary had spent the night next to Rusty, who curled up in a large ball by her side and took up too much of the bed.

These were the thoughts that filled Mary's mind as she descended the stairs into the kitchen, Rusty trampling along at her heels, for her first day as Mrs. Jefferson St. Just.

And that's when she noticed a faint scent of smoke rising to her nostrils. Violet was standing over the stove, covering her mouth with a handkerchief and stirring something that looked almost inedible.

"Turn off the heat!" Mary called, rushing over to her and quickly removing the pan from the woodburning stove. "Open the windows! We'll choke," she commanded William, who obeyed quickly.

Violet flopped herself onto a chair in the kitchen.

"I'm sorry!" She cried, "I just wanted your first breakfast here to be good."

"Yeah! We usually eat grits," said Maurice, "so she was gonna make flapjacks and eggs, but they stuck to the pan and got all black. I think grits look better than that."

Violet laughed and admittedly said, "It's true my cooking skills have not improved much,"

"Her venison tastes like a leather boot!" William cried. "Mamma used to make it so tender you didn't even have to cut it."

"It's true," Violet admitted. "Unfortunately, Rose did not leave anything but a list of ingredients in her recipes. I just haven't been able to figure out how she made her food so delicious. Everything I make seems to do this," she said, waving her hand toward the direction of the wood-burning stove." Mary laughed gently.

"Not to worry, dear. I'm a decent cook myself," she said, scraping burned flakes of flapjacks from the pan to the floor, where Rusty happily gobbled them up. "William, will you bring me the flour and sugar? Oh, and a bit of yeast and some vanilla, if you have it? Thank you, that'll do," and she whipped up the batter and poured it onto a clean pan in perfectly rounded, fluffy circles, flipping them to reveal evenly golden cakes.

"The trick is the level of heat and the thickness of the cake," she smiled as she flipped them onto plates and passed them to the children. Maurice grabbed his plate excitedly and Anna reached her arms up for one of her own.

"Mother used a bit of nutmeg and cinnamon in *hers*," William said, sounding none too impressed. But he grabbed a fork and some maple syrup and gobbled them up in a few seconds flat while Mary smiled on. It was okay. He missed his mother. Just as she missed hers.

Mary turned her head toward the stairs, which creaked under the weight of Jefferson's thumping boots.

"Why does it smell like smoke in here?" he asked, grumpily.

"Oh, I burned some flapjacks, but no worries! Mary came to the rescue. Would you like some?"

"Cereal is fine for me, thanks,"

"Heaven forbid you enjoy yourself," Mary whispered to Violet, who stifled a snicker. Jefferson glared at them, but helped himself to some cold cereal before standing, putting on his hat, and heading out to the fields.

"Is he *always* so unpleasant?" Mary asked, when the children had scraped their plates and scrambled out of the kitchen.

Violet smiled, "I'm sorry I described him as kind-hearted. That wasn't fair. But it wasn't a lie. I truly believe that he *is* kind-hearted. It just takes some time to see it."

"I'm not sure time is the problem," Mary said cynically, but the smile on her face told Violet that Mary was up to the task, ready to take on life here at Redwood Ranch, however unpleasantly Jefferson behaved. And she felt certain that Mary would eventually see what she saw in her brother.

Mary cast her a skeptical look. "Anyway," Violet continued, "you already showed me up with your cooking this morning. So you have that going for you," she laughed.

"And you do not. Does the kind doctor happen to know what he's in for when you start cooking for him?" Violet laughed heartily.

"Of course he does! One of the first times I talked with him, I asked him what he likes to do for fun. And you know what he said? He said he likes to cook! Said it makes him feel calm and relaxed. I decided right then and there that I would get this man to marry me." Mary laughed.

"Oh, stop. You can't be serious."

"Oh, there were other reasons, of course. But that certainly piqued my interest." As they laughed, Rusty came bounding up to them, wagging his tail, apparently looking for more table scraps.

"I'll have to get him some proper food."

"I'll go to Henley's Feed tomorrow," Violet said. "But you're here now, so I suppose it's time I leave you here. I won't be needed here quite so much anymore." She said this with an air of sadness mingled with relief.

Mary felt a little stunned for a moment. She'd taken to the children quickly, but Violet had always been there to oversee things. She was merely along for the ride. But Violet was right. Mary would have to step into a bigger role at home now, and the sooner the better.

No sooner had Violet walked out the front door than Mary heard a shrieking sound coming from the next room, followed by a loud wailing. *What on earth?* She wondered as she hurried through the kitchen door.

She came upon the unpleasant scene of William holding Maurice by the hair, Anna wailing, and Maurice shrieking. For a baffling moment, she looked around to see whether anyone would intervene. And then, all at once, she realized that no one was there to help her. She alone was responsible for intervening.

"Just *what* do you think you're doing? Let GO of him!" she shouted, advancing toward them.

"I will NOT!" William retorted. "He broke my fishing pole, and he won't tell me where he's hidden his unless I take him with me." Maurice continued shrieking and flailing. Mary advanced, taking William firmly by the wrist and looking directly into his eyes.

"I said let go, and I mean it. We'll talk about this calmly, like the young adult that you are." The authority in her own voice surprised her. William released Maurice, who stumbled backward and tripped over Anna, who had only just ceased crying and immediately resumed upon being tripped over.

"Now, I'm going to hear you both out here, and we're going to decide together what to do about the fishing pole. But neither of you will be doing any fishing on a school day until your lessons are completed. Now, let's talk about this. Maurice, you can tell your side of the story first."

"I never meant to break his fishing pole! I only wanted to go with him, and he wouldn't let me. Said I scare the fish away. So I went all by myself. And Dad didn't line mine yet, so I had to take his. And I never meant to break it anyway. So I don't want to give away mine. I never even used it." Mary nodded with a look of understanding. Then she turned a sympathetic gaze to William, before turning back to Maurice.

"Now, Maurice. You should not have taken something that did not belong to you without asking. Just because something of yours isn't working does not give you the right to someone else's. What would you think if I took your Aunt Violet's reading glasses without asking because I don't have a pair of my own?" Maurice let out a giggle. Encouraged, Mary continued, "and then let's say I broke her glasses. Do you think that would be okay that I did that? Because I didn't have my own, after all, and I really wanted some." Maurice laughed out loud at this.

"No!" He said, "Of course you wouldn't do that!"

"Why not?" asked Mary.

"Because they are *her* glasses. You would have to get your own."

"Exactly," said Mary. "As adults, we respect other people in many ways, but one of those ways is by respecting their things. If I stole something from Aunt Violet, she would think that I don't care about her very much, wouldn't she?"

Maurice's face dropped, and Mary could see as the understanding came over him. He shook his head, "Yeah, I guess so." He scuffed his toe on the ground.

"Next time you want to use something of William's, please ask him. And if he doesn't want you to use it, come to me and we will see what we can do about getting you your own, okay?" Maurice nodded. "Why don't you take Anna out into the yard now?" Maurice obeyed, and Mary turned to William.

"You know he wants to be like you, right?" she asked William. He rolled his eyes, but Mary continued, "You know, I always wanted a sibling."

"They're not all they're cracked up to be," William clapped back. Mary chuckled.

"Maybe not now. But I'm thinking of adults. I had a friend with three sisters, and they were just the best of friends. They did everything together. It was like they just had a built-in friend to go through all of life with them from childhood on up. I was always so jealous of that. Maybe that's why I like your aunt so much. I always wanted a sister. It might not feel so lucky to have a brother right now, but you treat him right, and you just might make a best friend out of him."

"I already got a best friend."

"Yeah? That's great. We all need friends, don't we? But I'm telling you, I see something different in siblings that are best friends. It's something deeper. It's like they are bonded not only because they share interests but because they have shared their entire lives. You may want him one day, so maybe just think about that before you alienate him now." The defiant look never left William's face, but the moments of silence showed Mary that she was getting somewhere, albeit slowly.

In fact, William had been feeling a sense of respect at having been talked to like he was an adult—like he was equal. Mary used big words with him, and he *did* understand them. So even though he had been determined to dislike her, he felt a tinge of respect and validation when she conversed with him like he was just another adult. It was the conversation he always craved. Still, she wasn't his mother, and he wasn't about to let her act like it, so he tossed his head and flounced out of the room.

Chapter Eight

"You know, I've been here some time and I have to ask about Anna. I thought maybe she was just shy at first, but she really doesn't say much, does she? And she's almost three, right?" Mary asked, and Jefferson glared at her from under his wide-brimmed hat.

"Nothing's wrong with her, if that's what you're getting at."

"Wrong with? No. No one said anything was *wrong* with her. Some kids just need a little extra help with..."

"She's fine," he snapped. "Not everyone has to yap up a storm every five minutes." Jefferson felt immediately regretful for the barb, and he knew he should say something to soften his harsh words, but anything tender he thought to say seemed to stick in his throat.

Mary turned her face away, and Jefferson knew she was hurt.

Ever since their wedding day, Jefferson had felt confused and irritated around Mary. She was stepping into her expected role quite well. She cooked and cleaned and looked after the kids and started their lessons.

But Jefferson was confused by his swelling heart, his nervous anxiety around her, the way his words stuck in his throat and came out only in short, harsh sentences which did not reflect his heart.

The problem was, he didn't understand his own heart. Not at all. He fought against his desire to gaze at her, be mesmerized by her. But no, he didn't love her. He couldn't love her. He still loved Rose. So every night, he went to his separate room and looked at Rose's picture for a long while before drifting off to sleep.

Mary was nothing like Rose. Rose, whose soft, warm smile had won his heart so many years ago. Rose, whose gentle countenance and soothing presence had quietly, easily, brought out the best in him.

Mary's fierce eyes were the opposite of Rose's. Her sharp language and prideful countenance annoyed him at times and amused him at others. Her wit kept him chuckling quietly to himself, and her vivacious ways brought a liveliness and constant chatter to the home.

Sometimes, Jefferson found that these attributes grated on him. But mostly, he enjoyed her presence. What bothered him the most was that he was drawn to her. To cover for this, he spoke to her more harshly than he otherwise would have.

But, as he was unable to admit this truth to himself, he simply continued in this way, leaving Mary feeling wounded, and Violet confused. He'd overheard Violet say, "I don't know what's come over him since..."

Mary had answered, "Since he was strong-armed into marrying me?" And the two had fallen silent in a rare moment of tension between them. He'd felt his heart throb at hearing this, and he longed to defend himself...to explain. But how could he make someone else understand him when he could not understand himself?

He loved watching her with Anna and Maurice. He had to admit they loved her and were thriving academically under her guidance. He also noticed that the fighting and arguing in the house had slowed down some, and there was quite a bit more laughter. He was happy and thankful for this but did not know what to say to show it.

He resonated most with his oldest son, who eyed Mary with the same suspicion Jefferson felt. He recalled a day, during the second week of Mary's arrival, when she had allowed

William a day off of lessons to help bring in the harvest. Jefferson and William worked alongside each other, father and son, in the glaring heat, working until they were tired and numb.

William had at least as much stamina as the hardest workers on the field, and almost as much strength. He wanted to prove his work in the fields, for he much preferred it to his studies. Jefferson felt a connection to William, who had been old enough to process the loss of his mother in ways the others could not. His memories of her were strong and vivid, and Jefferson reveled in hearing William reminisce.

So, that day working side by side in the hot, golden fields, he asked his son, "What do you think of Mary, really?" Somewhere deep inside, Jefferson was looking for permission to like her. If William could like her, perhaps he could, too.

William stopped, looked up, inquisition in his eyes, and said, "She's not Ma. She will never be my mother." And Jefferson felt his words resonate within his soul. Mary was not Rose. She was nothing like Rose. Her personality and features were the direct opposite of the very essence of Rose, and that was a constant reminder of how much they missed her.

Unbeknownst to himself, Jefferson longed to open up to her, to get lost in her laughing eyes, to smile at her witty humor, to laugh with her. But he could not, for every time he felt himself move toward her, he imagined that he was simultaneously moving away from Rose, and he would retreat into himself, into his memories, climb the stairs, and hold the picture of her.

This was the pattern Jefferson had established, and he hardly understood why. All he knew for certain was that he felt himself drifting away from Rose whenever he was in

Mary's presence, and he could not bring himself to betray her.

Had William been willing to embrace Mary, perhaps Jefferson would have opened up a little more, too. But now, he couldn't bear the thought of leaving William alone to cherish the memory of his beloved mother.

Jefferson had loved Rose with all of his heart, but he had a life before Rose, too. He felt that allowing himself to get lost in Mary's eyes would be to abandon William to grieve alone. Anna had been too young to remember her mother at all, and Maurice had been young enough that his memories were scarce.

But William, Jefferson thought. *I can't let him feel abandoned to grieve alone.*

The more Jefferson was with Mary, the more he was drawn to her, in spite of himself. He told himself he was busy, far too busy to spend much time in the house. He often took William with him, leaving Mary to read with Maurice and care for Anna.

She cannot be too lonely, he reassured himself. *Violet is still here with her anyway. Mary prefers her company to mine. I'll spend more time at home after Violet's wedding.* And in this way, he went on convincing his mind of all the things his heart knew to be false.

And yet, I should be spending more time with my other children, too. Not just William. They will get to feel I'm choosing favorites. I will take Anna out riding tomorrow. She's never been. Anyway, at least Ill spend enough time with her to see for myself how she speaks.

He mentioned it at breakfast the next morning.

"I assume you'll be riding with her," she said.

Jefferson, annoyed at her presumption that she knew more about his own children than he, replied, "No. I will put her up to ride. She'll have to learn some time. I was up on a horse at her age."

"Well, yes, maybe..." Mary replied.

"I think it's a terrible idea," Violet joined in. Jefferson felt his cheeks go red. Who were *they* to tell him what he could and could not do with his *own* children? Rose, he felt certain, would have trusted his judgment. He felt their condescending gazes and seethed under them, for he knew his children. *He* was their father, and his authority was not to be trifled with.

"No one asked you," he snapped at Violet. Then, turning a fierce gaze back on Mary, said, "I will take my own daughter riding today."

Mary stammered then said, "You don't see her balance. I mean, she does not seem to balance like other girls her age..."

"She can't speak! She can't balance..." Jefferson thundered, his eyes flaring. His broad jaw twitched beneath his beard. He stood to his full height and towered over them. "What else *can't* she do? What else do you think is wrong with *my* daughter? Go on, tell me! No, I'll tell you what's wrong with her. She's cooped up in the house all the time with you two, who coddle her and won't let her do anything for herself—"

"Now, hold on a second," Violet tried to interrupt.

"I don't want to hear another word out of either of you. I'm taking her riding, and it's final."

"Perhaps you could take the lead, and I could make sure she—"

"Enough!" He shouted, "I said I will do as I please."

They fell silent, then resumed their breakfast to the sound of the clinking of forks until Maurice interjected, "When will you take me riding?"

"Come along with us," he answered. Maurice, satisfied with the answer, ate his breakfast in eager anticipation, unaware of the tension that hung in the room. He was only happy to be going with his father.

"William, you can stay and work on your lessons today. Maurice can begin when we get back."

"But dad…"

"No arguing," he snapped. And William fell silent, too.

***

Anna's jolly smile spread across her face when Jefferson lifted her tiny body into his strong arms and walked out the door, Maurice following behind. Rusty, always up for an adventure, slipped out behind Maurice before they could shut the door.

Jefferson looked at his baby girl, black curls all clustered around her head, big blue wondering eyes gazing up at him, and he smiled.

Why don't I do this more often? He thought. He lightly pinched her cheek and she giggled, making him laugh.

"You keep an eye on her, while I saddle Nelly," he said to Maurice, handing her down to him. Anna whined and squirmed. She'd been enjoying being in her father's arms. But Maurice did his best to hold her.

"Look, Daddy is getting the horse!" he said, pointing as Jefferson called Nelly in from the pasture. He checked her shoes and saddled her quickly.

I'm her father, he told himself. *They'll not think they can order me around and I'll just tuck my tail between my legs and obey orders. They are in my home, and these are my kids.*

He spoke to himself in this way until Nelly was saddled up. She stood stamping and swooshing flies away with her long, white, tail.

Jefferson smiled at Anna as she squirmed away from Maurice and ran, toddling to him, reaching her arms up. Her thick black hair all clustered around her chubby, round face and her big, round, dark eyes were full of excitement. A feeling of warmth came over him.

"Come here, sweetie," he called, scooping her up into his arms as she wrapped her own little arms around his neck. He pressed his forehead to hers and said, "You are Daddy's little girl, aren't you?" She giggled.

"You want to ride a horse?"

Chapter Nine

Violet and Mary paced and tried to keep up the small talk after Jefferson headed out the door with Anna in tow, but an unnerving feeling bubbled up in Mary and refused to leave her alone.

"I'm going after him," Mary said. "I've got to talk some sense into him."

"He said not to…"

"I don't care," snapped Mary. Then, turning to William, she said, "finish that page of arithmetic and then you can join us." She fastened her bonnet and closed the door quietly behind her.

She began to pick up pace as she made her way to the stables and arena. First she walked, then broke into a trot, and then a long-strided run. Something was driving her to go faster, and she heeded that push.

She had just rounded the bend, and saw Anna on Nelly, their oldest mare. *At least he hasn't been a total fool and gone and put her on Ajax.* She said to herself indignantly. Having them in sight, she slowed to a brisk walk.

"Hey! Wait up!" She heard. She turned to see William following her against her orders.

"I told you to finish your arithmetic," she shouted. Then she turned and picked up her pace toward Jefferson.

Mary could just make out the figure of Anna, tiny and perched atop Nelly like a bird.

When she was no more than twenty feet away, Jefferson looked up and, noticing Mary, turned his gaze to her. By unfortunate coincidence, Nelly was spooked by something at the exact moment when Jefferson had turned his attention to the advancing figures of Mary and William.

Mary watched in horror as Nelly sprung forward, and Anna toppled to the ground. Jefferson reached out his arms to catch her, but he was moments too late.

Mary broke into a full sprint, William running behind her. She could hear Anna's wails growing louder with every step.

Anna held her leg and screamed in such pain that Mary thought her heart would break. She turned helpless eyes up to Jefferson, but the moment her gaze settled on his face, anger burned within her, for she had *told* him she was too young. She had begged him not to take her.

You brute of a man, she thought. She wanted to say something, *anything,* but the words were stifled by her fury.

She turned glaring eyes on him, and he looked away, ashamed. This infuriated her all the more.

You should have backed down before it was too late, she thought, and the images of what *could* have happened flashed before her mind until she was blind with rage. In one, thoughtless instant she lifted a shaking hand and slapped Jefferson hard across the face. He seemed stunned, but did not respond.

"I told you!" She shouted through tears, her voice shaking. "You never *listen.* Well, look where that got you!" She knew her words cut deep by the look of shame and horror that crossed Jefferson's face. She might have even felt sorry for him under different circumstances. She scooped up Anna in her arms just as William caught up to her, panting for breath.

"What.... happened?" He asked.

"Take a horse, and run for doc Blanks," Mary commanded. When he did not move, she shouted, "Go! Hurry!" and she began to carry Anna back to the house.

Jefferson came up silently behind her.

"She's heavy. Please, let me," he said, reaching his strong arms out for Anna. Mary scowled, but he was right. She was breathless and her arms were aching. She handed Anna over into her father's strong arms.

As they made their way up the winding gravel road, Mary stole curious glances at Jefferson. One cheek was bright red above the line of his beard, and Mary began to feel a deep sense of regret.

What on earth came over me? She wondered. She'd never done anything of the sort before, and though she was primarily concerned with Anna, who still wailed and held on to one leg, she could not help but wonder what Jefferson would do once things settled down.

He's not the sort of man to put up with being slapped, she thought. *Would he turn out his own wife? Perhaps he has that right.* She wished more than anything that she could go back in time and control her anger or fight harder against his taking Anna at all. But it was too late. Anna wailed and held her leg. Jefferson's cheek grew redder by the minute, and Mary's heart sank with fear and regret for both herself and little Anna.

***

"Well, it's just a sprain, but a bad one," Doctor Blanks said after he'd examined and wrapped Anna's ankle and rewarded her with a stick of peppermint. She sat now, licking it, and paying no attention whatsoever to her ankle.

"The good thing about little ones is they're quite bendy, and they heal up right quick. I wouldn't let her walk on it for several days at least, though. I'll come next week to check on it. Until then, you'll have to make sure she doesn't try to stand on it. That's going to be the trickiest part with a little one like this. She isn't going to understand why she isn't allowed to do all the things she used to do. Soon, she'll be able to get around on crutches, but until then..."

"I'll make sure," said Mary. "I'll keep her entertained and won't let her stand on it."

"I'm sure you'll do a fine job," said Dr. Blanks.

William sat on Jefferson's chair across the room, scowling at Mary as Dr. Blanks talked. Violet, who was standing quietly behind the chair William occupied, spoke up, "I'll be here, too. Whatever you need. We'll work together."

William turned a furious gaze on Violet and said, "We don't need *her* help. You and I can take care of things, just like we used to."

"Hush and don't be ridiculous," said Violet. "I have no mind to do this without Mary's help, and anyway, why shouldn't she? She's here, after all."

Mary smiled at Violet gratefully, but William only retorted, "We wouldn't even *be* in this situation if it weren't..."

"You keep your mouth shut, son," Jefferson's low deep voice reverberated throughout the room. William did hush up, but he did not stop casting angry, sidelong glances toward Mary.

He thinks it wouldn't have happened if I hadn't called out to Jefferson, Mary deciphered. The same thought had crossed her mind. Even though she blamed Jefferson for having taken her in the first place, the moment of the fall flashed through her mind. Jefferson had turned to see Mary, coming after him, and that's when it had happened. Mary knew William had seen this, too.

Dr. Blank walked over to where Violet stood, took her hand and pressed it to his cheek.

"I'll be back as soon as I can, my dear. I have quite a few appointments this week, or I would stay longer with you. I'll miss taking you along to see my patients, but you'll be needed more around here these next couple of weeks."

"We'll be okay, here," she answered. "You worry about your other patients. I hear poor old Mrs. Halsworth has a nasty cough."

"Well, I don't know if there's much I can do about that, but I have three babies due any day now, and the midwives are concerned they'll need me for at least one of them." He pecked her on the cheek and slipped out the door. Jefferson quietly followed.

"Jefferson?" Violet called after him, but he either ignored her or did not hear her.

Anna, exhausted, had fallen asleep with her fist tightly gripping the peppermint stick, several strands of black hair stuck to her sticky face.

"I'll make her a bed here by the fire," Violet said, "And we'll take turns sleeping out here. It will be closer to the kitchen. That way, if she wakes up in her bed, we can catch her before she tries to stand up."

"Good idea," said Mary. "I'll get her cleaned up while you make up a bed."

***

Later that night, Mary and Violet sat by a crackling fire; it was an oddly cold night for a Georgia summer. Anna lay, still asleep, on a makeshift cot near their feet.

"She sure slept a lot today," Mary noted.

"Pain can take a lot of energy," Violet replied. They sat silently, looking at her, both thinking how very narrowly they had avoided tragedy.

"Violet," Mary said after a long pause. "I...I slapped him," she confided.

"Who?" Violet asked.

"Jefferson. I slapped him. I...I don't know what came over me. I was shaking all over. I couldn't speak. I just...I slapped him."

"He probably deserved it," Violet chuckled, "my brother can be stubborn as a mule." Violet's light-hearted response did not comfort Mary. She still felt certain that the repercussions were still looming.

"What do you think he'll *do*?" Mary asked, her earnest eyes searching Violet's face for an answer.

"Do?" Violet responded. "Nothing, I suppose. He's not going to slap you back, if that's what you're thinking. He's never raised a finger to anyone."

"No, not that. I just.... I wondered if he might turn me out."

Violet paused and seemed to be thinking about that for a moment.

"No, I don't think so," she said slowly. Then, more definitively, "No, not a chance. He may not know what to do with you, but you're his wife now. He protects his own— always has. No, he wouldn't turn you out. I don't know how he'll respond to that, but I don't think you need to worry that your home is at risk. This is where you belong now. Anyway, I would never hear of such a thing, and he'd do anything for me."

Mary sighed in relief. In that sigh, her fear left, but regret grew. She felt a deep sense of guilt at having laid a hand on him—big and strong though he was. She believed Violet, that for all his grunting and sharp words, he never would lay a hand on another human being. But she had, and the guilt of it rested heavily upon her shoulders, for she didn't know how to make amends, or even how to apologize.

Even though Violet reassured her that Jefferson would never turn her out, Mary felt that she could not rest until she had made a proper apology.

I was so far out of line, she thought, *but I can ask for forgiveness. I must apologize as soon as the opportunity arises.*

"Can we talk about happier things for a while?" Violet asked, interrupting Mary's thoughts.

"Most assuredly," Mary answered.

"Come on," said Violet, "The children are asleep. Let's take a walk in the garden."

Arm in arm, they walked in the garden. Though it was dark, the full moon provided enough light by which to walk, and they admired the produce. Mary's eyes scanned the vast fields, rows of corn, and pastures. In the moonlight, she could just barely make out brown and white cattle dotting the fields in the distance, grazing leisurely without a care in the world.

"Do you think you might be interested in helping me plan my wedding?" Violet asked, with eager anticipation in her voice.

"Oh, yes!" Said Mary excitedly, turning her attention from the cattle back to Violet.

"I know it's a lot to ask. We hardly know each other, and you've just arrived. Since Rosie died, I haven't had much time to develop friendships with any of the women from town. Rosie was my best friend, and now my life is consumed here. I've tried to plan, but I don't have anyone to talk to about it."

"I'm happy to. It'll give me something to look forward to." They had reached the edge of the garden and continued around the perimeter of the yard as the sun slowly sunk toward the horizon.

"Oh, thank you, Mary. This means so much to me," Violet said, clasping her hands to her chest.

Mary smiled. "Tell me about your fiancé. I've met him only briefly."

"Rupert is the happiest man I have ever met." Violet's expression, which had been light as she spoke of the wedding, darkened slightly. "I've had a difficult life. Our parents died when I was young...oh, but you don't need to hear my life's story. Rupert brings a happiness to this somber soul. He's made me feel lighter and more hopeful since the day I met him."

Mary felt honored to be invited into such a beautiful story. Her own marriage had not turned out to be as romantic as she'd once hoped, but she could find delight in the romance of Violet's life. She had already come to like Violet very much, and was happy to be a part of her wedding.

"How long have you been engaged?" Mary asked earnestly.

"For over a year," Violet replied, and Mary's jaw dropped. She'd never heard of anyone being engaged for so long without being married.

"My mother disdained long engagements," Mary said, "'Too much time for impropriety to brew,' she used to say."

Violet burst into laughter. "Your mother had a point. It has been quite strenuous, being engaged so long and not having a wedding date set."

"Why not just set a date then?" Mary asked. Violet's face brightened.

"I can now, thanks to you."

"Thanks to *me*?" Mary asked, astonished.

"Yes. It's why I wrote the ad in the first place. It was very selfish, I know, but I was getting tired of waiting, and ready to be married. And poor Rupert has waited patiently all this time, wanting to be married but respecting my wishes. I couldn't marry Rupert and be the wife he deserves if I was still needed here. I didn't want to think of what would happen to Jefferson and the children if I just abandoned them. It will be hard enough as it is to leave them, but to leave them with no one to fill in my place—well, that was simply unthinkable.

"Jefferson wouldn't think of looking for a wife, and this is such a small town, with miles of farmland between neighbors; all the women for miles around are already married, or else too young. I knew Jefferson needed a woman who had lived some, who had been through some things just like he has. That's why when I got your response and heard about your parents, I thought you would be perfect for each other."

"Well, I understand why you might have thought so, though I do not believe I am perfect for him. In fact, I have come to believe I am quite irksome to him."

"Oh, don't be silly. You are no more irksome than anyone else. *He's* simply irritable, and that has absolutely nothing to do with you." Mary only shrugged her shoulders, not at all reassured.

Violet continued, "Mary, I know I should have been honest with you and with Jefferson, but I was desperate. I felt trapped. Rupert and I are in love, but I was about to set him free to find another woman who could truly be his wife. Just when I was about to break off the engagement, I thought of the ad. When I got your response... well, I just began dreaming... I'm sorry, Mary. Have I ruined your future happiness to secure my own?" She asked this in such earnest, with dark, sorrowful eyes that Mary's heart went to her.

She leaned across the sofa and took Violet's hands into her own.

"No," she said firmly. "You did no such thing. If anything could be blamed for ruining my happiness, it would have been my father's mishandling of money, but not you. No. I am quite determined to be happy, come what may. You saved me from a man who most certainly would have made me unhappy. Jefferson may be unpleasant...but this man...you didn't see the look in his eyes. He has a mean streak a mile wide. And he wanted me for a wife. My father owed him a large sum and...apparently promised this man that I would be his wife."

Now it was Violet's turn to be surprised,

"You never said anything about another man..."

"Of course I didn't. He's of no concern now. I've eluded him."

"What was he like?"

"He's not someone I wish to remember, so let's not talk about him."

"But your father...why would he...?"

"Thought it would ensure my future, I guess. My father was a good man, don't get me wrong. He was. He was so full of life. Everyone wanted to be around him. He saw the good in everybody. The problem was, he never saw any bad even if it was there.

"Now my mother," she said, a look of pleasant reminiscing coming over her face, "My mother had a discerning eye. She always knew if someone was trying to pull the wool over her eyes. I never got away with even the whitest lie with her. Father, I could have fooled him all day; he'd always see the best anyway. I'd bet anything my mother knew nothing of the arrangement, and my father thought he'd done a right good thing."

Violet looked at her with sympathetic eyes that seemed to see right through to her soul.

"Sounds like they were quite the match, your parents," said Violet. "They'd have been proud. Watching you pick up and put a life together for yourself," said Violet. "They'd have been glad to watch you rise up out of the pain to smile again."

Mary nodded and smiled thoughtfully.

"You know," Violet continued, "I think Rose would have wanted Jefferson to grieve her loss and then live, just like you're doing. He's grieving in his own way, I guess, but mostly he's withdrawn. The night you got here was the first time he ever cried with me." She paused. "I miss her, too. She was my best friend."

"What was she like?"

"Rose...she was soft, kind, and gentle. When you were with her, you were home. Everything about her was so gentle and approachable. Even her laugh was soft."

"She sounds absolutely lovely," said Mary, and then thought, *It's everything I'm not. No wonder he can't love me.*

Mary was acutely aware of her own self-centeredness. She had asked about Rose, and then could only think of her in contrast to her own self. She could hardly help it. Violet's description of Rose stood in stark contrast to herself, and it was not lost on Mary that Jefferson had chosen Rose, while she herself was thrust upon him.

"I can't believe I get to live here," she said.

"It's beautiful, isn't it?" Violet asked. "I forget sometimes how lucky I am to live out here."

"I think this is the first time I've seen the cattle," Mary said.

"They've been in the far fields. They just moved them into the near field today. The far field is all grazed over. Greg and Jack...have you met them? They're our most trusted hands."

"No, I don't believe I have. It's about time I get to know some of the workers, though. I think I'll ask Jefferson if he can take me out to tour the fields."

"I think he would love that."

They walked on, arm in arm like old friends. A large cloud moved over the moon, casting them into complete darkness.

"We better go on in," said Violet.

They walked toward the house, and the moon shone so bright that Mary could see the white pillars gleaming on the porch.

The reddish-brown bricks of the building could be seen in the dim light, and Mary thought, again, that the home was both quaint and beautiful, but the landscape itself was what took her breath away. The home, nestled between the green hills, had a backdrop of sloping hills, spotted with cattle and patchy grass where they had grazed. Beyond that, the fields and rows of corn reached to the horizon.

Chapter Ten

Mary woke early that morning and went out to collect the eggs from the henhouse while Violet slept next to Anna. The cold dew brushed her ankles, and soft orange light rose to touch the horizon over red and gold lined fields. She stopped for a moment and breathed in the fresh morning air.

I thought I loved Texas, she thought, *but Georgia...this is truly God's country. The red earth, the lush ground, the lingering scent of peaches and apples that hangs in the air after a rain.*

In that moment, she thought she might come to love the red Georgia soil even more than she'd loved the dusty brown Texas earth.

She ducked her head into the chicken coop, despite chickens who eyed her with antagonism. She waved them off and grabbed a hold of one warm, brown, egg after another. She didn't much mind the Dominique chickens. Their black and white feathers were beautiful, and they never jabbed or pecked at her when she reached in for the eggs. It was the Old English Game chickens she could hardly stand. They were by far the most beautiful chickens in the coop, with their purple, green, red, and white feathers glistening in the sun.

It's as if they know they are beautiful, Mary thought. *They think they run this place!* She reached in for another egg as one of the Old English Game chickens ran toward her aggressively, clucking and jerking its head back and forth. She pulled her arm out of the coop just in time.

She wished they could keep just the Dominique breed. They were far better egg layers. She got about five or six beautiful brown, blue, and white eggs from each Dominique chicken every time she went to collect. The Old English Game chickens laid only one or two small, white eggs per day.

She knew they were better eating chickens, though, and when the rooster would breed with them, they'd have cute little fluffy chicks they'd raise for a year before having plenty of chicken to eat. She could see why they kept both. So, she gathered her courage and ducked her head into the coop one last time to make sure she hadn't missed any eggs. She just barely missed being pecked in the face, but she did successfully gather all the eggs.

Excellent, enough for everyone's breakfast and my pie crust, she thought as she placed eleven fresh eggs into her basket.

Violet was tending to Anna, and the boys had both started on their literature lesson, so Mary decided to work on the apple pie. The apple tree in the backyard was ripe with tart apples, and she wanted to make use of them; they were falling faster than they could eat them.

She was kneading the pie crust dough when she heard the door open and heavy steps. She turned to find Jefferson.

"Boys, can you give us a minute?" He asked. Happy to dessert their lesson, they dashed out without question.

Oh, boy. Here it goes, she thought. *He's going to reprimand me for slapping him. I'll take it the best I can; I deserve it, after all. I only hope he will accept my apology.*

"Mary," he said, his voice softer than she was expecting. She turned, wiping the dough from her fingers. "Mary," he repeated, then continued, "I'm so sorry. I wanted to take Anna out riding because I had been feeling that I was neglecting her. They remind me so much of Rose. William is basically my younger self. I connect with him so easily. Maurice will insert himself easily into any conversation. I felt I'd been ignoring Anna. I thought if I took her out and taught her to ride, it would be...oh I don't *know*...something I could do with her.

"And then, when you and Violet told me you thought I'd better not...I just felt so...like I wasn't their father anymore. I *needed* to be their father again. I didn't think anyone should tell me what to do with my own kids, so I couldn't see that what you were saying made sense. Anyway, I just want to tell you that I am so sorry."

Mary stood, stunned. Of all the things he could have said, she was not expecting *that*. Now was her chance to get the guilt off her chest.

"Oh, Jefferson, *I* am sorry. You must have already felt terrible, and the way I...the way I slapped you like that..."

"I deserved it," Jefferson chuckled. "Anyway, I saw how much you care about my little Anna, and you've only known her for a short time. You've already taken her into your heart, haven't you?"

Mary smiled, acknowledging that what he said was true. "From the moment I laid eyes on her."

"You are so open, so full of hope and life...even after losing everyone and everything you ever knew. I admire you, Mary Margaret. I really do."

Mary felt herself blush. Here was this man, whose approval she had never hoped to gain, telling her that he admired her. Here was a man who she had thought was proud and arrogant and boisterous, apologizing to her in humble repentance. She hardly knew what to say or think.

Thankfully, he changed the subject.

"Maurice mentioned that he saw Tom Sawyer in your collection. I was hoping I might get my hands on it."

"Why, yes, of course. Father gave me a first edition for my birthday when it was first published. I loved it instantly."

"Yes, it's made quite a ripple, hasn't it? I've wanted to read it since it first came out."

"You're more than welcome to it. I'll go get it for you now." She wiped her hands again and mounted the stairs, two at a time, heart beating fast. Was it the physical exertion of climbing the stairs? No, she did that every day. Why was she feeling this way? Her heart was pounding, her face flushed, her hands shaking as she pulled the title from the shelf.

She composed herself and descended the stairway with an air of calm masking her fluttering heart.

"Here you are," she said.

"Thank you," he said, slightly bowing his head to her and turning to go.

"Wait. Jefferson?" The words seemed to tumble out of her mouth before she could stop them.

"Yes?"

"There's so much about the book I never got a chance to discuss with anyone. It's so full of ideas. Maybe we could talk about it?"

"I'll let you know when I'm finished with it," he said, his white smile splitting his beard, his blue eyes glistening. "Let's wait 'til then. I wouldn't want you giving away the ending," he said.

"Sure," she said, but laughed to herself, thinking how disappointed he probably would be in an ending that didn't seem an ending at all, and then they would talk about *that*.

She could hardly wait for him to finish it. She had been alone with her books and ideas for so long. She loved conversing with Violet, but she wasn't much into literature, and they hadn't found anything they'd both read and wanted to talk about. Mary was often left alone with her thoughts, and she was eager to have someone push back on them and validate them. Of all people, she never imagined that Jefferson would be the one to want to read and discuss with her.

Well, she thought, *he is my husband after all, and I am grateful we can connect on literature, if nothing else.*

"Come to think of it, I don't have to get straight out to the fields. My workers can cover things for a while. I have a little time. Come with me." Mary followed him out of the kitchen and through the living room, past the entryway, and to a door. It was a room she knew existed, but had never been in. Jefferson swung open the door, and she stepped into a room with bookcases from ceiling to floor.

"Was this Rose's library?" she asked, mouth agape.

"This is my library. A few are Rose's, but she never did enjoy books the way I did." Mesmerized, she ran her hand gently along the edges of the books.

"Maurice said he hardly had any books to read," she said as she perused the titles.

"He's not so interested in these," Jefferson laughed. Someday, maybe. These are the writings of Thomas Paine and collections of William Wordsworth poems..."

"Ohhh...." She gasped, interrupting, "my favorite poet."

"Is he?" He asked excitedly.

"Oh, yes, so very often I have recited 'We Are Seven' in my head after..."

"I read that poem when I lost my Rose, too, and when we lost our baby..."

"It is somehow comforting and uplifting at once, not like someone who *tries* to lift your spirits when you've lost someone dear, but someone who just *does*."

"I know exactly what you mean. I think of Anna when he says of the little girl that 'her hair was thick with many a curl that clustered about her head'"

"Oh, yes, most certainly, that describes Anna well."

"But when he said that she had 'a rustic woodland air', that reminds me of you. You have life in your eyes, Mary." He took a step toward her, and she stood still. She was surprised to find that she wanted him to take another step, to take her by the hand.

But he stopped, took a step back, placed the Tom Sawyer book on an end table next to a chair, and said, "You're welcome to borrow any of these at any time. Just help yourself."

"Thank you," she said, and her voice did not sound like her own. He walked past her, his hand brushing hers lightly. A chill went through her, and then she felt warm all over.

He is my husband, she said to herself. *He is mine, already.* She had only ever felt this way one other time, and she was but a schoolgirl, fancying herself in love with an older boy who did not notice her.

This was something different, and yet the same. He was hers by law, and yet she had never hoped to have his heart. What's more, she'd never imagined that he would have hers.

***

Over the next few days, Mary found herself hoping to catch Jefferson's eye, moving to be closer to him, brushing his hand as she walked past him. She felt a heightened sense of awareness of his presence, and when his eyes were on her, her cheeks burned. At times, she felt the condescending gaze of William during these moments, as if he was saying, "I'm on to you, and I do not approve."

In spite of this, Rusty had taken to William as his own. Every time William grabbed his fishing pole, Rusty started wagging his tail and spinning circles by the front door. He was too big now to sit in William's lap, but he nearly always laid at his feet under the kitchen table during meals. He even slept at the foot of William's bed. Rusty had clearly decided that he was William's dog.

Even though Rusty had been a gift to Mary from her father, she did not begrudge this. In fact, she felt that Rusty's taking to William was meant to be. She recognized almost at once that William did not want *her* around. However, he did want Rusty around. He began training him the moment he realized Rusty had been following him everywhere he went.

William had just begun training Rusty to recognize the scent of blood. He'd gotten a bow and arrow for his birthday, and he said he planned on getting a deer this year and he might need Rusty to trail blood.

"That's what bloodhounds are for, anyway," he had said. Mary told him he was free to do whatever he liked with Rusty, as Rusty seemed to prefer him to anyone else. William liked this, despite himself, and took to training Rusty to trail deer. The neighbor two farms away had gotten a deer, and he let William have a leg. William tied it to a string and let Rusty sniff it.

"Would you look at that?" William said excitedly to Violet. "He's just going nuts over it. He'll make a good blood dog. I just know it." Then, he asked Violet to keep Rusty in the kitchen while he dragged the leg all around the yard and hid it in a bush.

"All right, Aunt Violet, let him loose!" William called. Rusty dashed out the front door, frantically sniffing all over the yard. William kept count by tapping his foot rhythmically.

Rusty pulled the leg out of the bush. "Thirty seconds!" yelled William. "He's a natural!" Mary had watched this whole scene from the window, unbeknownst to William. She came to the doorway.

"Good work, William. You really have a knack for training." William, who was usually standoffish with Mary, could not help but revel in this compliment.

"Well, it ain't hard when you've got a dog as smart as Rusty," he said, patting Rusty on the head.

Mary knew that William didn't accept her, but he did accept Rusty, and that was good enough for now.

Maurice sat on the porch reading Tom Sawyer aloud to Anna, though she couldn't understand it.

I wonder if I could write something for Anna to read, Mary thought. She turned her attention back to William. Rusty was eager to be trained and eating up the attention. She realized that these children had her heart, and it certainly hadn't taken long. She knew Maurice and Anna accepted her, but William was taking his time.

Time, Mary told herself, thinking of her own mother, *It will take time.*

The children were occupied for the moment, so she went up to her desk and sat down to write down some ideas for a book Anna might connect with.

She'd noticed that although Anna remained silent most of the time, she seemed interested in the animals around the farm. She would point and smile whenever she saw a rabbit in the garden, and she wanted to pet the baby calves when they were born. She jotted down a few ideas, set it aside, and went in to make dinner.

Maurice came into the kitchen while she cooked.

"Hi Mary!" he said cheerfully. "Can I help?"

"You sure can! Here, mix up this bread dough and add flour until it isn't sticky, then knead with your hands. Are they clean?"

Maurice looked down at his hands.

"I've been fishing," he said. Mary laughed and gestured toward the porcelain basin.

"I've just brought fresh water, and there's a bar of lye soap next to the basin."

Maurice scrubbed his hands for a while before coming back over to help with the bread.

"Mother used to make bread," he said.

"I bet it was delicious," Mary answered.

"It was," he said matter-of-factly as he added a handful of flour to the mixture.

"How do you like Tom Sawyer?" Marry asked.

"I think he's funny," Maurice answered. "I'm right to the part where they decide to go to their own funeral! I can't believe they just let everyone worry about them for so long!" Mary laughed.

"What would you have done?" She asked. "If you'd heard they were going to have a funeral for you and only you and your friends knew you were actually alive?"

Maurice thought about that for a while.

"It'd be kind of mean to let you all cry and be sad for a few more days," he said. "But I would like to see how much everyone said about me. But see, Tom must not have had anyone he loved die. If he did, he couldn't have done it, you know?"

Mary knew what he was getting at, and thought he was wise beyond his years. Grief and loss had a way of doing that.

"I remember how it felt when Mama died," Maurice went on. "How it still feels," he added. "And I couldn't let someone feel that way just so I could surprise them at my own funeral. But I don't blame Tom, you know? From the way he talks about it, it's like he just doesn't know. He doesn't know what it feels like for someone he loves to die, so he thought it would be a fun prank to surprise everyone. And maybe Tom didn't really know if people loved him. Maybe he thought he'd go hear his own funeral just to make sure."

"Ahh, Maurice, you are too insightful for a nine-year-old, you know that?" Maurice blushed.

"I just love reading."

"Good books have a way of giving words to how you feel," Mary said, sensing she understood what Maurice was feeling as he read Tom Sawyer. She'd felt the same thing, only she wished she'd had the chance to read the book as a child. As it had come out only recently, she'd read it as an adult, and she envied the children who would get to read that book with the heart and mind of a child. Talking to Maurice about it was like getting to experience that second-hand. She loved his innocent insight, which seemed wise beyond his years, and yet somehow still fresh and young.

Chapter Eleven

The sun beat down on Jefferson's broad back as he and his men gathered the last of the harvest. Thankfully, the first few crops had been gathered in time, and this last one looked like it would be too. And it was a good year. There would be plenty of grain to feed the animals, plenty of sweet corn to eat and store, and even more to sell and use the proceeds to pay his men well and grow the farm. He might even have enough extra to help Violet with some wedding expenses.

His thoughts turned to Mary.

She never uttered a word about our own wedding being small and hurried, he thought. *Perhaps, one day, I'll take her on a honeymoon. We'll go up north—up the Mississippi River— and talk about Tom Sawyer.*

He thought of her green eyes often these days. They seemed to be inviting him. *She's my wife,* he often thought in amazement. And yet, he'd never been to her room.

What would she do if I came to her room tonight? He thought. But he'd had this thought before, and always, he'd been too filled with apprehension. Once, he even walked halfway down the hallway toward her room before he stopped and turned back around.

At last, he could admit that he was attracted to her. He had noticed her beauty objectively on the night she arrived, but it was not her beauty alone that drew him in. It was the happiness in her eyes, which seemed more than surface deep—eyes that had seen pain, eyes that had cried, eyes that had chosen to laugh again.

Her smile, her dimples, her freckles, her laugh—it was all contagious. Life flowed out of her and touched everyone in

117

her path. It was a quality that Jefferson utterly lacked. He had come to find comfort in the joy that Mary brought to his home. He had found that he could look into her eyes and feel understood.

"Dad?" A voice broke into his thoughts.

"William! What's the day's catch look like?" William only shook his head. Rusty played at his feet and tugged at his pant leg.

"Not fishing today," he said.

"Oh?"

"Dad...I don't think this is working out."

Jefferson shoved the end of his sickle into the ground, leaned his arms on it, and stared hard at his son. Finally, he said, "What's not working, son?" William shuffled his feet, prompting Rusty to come after his pant leg again. William nudged him away gently with his foot and said,

"Mary."

"Mary?" Jefferson questioned.

"I don't think it's working out with her here."

Jefferson looked at William harder through squinting eyes.

"She's my wife, William. This is her home. Sending her away might have been an option before we were married, but it's far too late for that."

"So, you made your bed, now we all have to lay in it, huh?"

Jefferson was taken aback by his son's cheek. He'd known him to clap back a time or two, but William said these words in such a vicious tone and with such resentment in his eyes that it caught Jefferson quite off guard.

"Look, son, I know you miss your mother,"

"Your wife," William interjected.

"My late wife."

"That's right. Mary is your wife now, isn't she?" William asked, the scorn heavy in his tone.

"She is."

"She might be your new wife, but she's never going to be our new mother."

"William, no one is trying to replace your mom,"

"You did."

"I did not replace..."

"You said it yourself!" William shouted, "Mom is your *late* wife. Mary is your wife. You replaced her, and you're forcing it on all of us. Did you ever think to ask me what *I* wanted before you went and married her?"

Jefferson tried to maintain composure, but William had struck a nerve—a nerve he had every intention of striking. Rose. His *late* wife. Mary. His *current* wife.

"Son," he said, stiffening, "I've told you that I will never replace your mother. She has my heart forever. You must trust me when I tell you that. As for you, I can't force you to open your heart to Mary. A heart can no more be forced than a feral cat. Your heart will open in your own time if you choose. I can't make it, but I will expect you to respect her."

"I want her out of here. I can't bear to see her face every day. I can't stand to see you with her."

Jefferson felt a twinge of guilt at this. He had become more enamored with Mary over the past week, and he had suspected that William noticed. Now, he knew for sure. He had been concerned about how William would feel if he should notice. In some ways, it felt like a lifetime ago when Rose was with them. In other ways, it felt like only yesterday.

He often felt himself being pulled back and forth between two desires. In some ways, he wanted to move on. He wanted to live and to move forward in life with Mary, whom he was, he finally admitted to himself, beginning to love. In other ways, he felt like moving on was leaving Rose behind. If life remained just exactly as it was when Rose died, he would feel closer to her. However, if he gave his heart to Mary, he would feel that he was indeed leaving Rose behind.

It was a long while before he answered William. William just stood there, scratching Rusty behind the ears and looking at his father accusingly. Finally, Jefferson said.

"I can no more send away my own wife than abandon my children. My family is mine alone to provide for and protect. I'll guard her as much as I guarded you, your siblings, and my sweet Rose. There's no more to be said on that matter."

"She's got no right to be in this family. Send her away. You can get me my own dog," William retorted.

"She has every right," Jefferson said firmly.

"I hate the way you look at her," he blurted out, and then looked up at his father in trepidation, as if he had never meant for those words to escape his mouth.

"The way I look at her?"

William shrugged his shoulders.

"Like you used to look at mom," he answered, and his voice cracked as he struggled to fight back tears.

"Oh, son. Come here," Jefferson pulled William to himself, holding his head with one hand, and letting the young man cry into his chest just like he had when he was a little boy and scraped his knee.

"I still don't like her," William said after he had cried in his father's arms for a few minutes.

"I know, son. I know."

***

It's not true, Jefferson told himself, *I did not replace her. Rose would have wanted...Rose...She would have wanted me to live.* But despite his self-reassurances, his son's words rang true in his own heart. He felt them as much as William did. Ever since he decided to wed Mary, he had had to fight back feelings of regret and shame. He'd had to fight the notion that he had tried to replace his beloved Rose.

And fight it, he did. He fought those thoughts valiantly until he heard them come out of his son's mouth. Then, when his own thoughts flowed out of his son, they struck his heart like a poisoned arrow. He felt the initial pain of it, and then the poison began to seep into every crevice of his heart.

With a heavy heart, Jefferson made his way behind the house, to his wife's grave.

Rose was buried in her favorite place. About twenty yards behind the rear of the house stood an enormous oak tree. Behind the oak tree, three lilac bushes stood bare, but when they were in full bloom, it was the most beautiful place on the land. Rose had planted the lilac trees because she adored the smell.

Jefferson remembered thinking it was a waste of time to take such good care of the trees which would only bloom for a few short weeks every year. But Rose loved those light purple flowers, and she loved the smell of them. Every year, when they were in bloom, she spent as much time as she could sitting against that oak tree.

Before they had William, she would sit out there for hours with her needlework. When each child was a suckling infant, she'd set out a blanket and sit against that tree feeding the babe. When the children were toddlers, she chased them around it. The child they lost was buried there, between two of the lilac bushes. And a little more than three years ago, he had laid Rose to rest in a grave between the third lilac bush and the giant oak tree. It had been Rose's favorite spot.

"Oh, Rose," he said aloud, as he approached the oak. "How he needs you." Slowly, he got to his knees and ran his hand softly over the ground. The sun was beginning to set, casting the shadows of tree branches on the grass growing over her grave.

Suddenly, he could not comprehend that Rose, his dear, sweet Rose, was lying lifeless and wasting away under the ground beneath him. It could not *be*. Even now, he still expected to hear her soft step and turn around to see her gentle eyes and kind smile. But no, he would never set eyes on that beautiful, sweet face again.

Hot tears fought their way to his eyes and flowed down his dirt-smeared face. He heard a step behind him. It was not the soft, gentle step of Rose. It was the quick step of Mary.

"You miss her." The sound of someone else's voice saying those words, acknowledging his pain, was more than his body could handle and it convulsed in sobs. She placed a small, white hand on the back of his shoulder.

"She must have loved you all greatly. That's why you feel her loss so much. You loved her, and you love her still. It's her love you are missing."

It's true, thought Jefferson. *I miss her love. I miss her touch. I miss her smile. I miss her voice. I can hardly believe that she is lost to me forever.*

And then, because his heart could not contain the pain, he said, "You might think it would get easier, as time goes on, but the longer she's gone, the more I miss her. The more the children grow, the more I'm reminded that she never got to see it."

Mary knelt by him and placed a hand on the ground next to his.

"Tell me about her," she said. Jefferson looked at Mary with a dirty, tear-streaked face, and he smiled.

"She was the gentlest soul you ever met. She smiled whenever I walked into a room, and whenever I was under that smile, I was the man I wanted to be. I became the man she thought I was. And she always thought more of me than was merited. But when I was with her, it was like I could become that person she already thought I was. I know that sounds silly,"

"No, not silly. Not silly at all," Mary said.

There was a long pause, and only the sound of the gentle breeze and Jefferson's labored breathing could be heard to break the silence.

Finally, Mary said, "This is the most beautiful resting place. On the day I arrived, the lilacs were in bloom, and the beautiful smell drifted in through the bedroom window. It gave me hope in one of my darkest moments. I was missing my own parents that night—missing them so deeply—and the smell lifted my spirits."

"Rose always said they smelled like hope," Jefferson said.

"Like hope. I like that. They do smell like hope." They both took a breath in, imagining the flowers in bloom.

"Jefferson," Mary said. "I see how William looks at me. I can only imagine how he must feel. I'm not his mother; he already has a mother. She's right here. And he's afraid if he lets me love him, he will be losing some part of his mother.

"I have no desire to replace Rose. I don't want to make you forget. Lord knows, I don't want to forget my lost loved ones. I want to help you remember. Talk to me of her whenever you feel memories of her. I want to hear. I want to become a part of this family, and that means becoming a part of keeping her alive. When you remember a funny story about her, share it. I will not be offended. I want you and William and Maurice and Violet to say her name to me whenever you please. I'm not here to make you forget. When you tell me about her, I will become a part of helping you remember."

Jefferson noticed a look in Mary's eyes that matched the pain in his own heart. He stayed on his knees. Mary, on her knees beside him, looked into his eyes, and they felt one another's pain.

"I've told you about Rose. Tell me about your parents…if you will," he said. Mary shifted on her knees to face him. He did likewise.

"They were beautiful people. My dad…he was the kind of man everyone wanted to call a friend. He lit up a room. His laugh was so loud and so contagious you couldn't help but laugh with him, even if his jokes didn't make any sense to you." Mary giggled, and Jefferson smiled. Then, he took both her hands in his and peered into her eyes.

"Tell me more," he urged.

"My mother was full of determination and grit. They made their way west before the railway was there, you know. The trip was grueling, but my mother's determination and my father's hopeful spirit got them to Texas. At least that's what they always told me. They farmed and had me. And the small town grew and grew until it needed a mayor. My father was the obvious decision. I grew up well cared for and well known. I could hardly have imagined that my father had accrued such debt to leave me penniless."

"That must have been quite a blow."

"Yes, it was. But it's not how I want to remember my father. He may have been imprudent, but he was the happiest, most hopeful man…"

"It sounds like you're a lot like him," Jefferson said.

"Oh," said Mary, blushing. "I certainly hope so, in some ways, I suppose. But I am like my mother, I believe, too. She had the fortitude of a soldier and the inner strength of an ox. Yet she was kind and gentle, too."

"She sounds lovely."

"Oh, she was…if I can grow into half the woman she was…"

"I've no doubt you already are."

They fell silent, and Jefferson held on to her hands. They felt cold and small in his. But her eyes were warm, and they let him in to see the deepest parts of her soul. And as he looked, he saw her in a way he never had before. And he felt that she saw him, too.

Chapter Twelve

Dark storm clouds formed over the big white house, casting shadows and making it feel like dusk late into the morning. Mary had just finished cleaning up the kitchen after breakfast, and she walked into the living room where everyone sat around the crackling fire, for it was one of those strange late summer days when the storm rolled in so fast and cold that they had to light a fire for warmth.

Violet and Dr. Blanks sat on the loveseat, talking in hushed tones. In the middle of the room in front of the fire, Maurice sat building a tower of blocks with the express purpose of letting Anna knock it down, which she did with enthusiasm. She sat on the floor with one leg still in a brace. She shrieked with laughter each time she punched the blocks with a fat fist and watched the tower come tumbling down.

In the corner of the room, William sat on a chair untangling a fishing line, with Rusty sleeping at his feet. Jefferson sat on his armchair reading Tom Sawyer. All was silent, save for the rolling sound of thunder and Anna's intervals of shrieking laughter.

"Looks like a twister," Jefferson said, looking up as Mary walked into the room. "We won't be getting anything done today."

The children all cheered. It was a rare occasion to have everyone home for a whole day.

"Well, I'm awfully glad I came today, then," Dr. Blanks chimed in with his usual chipper voice. "Would have been a shame to be shut in alone today." He smiled at Violet and the two resumed their private conversation.

Mary smiled at them. They truly were a perfect match. Violet had a warm heart and a big soul, with dark, somber eyes, while Rupert had a light step to match his light-hearted personality. He smiled often, and his hair, which he said was too long, curled up in blond waves about his forehead. Mary wondered how a man with such a harrowing profession could maintain such a light manner.

Perhaps his light heart makes it possible for him to bear to look on the pain of others and still see the good in the world, she thought as she observed him running a strand of Violet's long black hair lightly through his fingers. She would have pondered this longer, but Jefferson interrupted her thoughts.

"Well, I've finished Tom Sawyer," he said as he closed the book and handed it back to her.

"Oh? And what did you think?" she asked.

"I don't think I'll forget that book, and neither will anyone else who reads it."

"I thought the very same thing. An instant classic. I told my father that when I first read it. I couldn't tear my eyes away."

"The way the author gets into the mind of a young boy is quite amazing, actually. I hardly remembered my own boyhood, and yet when I opened the pages, I found I could remember thinking in just the same way. Oh, it was all about glory and attention. The way he glories in the idea of showing up at his own funeral without a care in the world for his mourning family! If that isn't just how a boy would think."

"I never thought of that," Mary confessed. "Though I never was a little boy."

"What moved you most?" Jefferson asked. "There must have been a reason you loved it so,"

"Oh, yes. There were so many things. I laughed out loud through most of it, I remember that. But really when Tom decided to tell the truth, even though it put his own life in danger and even though he was breaking a promise to a friend...well...when I read that, I said to myself that I would be like Tom Sawyer. If it ever came down to it, I'd choose to tell the truth too."

Jefferson smiled and said, "That's an interesting point. I thought about that. You know, he thought maybe he was doing the wrong thing by breaking his promise to his friend. He was certainly afraid. But in the end, his conscience won out. That's the thing about kids, too, you know. Their conscience hasn't been so marred by the world yet...they haven't had as much chance to dull it. They still feel it strongly. I think if there's anything the author was trying to say, maybe it's that we could all learn something from the innocence of children."

"Oh certainly!" Mary gushed. "Do you remember how he describes the school at the beginning? The way the adults were behaving in front of the important guests? Doing things they normally would not...like it was all a show. And Tom saw that. He saw that adults are just as silly as kids sometimes. You know I laughed out loud when he was showing off to Becky, but then, everyone was showing off. The adults too. The kids were just smaller versions. But you're right... I think the children were more obvious in their antics, but they were also more innocent, in a way."

"Ahh, that's so perceptive."

At that moment, they both looked up and noticed everyone looking at them. Violet had a glint of elation in her eyes. Rupert's laughing eyes seemed to say, "I know what you two are up to," and William glared at them. Only Maurice and Anna seemed not to notice.

"What?" Jefferson said, sounding irritated.

"Oh, nothing," Rupert said good-humoredly, a look of feigned condescension in his eyes.

"Two people can't discuss a book in this house?" He asked, seeming even more irritated, but Mary only laughed it off.

"Apparently they have nothing interesting of their own to say so they must let themselves in on our conversation," said Mary with an air of feigned haughtiness.

"I don't believe we were welcomed into your private conversation at all," Rupert chimed in. "The two of you seemed rather engrossed."

"As opposed to you and Violet, I suppose," Mary joked. Everyone giggled, Anna and Maurice joining in just to be a part of the laughter. William threw his tangled line and pole to the ground forcefully as he stood up and knocked the chair over as he stormed out of the room. Rusty woke, stretched, and followed him.

"William?" Jefferson called after him, making a motion to get up.

"Can I go talk to him?" Mary asked, putting a hand on his arm. Jefferson nodded and Mary followed William through the entryway and out the door onto the porch.

He was standing in the front yard looking up at the dark clouds as the wind swirled around him. Rusty stood under the shelter of the porch roof, barking at William, but would not leave the porch for fear of the storm.

"It's okay, boy," Mary said soothingly, patting his head as she walked out onto the yard toward William.

"William?" Mary called. She was but ten feet from him, but the wind drowned out her voice and she had to shout. He did not turn around. She approached him.

"William," she said. Compassion filled her voice, and when William turned to face her, she saw that tears were running down his cheeks. "What is it, William?"

"Everyone's happy," he nearly screamed the words, choking them out through tears. "Everyone's happy and no one even cares to remember that tomorrow is the day Ma died. We all celebrated Anna turning three yesterday, and no one mentioned mom. No one cares that she died two days later. Well, I care. I'm not about to sit around and laugh with you all."

Mary's heart ached for him. She missed her own mother, and she could only imagine the breaking heart of nine-year-old William. Old enough to know, but too young to understand. It was the kind of pain a child should never have to endure.

She saw the pain in William's eyes, and she felt that pain, too.

He doesn't know that he will laugh again one day, if he will grieve her, Mary thought.

"William," she said, having to shout above the sound of the wind. "Tomorrow, we celebrate your mother's life, and we mourn her passing. You and your father knew her better than any of us. Tell us about her. What was her favorite flower? Let's pick them. What was her favorite thing to eat? I'll do my best to make it. When this storm passes, we'll gather around by her grave and you can tell us all your favorite memories of her. I wish I had known her. She sounds like the most amazing mother."

William let out a sort of wail, which could be heard about the roaring winds, and he bent over slightly, holding on to his stomach as if he were sick. Mary put a hand on his shoulder, and when he turned and hugged her, she felt a glowing warmth fill her chest.

"Would you like that?" she asked. William looked up at her, nodded his head, and hugged her again. Mary put an arm around him, guiding him back to the house.

Chapter Thirteen

The next day was the kind of calm after a storm that stills your heart. The air felt heavy and still. It had that fresh smell that always comes after a storm, like the old stuffy air had all been wiped away, and new, fresh, air had settled in. Mary breathed in deeply, closing her eyes and soaking it in.

Today was a day to celebrate Rose, but Mary couldn't help but take a few moments to think about her own mother. That strong, determined, graceful woman had always been her rock, and Mary had not realized it until she was gone. Mary could be free and wild because her mother was there, like an anchor, holding her down and making sure that she didn't fly too far off.

Mary could laugh and live, and push the limits, because her mother was there, providing a framework for morality and guiding Mary through life. Without her mother, her anchor, she had felt so lost. And yet, the memory of her mother's words and the story of her life began to work on Mary's mind and heart, anchoring her in so she would not float away. That is how Mary began to see it.

And her father? In the back of her mind, it bothered her greatly that her father had promised her in marriage to Kit. Of course, Kit could have been lying. In fact, he probably *was* lying. And yet, there had still been the debts, confirmed by Mr. Whalen and all the bank records.

Her father had always been her favorite. He was wild, like her. His energy matched hers. She even looked like him. She wanted to do everything with him. He had taught her archery and how to shoot a shotgun and she had shot a deer off the back of a horse because he had taught everything from how to shoot to how to ride, to how to make a deer call.

As a child, she'd always thought her mother was the boring one, always sewing and mending, cooking, cleaning, and bookkeeping. She wanted to be like her father, and she felt that her mother was always getting in the way of her fun. But now...oh now, she felt so differently. She wished her mother was here so she could tell her, show her, how much she loved and appreciated her. How she wished she could tell her how sorry she was for all those times she'd said her mother was ruining her fun.

Because her father—the person she'd loved most in the world, may have promised her in marriage to someone she did not consent to marry. Even if he hadn't, he most certainly had squandered her inheritance. No, now he did not seem so fun. Although she cherished those memories, now she could only see him as irresponsible and foolhardy.

She didn't want to think of him this way, because he was gone and it was confusing to miss him and to be angry at him all at once. When these thoughts came to her mind, she told herself she simply couldn't think about her father. Not now.

Today, she would remember her mother and she would learn about Rose. Today, she would enter *their* pain. She would mourn the loss of their loved one with them. And quietly, she would think of her mother, and let all the memories of her swim into her head and make her cry or laugh and have their way with her. Today was not a day for being strong. Today was a day for feeling.

She had an early start that day. It was just about five in the morning, and she walked around to the east side of the house just in time to watch the blood orange sun creep up to touch the horizon. She breathed in again and the fresh after-rain smell filled her nostrils. The morning air was growing cooler by the day, and she pulled her shawl up and wrapped it more tightly around her.

Mary heard heavy footsteps behind her, but she was too engrossed in the sunset to turn around. She knew Jefferson's step by now—heavy and sure. He came to stand beside her.

"The most beautiful place in the world to watch the sun rise."

"Mmm...." Mary let out a satisfied hum of agreement. She was engrossed in the splendor of the early morning sun touching the dewdrops on the grass and the light fog that drifted across the fields of gold and brown.

"Truly, a piece of paradise," Jefferson continued. "Mary, thank you. Thank you for understanding William, and for taking the time to remember Rose today. William was wrong, of course, to think that I had forgotten. I could never forget how she clung to life for those two days."

"Of course not," said Mary, turning to him and looking up into his somber face. "Of course you could never forget. It is not something one forgets."

"But I haven't been fair to William in these past couple of years," he confessed. "I haven't remembered her this way. Not openly. I've never even cried in front of William. Only in my room, by myself, clinging to her picture. I never gave William the chance to see that I could never forget this day."

"Well," she replied after a short pause, "that can change today."

Then, she felt a large, strong arm around her shoulder. Jefferson squeezed her to himself briefly before letting go. Then, he turned to walk back to the house, and Mary's heart swelled with feelings she could not quite name. Compassion mingled with intensity and morphed into something she had never felt before.

Was this love? She didn't know.

***

By late morning, the sun was warm and bright, but the air still felt fresh and cool. Maurice and William were busy carrying items from the house to the yard. They set out a picnic blanket on the ground near Rose's grave. Maurice arranged a vase full of flowers Mary and William had picked. Mary watched them from a kitchen window as she baked a raspberry rhubarb pie. Jefferson prepared to fry up some walleye William had caught earlier that morning, remembering how Rose had enjoyed a fresh caught fish dinner.

Violet had been in her room, getting ready for the day and waiting for Rupert to arrive. He'd promised to come by over lunch and spend a couple of hours with them. Now, Mary heard her step on the stairway and soon she was in the kitchen.

"Can I help with the pie? I'm afraid I've slept in."

"Not to worry. You are well rested," Mary said, smiling.

"I think it's brave of you to do this."

"Oh, I've made plenty of pies before," Mary joked.

Violet laughed. "You know what I mean," she said. "It's brave of you to ask for this—to remember Rose this way. I'm ashamed to say I was always too scared to. Too scared to even ask William about his mother. I always thought it would be best not to bring her up if someone seemed to be having a good day. But you know, they were probably always thinking of her just the same, just like I was. I think the real problem is that I was afraid to ask myself how I felt. I just miss her so much."

"I know you do," said Mary. "You were a good sister to her. From what Jefferson says, it sounds like the two of you were the dearest of friends."

Violet nodded, tearing up. "Oh, come here," Mary said, quickly placing the pie in the oven and turning to Violet to pull her to herself in an embrace. "You can cry. Go ahead. You loved her, too."

"I've hardly thought about how much *I* missed her," Violet confessed. "I needed to be there for everyone else. They had lost a wife and mother. They needed me to be the strong one—to step in and fill in her roles and take care of everyone. But, yes, I miss her, too. She was my closest friend."

Mary squeezed her more tightly and said, "You did Rose the greatest kindness by caring for her children. You truly are the best friend a woman could have, Violet. But now I am here. I can carry the load with you. And you can be free to feel and to cry." At that, Violet began to let out small sobs as the tears fell.

"She was a wonderful woman," she said after her tears had slowed. "Let's go join the boys outside. I think you'll feel like you knew her after today."

Outside, the boys had spread a beautiful picnic. A vase full of flowers sat at the center. They had placed Anna, still in a leg brace, on one corner of the blanket and Maurice and William took opposite corners, pulling it tightly. Anna laughed as the vase tipped over. The boys were already talking to Rose as they straightened the blanket and tried to keep the vase from tipping. They spoke lovingly to Anna, telling her all about the mother she never knew.

Violet and Mary joined them.

"Here, I'll take this corner," Violet said, stooping to pick up one end of the blanket. Mary scooped up Anna, who was not doing a sufficient job in keeping her end of the blanket straight. Together, they straightened it out, placed the vase and flowers back in the center, and each took a seat.

Shortly, the low voices of men could be heard rounding the corner to the back of the house. Rupert and Jefferson approached with a pan full of freshly fried fish and a stack of tin plates to go around.

"Lunch is served," said Rupert, happily placing the tray of fish down.

"Oh, my pie!" Mary said, jumping up and heading into the kitchen. She returned with a piping hot pie and sat down next to Jefferson.

"Let's pray," Jefferson said. They all took hands and bowed their heads.

"Father in heaven, we thank you for this beautiful day. We thank you for the means to feed ourselves, to survive. We thank you for friendship. We thank you for Rose. We thank you for the time we had with her, for the way her beautiful heart touched and shaped us all. Amen."

"Amen," everyone echoed in unison. The mood was somber, but peaceful, as Rupert passed the fish around.

"I didn't know Rose like the rest of you," Rupert began. "As you know, Violet and I began to show interest in each other after her death. But I knew her in passing, just like I know anyone else in town. I remember seeing her in church. I always thought her reverence was something to behold. Our seats were positioned just so that I could see her and Violet's faces best if I were to scan the room.

"I remember one Sunday, we were singing *Nearer, my God, to Thee*. I was singing the words, but my mind was elsewhere. I happened to scan the room and catch sight of Rose. Tears gathered in the corners of her eyes, and the reverence on her face struck me. I remember realizing at that moment that she had something I was missing in my life. Reverence. I had always treated life so flippantly. And still, I do...at times. But the reverence I saw in Rose's face that day told me that she had something I lacked. Something I wanted. And that began to work on me in some way."

"She was reverent," said Jefferson. "But not pretentious. That was something I found so striking about her when I first met her. Sometimes, when you meet reverent people who love church and read the Bible, you find that they are pretentious. Rose was never so. She never considered herself better than anyone else, no matter who they were. Somehow, she was able to keep a pure heart without ever comparing her own purity to the impurity of others around her. She saw the good in everyone. To be sure, she saw the good in me. She made me want to become the man she thought I was."

"Can we sing that song?" William asked. "I remember mom singing that one to me at night as I fell asleep. And she used to sing *What Wondrous Love is This*."

Their voices rose, shaky at first, but stronger as they raised their voices up.

What Wondrous Love is this, Oh, my soul, oh my soul? What Wondrous Love is this, that caused the lord of bliss to bear the dreadful curse for my soul?

Mary had fully intended to keep her focus on Rose and the others today, but at these words describing Rose, and as the words of the song filled her soul, images of her mother flooded her mind, and she could not help but picture her own mother's face. Every description of Rose only reminded her of her own mother. She began to choke up and could only mouth the final words of the song.

And when from death I'm free, I'll sing on, I'll sing on. And when from death I'm free, I'll sing His love for me.

Chapter Fourteen

"Oh, she's healing up just fine," said Rupert, as he ran his hand firmly up and down Anna's ankle. "It looks like she's ready to put some weight on it."

"That's a relief," Mary said. "She's been impossible to keep still. I have to carry her everywhere or she tries to walk."

Jefferson looked at Mary with eyes full of gratitude. What would he have done without her? She had watched Anna like a hawk, making sure her every need was attended to, picking her up whenever she tried to walk, keeping her spirits up even as her mobility was limited.

Will she ever know how much this means to me? he wondered. She had attended to her as lovingly as Rose would have.

"Does it seem painful when she tries to walk?" Rupert asked.

"A little," Jefferson answered. "She does seem to favor it and lean to one side. I've been working on a set of crutches. They're almost done."

Rupert smiled as he stood, his curly hair bouncing atop his head. "That'll be perfect," Rupert responded. "I bet she will take to those quickly, and she should be able to put more and more weight on it over the next couple weeks until she doesn't need the crutches anymore. She'll know, so when she tosses the crutches aside, let her. I can come check on her to make sure, but she's well on her way to being good as new."

"You are just the best doctor I ever knew," said Violet.

"I believe you've only ever known two," he responded with a glint in his eye.

"No matter," she said, laughing. Then, turning to Mary, she said, "I'm attending Rupert on his visits this week. Now that Anna is on the mend, I assume you'll be okay without me?"

"My schedule is impossibly full this week," said Rupert. "And that's not including any potential emergency visits. It would really help if Violet could attend with me."

"Of course. We'll be just fine," Mary replied. Jefferson thought he noticed disappointment come over her face, or maybe it was sadness. He didn't know. He resolved himself to ask her the next time they were alone.

That opportunity came soon enough. After the kids were in bed, Violet was still attending patients with Rupert, and Jefferson and Mary had the evening to themselves.

When Jefferson came in for the night, his back was aching. He tried to bend down to take off his boots, but a sharp pain shot up his back and into his neck.

"Let me help," Mary said, guiding him over to the couch and crouching down to take his boots off for him. Back pain was no stranger to Jefferson. Rose used to help him with his boots when it got bad, and this gesture of kindness took him by surprise.

"You've cared for the children all day," he said. "Now you care for me."

"You're hurting. I can see that." She was right. His hands ached from hours of sanding as he worked to finish Anna's crutches by the festival on Saturday. His back ached from the extra hours he'd put in working in the fields so he could have a full day off for the festival. Every part of his body was worn down. He had worked until he had nothing left to give, and he could barely drag himself back to the house.

"Rupert says it's my height that's to blame...says he's seen many a tall man suffer from back pain like this."

"You look as if you might collapse. Here, lie down. I will do what I can." She worked rubbing the sore muscles up and down his back.

Jefferson could feel the pain releasing with every firm stroke. Her hands were surprisingly strong, and he felt the stress of the day melt away under them.

"Where did you learn to do this?" he asked.

"My dad taught me how to rub down a horse after a hunt," she said. They both laughed.

"Well, apparently it works on me, too."

In truth, he'd never felt more relaxed in all his life. It was like she had a magic touch that could melt away all his pain and fears.

As he lay there, letting her care for him, his heart ached to be nearer to her. He wanted to tell her all his heart's desires, his pains, his worries, but did she want that? He worked up his courage and spoke.

"Mary, can I ask you something?"

"Of course."

"When Violet said she'd be attending with Rupert this week, you seemed disappointed. Was something wrong?"

"Oh, yes, well, I was a bit disappointed, I suppose. The few days when Violet attended with him just felt so dreadfully long. I love the children. Please don't misunderstand that. It's just when you work so long into the night, I get so lonely for conversation with another adult."

He understood. He'd felt that way before, too. And yet, he was surprised to hear that she craved *his* company. As it was, he had been longing for her company as well. There were so many ideas in his head, and he wanted to talk about them. Somehow, Mary seemed to be able to help him put words to his thoughts.

It made him feel alive when she did that. It was true; when Violet was gone on visits, he came to the house less. He tried to make himself busy in the barn or in the fields, or he would take the boys fishing. He *wanted* to be with Mary, but he had been unsure if she wanted him around, especially when they were alone.

He had not forgotten what she'd said on the day she arrived. That he was the last man in the world she would want to marry. Those words still rang in his ears. The more he felt himself drawn to her, the more he felt the bite of those words. Since then, she'd clearly warmed up to her role as mother, but Jefferson was at a loss as to figuring out how she felt about her role as his *wife*.

Is she trying to ask for my company? He wondered. *Is she saying that she wants me around? Or merely that she wants Violet around?* He decided to take the chance and ask.

"When Violet is away, I will come back to the house earlier if I can. Would you welcome that?" As he said this, he twisted around to get a look at her face. She stopped rubbing his back and smiled.

"I'd like that very much."

***

Saturday morning finally arrived, and everyone was bustling around getting ready for the festival. Mary worked busily at her cherry pie; it was her mother's recipe, which had been renowned in her hometown, and Mary wanted it to

143

be perfect. It was the first time since her mother's passing that she'd made one of her mother's special recipes. Kneading pie dough always felt restful to her, and she worked her palms over the dough until it was flat and smooth.

Then, she laid it in the pie pan and carefully pinched the edges. She tasted the filling, which she'd made earlier that morning. It was the perfect mixture of sweet and tart. She closed her eyes, allowing the delectable flavor to melt in her mouth. The burst of flavor brought a flood of memories.

She could remember that very same flavor from when she was a small child, pulling on her mother's apron and begging for a taste of her famous cherry pie. Mother made the pie only on special occasions, and she always indulged her daughter in the first taste of the filling.

"Just to make sure it's fit to serve," she would say, winking at Mary.

Well, Mary thought, *I believe I have done well by your recipe, Mama.* She dabbed at the corners of her eyes with a kitchen towel.

Now's not the time for this, she told herself. She knew the pie would remind her of her mother, but she had not been quite prepared for the flood of memories that would come with that burst of flavor. Mary put the pie in the oven, removed her apron, and brushed the flour off her dress.

***

Rupert and Violet were hitching the horses. Jefferson led Ajax, his stallion, out of the stall. He planned to enter him into a contest, and he wanted him looking pristine. He rubbed him down, glossed his hooves, and brushed him ten times over. He used whale oil on his mane main and tail to make them it shine like a gems. Ajax looked quite proud of himself, almost as if he knew he was breathtakingly beautiful.

The boys ran around the yard, chasing each other. Anna was on her crutches, having taken less than a day to learn how to use them.

Mary stepped out of the house, and Jefferson could not take his eyes off her. She was wearing a lightweight, pale blue dress. Her unruly curls were pinned on top of her head. She flashed a dazzling smile, her green eyes dancing with delight. Jefferson thought he'd never seen a livelier soul in all his life.

He hardly ever looked forward to these types of events, but today was different. Jefferson often felt overwhelmed in crowds, and he much preferred long conversations with his closest friends to small talk with dozens of different people in one day. Today, however, he was with Mary, and Mary could talk to anyone. Her very presence drew him out and made him laugh. So naturally did she draw him into conversation that he felt at ease with her, even in a crowd.

Today, Mary looked as if she might burst with excitement. She seemed to flounce everywhere she went and smiled as if she had not a care in the world. She seemed to have shed the sorrows of the past year. She walked with a bounce in her step, and she smiled with a gleam in her eye.

"Will you ride with me?" Jefferson asked Mary, as she alighted the carriage. "Ajax is saddled up and ready to go. I think he'll be the finest stallion there. Violet and Rupert will take the carriage with the children, and William wants to know if he can bring Rusty."

"I would love to ride Ajax with you!" she responded. "I've just let William know that Rusty can come along, so long as he can keep track of him."

Jefferson's heart swelled. Though she'd been his wife these past few months, he still feared her rejection. Jefferson mounted and clicked his tongue, pulling Ajax up alongside the carriage. He looked up at her, standing there in the carriage with her wide grin, and his eyes were drawn to her dazzling eyes, her infectious smile, and her small, strong build. Everything about her lured him.

He reached out his hand and Mary took it, lightly stepping from the carriage and jumping rather smoothly onto the stallion's back.

I think I'm falling in love with her, he thought. He badly wanted to win her heart. She had admitted to him that she enjoyed his company, and their conversations and a shared love of books had convinced him that she did not hate him. But could she love him? He longed to know the answer but dared not ask, for fear he would discover that she did not love him. He welcomed her into his life, a little at a time. He was always surprised to find that she accepted the invitation to be with him.

Many nights, when they went to their separate rooms, he'd wanted to go to her room, or invite her to come into his. Always, the words stuck in his throat. What would happen if she said *no*? How could he go on from there? Married to a woman he loved but who could not love him? That felt like it would be more than his fragile heart could bear. That's why he never asked, and night after night went to his separate room.

He was satisfied, however, that they were getting along. Their many deep conversations about characters, poetry, and the human condition convinced him that they were at least intellectually compatible.

Many times, after one of their long conversations, he had longed to take her hand, to lean over and kiss her. He could not. Fear proved stronger than passion.

The chaotic noise of children screaming with glee interrupted Jefferson's thoughts.

"Dad! Are we going yet? Are we? Rupert says the carriage is ready. Can we go now, *please*?" Maurice jumped up and down with each word. William tried to remain more composed, but Jefferson knew his son and could see that he was brimming with excitement.

"Are you sure you want to go?" Jefferson teased. "It'll be hot, and there will be way too many people. I'm not sure you'll have any fun at all."

"Dad!" both boys teased back in unison.

"Okay, get on up into the carriage then! Where's your sister?"

"She's already with Auntie," William answered.

"I can't forget to pack my pie!" Mary said, sliding off Ajax's back and running back to the house where the pie was cooling. Jefferson watched her running and smiled at her excitement over a cherry pie.

She sure can find the joy in the little things, he thought, as he pulled the bridle over Ajax' ears and fit the bit into his mouth.

He led Ajax over to the carriage and peered in. He saw the faces of his three children, who were hardly able to contain their excitement. Violet and Rupert looked equally pleased.

"It's been a long, hard week for you, Rupert. Let's hope you finally get a day off."

"No getting hurt today," Rupert said. "That goes for you three, too," he said, waving a finger at the children. "I'm off today." Everyone laughed. Mary came out of the house with the box that held her prized cherry pie. She placed it on Violet's lap.

"Guard it with your life," she joked.

"Upon my honor," Violet said, placing her hand mockingly over her heart. Mary let out a full-throated laugh that rang through the air. It was a pleasant sort of laugh, loud but enjoyable and contagious. Jefferson couldn't help but laugh with her, though he couldn't have told anyone what he found so funny.

"Come on, I'll give you a lift up," he said. Mary placed a hand on his shoulder and a boot in his hand. In a moment, she swung herself up onto the stallion. She was small, sturdy, and strong. Jefferson couldn't help but notice that her physical characteristics matched that of her spirit. She was as resilient a person as he had ever met. In the months she had been at Redwood, she had melded into her role so well, it was almost as if she had always been there. Jefferson forgot, at times, that she had another life, a past, another identity almost.

I will ask her to tell me all about that, he thought. *Whatever she is willing to tell me, I want to hear.*

He mounted so that he sat in front of Mary, who wrapped her arms tightly around his waist. Jefferson felt his heart leap, and he wondered if she could feel how hard it was pounding.

***

The festival was crowded with the townspeople and visitors from neighboring towns and villages who had made the trip for the festival.

148

"This is so exciting!" Mary said, and Jefferson nodded. He felt like everyone besides him was drawn to festivals and crowds. He was excited to enter Ajax into the competition, and he was thrilled to have Mary there with him. He never did enjoy crowds, however. He knew that as excitement grew in everyone else, dread grew in him. He was determined to have a good time, despite the crowds. He knew from past experiences that whenever he was feeling overwhelmed by a crowd, he had only to look into his children's faces and see how they were enjoying themselves. That was worth it. Mary's outgoing nature made him feel more at ease in this crowd than he ever had before, and he took comfort in her presence.

Chapter Fifteen

Mary clung on to Jefferson, partly from fear of falling off the tall stallion, and partly to take full advantage of the opportunity to be near him like this.

If she was being honest, it had caught her off guard to fall in love with him the way she had. She tried to pinpoint the day and time when she had first realized she loved him. She couldn't be sure, because her heart began skipping a beat when he walked into a room long before she recognized it. She knew, however, that when he told her that his favorite poem was *We Are Seven* by William Wordsworth, she was sure of her love for him, but it was not because of the poem. It was just the moment when she realized.

Since then, she'd yearned for the evenings spent alone after the children were asleep. She wanted to know his heart, his mind, his past. She wanted to know everything about him. She could hardly believe that when she had first met him, she thought he was dull.

Goes to show how wrong I was, she thought. She shook her head in indignation at her own past self.

How could I have been so sure that he was dull and angry? She recalled the way Violet had first described him and came around to the belief that Violet had not lied after all. At least not regarding his character. The version of Jefferson that Mary had been introduced to the night of her arrival was just a glimpse of the real man. Her presence had been unexpected. He had been under the stress of the harvest. He was still grieving. All these factors played into the person she thought Jefferson was the night of her arrival.

I was so foolish, she thought, *to assume I knew all about him.* She thought about some of her worst moments. She, too, had lost her temper in moments of rage. She'd made ignorant comments in conversations. She had come off haughty and arrogant.

I would not want my character judged by my worst moment, she thought. She resolved to believe that the night she arrived was indeed one of Jefferson's worst moments. Since then, he'd only grown in her esteem by the day.

"Well, here, we are!" Jefferson announced. The festival was bustling, and she could hear the low murmur of voices though they were some twenty feet away from the crowd. "The carriage should be here shortly." They rode into the crowd, toward the round pen where the horses were being lined up and held until show time. Mary looked around at all the faces, recognizing several, and noticing many new ones.

She saw a red-haired woman and thought for a moment that she might be Georgia. She was not, but Mary made a mental note to fulfill her promise to write to her. She had so very much to tell her. How surprised and happy she would be to find out that she had, in fact, fallen in love!

Mary let go of Jefferson's waist, and he dismounted and helped her down. She stood, still looking around in wonder at all the people, while Jefferson signed Ajax up for the competition and tied him up.

"Come on, let's go look for the rest," he said. They set off on foot and found the carriage parking right outside the entrance.

They watched from a distance as Violet handed Anna out of the carriage and into Rupert's arms. Maurice and William scrambled out of the carriage and were running toward them at full speed, with Rusty stumbling at their heels. Rupert held Anna, and Violet carried the crutches under one arm and Mary's pie under the other.

Rupert set Anna down and got her situated with her crutches.

"The children are hungry already," Violet said. "I thought I'd take them over to the food stalls, so I may as well enter your pie. You and Jefferson can enjoy some time to yourselves for a while."

"That would be nice," said Mary.

"Let's go catch up to the boys," said Violet. She and Rupert walked off after the boys with Anna moving along on her crutches between them. Rusty kept dashing back and forth between the boys and Violet and Rupert.

Jefferson and Mary were left to walk alone.

"It's a perfect day for a festival," said Mary, turning her face up toward the warm sun. Even though they were surrounded by crowds of people from every neighboring town, she felt alone with Jefferson, and she basked in it. They walked past the stables, where the ponies were being saddled in the round pen for children's rides. Then they passed the food stands, where all the heavenly smells rose into the air and mingled together. After that came the games, where people were already practicing for the three-legged race and horseshoe toss.

"There's no one I'd rather be here with," Jefferson said, smiling down at Mary. She blushed and looked down at her feet.

"I'm happy to be here with you, too," she said. "You deserve a day off. You work so terribly hard. How does your back feel today?"

"Better than usual, actually."

She smiled. "Good. You deserve to have some fun today."

"And so do you. You've been working every bit as hard, keeping up with the house and the children's studies."

"I must admit, I have really been looking forward to this day off," she said.

They walked around the grounds a second time, sometimes talking and other times in silence, soaking in the noise and the bustle around them and enjoying each other's company.

Mary pulled a newspaper clipping from her waistband and looked at the printed schedule of events.

"It's time for the pie sampling! Let's go!" said Mary, excitedly, wanting to see how her mother's famous cherry pie recipe would fare.

Jefferson smiled at her, and Mary thought it might be the first time she had seen him looking truly happy since she arrived. She smiled back, delighted to see this side of him. As they walked on, she felt him slip her hand into his. Blood rushed to her face, and her heart leapt. His hand felt big, strong, and calloused against her small, smooth one.

They walked quietly. Mary soaked in the bustle of the chaos around them even as she melted into her own separate world with Jefferson. He was holding her hand. She gave his hand a little squeeze, and they walked on.

By the time they reached the tables, the judges had finished their tastes of pie and placed their scores on the table in front of them. The man with a long black beard stood on a pedestal and shouted out to announce the third and second place winners, names Mary thought she recognized but couldn't put a face to. "And, last but not least, the first-place winner is Mary Just!" Mary turned to look at Jefferson, eyes full of delight. If only she could tell her mother that her famous cherry pie won first place! She jumped for joy and walked up to receive her first place ribbon.

They sampled every delicacy, from scones and crepes to meatloaf and cheese.

They were finishing off the samples with pound cake when William and Maurice ran past them, chasing Rusty.

"Wait right here," Jefferson said. Mary finished her cake, looked around her and concluded that she was awfully lucky.

Jefferson returned carrying a long, leather strap in his hands.

"It's a leash and collar," he announced, handing it to Mary. Mary took it and felt the smooth leather. They couldn't have been cheap, and she couldn't believe he would spend that on her dog. She didn't know what to say.

"Come on," he said, "let's go find the boys. They'll be needing this."

They found them near the horse stables. William had caught hold of Rusty and was trying to keep control of him. A little crowd had gathered to help the boys catch Rusty, and everyone was petting his head and scratching his ears.

"Want to see him do some tricks?" William asked. Mary was surprised. She'd never taught Rusty any tricks at all.

"Sit," William said. Rusty obeyed.

"Shake," he commanded. Again, Rusty obeyed. Mary's jaw dropped. William smiled at her.

He proceeded to show off all of Rusty's new skills, which included rolling over and playing dead when William pretended to shoot him with his finger. Everyone clapped, but no one more enthusiastically than Mary.

"When did you teach him?" She asked.

"Oh, whenever I took him fishing and nothing was biting, I just fed him some of my packed lunch in exchange for a few tricks. Never did hear of a bloodhound learning so fast," he said as a look of pride came over his face.

"Your father bought you something," Mary said, handing him the collar and leash. William looked up at his dad with big eyes.

"Thank you!" He said, slipping the collar over Rusty's head and adjusting the size. He clipped the leash on.

"This will be much easier!" said William. Everyone laughed, and Mary looked up at Jefferson, who was smiling at his son with a look of admiration.

"Can I take a look at the schedule?" Jefferson asked. "The horse show should be coming up."

He scanned the paper. "Looks like they're starting now." His tone was even as usual, but Mary sensed the excitement in his voice.

When they arrived at the arena, they saw that Rupert and Violet were already there with the children and had saved them front-row seats.

Mary felt the warm bench through her cotton dress when they all sat down together. They watched one villager at a time walk their horse around the round pin. When Jefferson and Ajax entered the pin, Mary thought they were both a striking pair, more beautiful than any of the others. The shiny, blueish black of Ajax's coat glistened in the sun. Jefferson's hair and beard were a softer black.

Ajax seemed enormous compared to the other horses, though it was probably less obvious to spectators who did not know that his owner himself was enormous. Jefferson's broad shoulders moved as he walked, his strong muscles moving beneath his shirt. Mary found that she was watching her husband more than the horse. She thought about how he had taken her small hand in his large one, and she smiled.

After hearing the announcement that Jefferson and Ajax placed first, they all cheered and jumped and hugged each other. Only Jefferson looked composed, but Mary knew his heart was leaping beneath his serious exterior.

They met Jefferson at the stables and Maurice and Anna fed Ajax congratulatory carrots and apples they'd bought at a stand outside the stables. Jefferson pinned his first place ribbon on Maurice, who smiled from ear to ear. William stood some ways away, trying to teach Rusty to walk on the leash, but the hound had other ideas at the moment, and pulled on the leash with all his strength.

"Looks like you have some more training to do!" Mary called. William yanked on the leash.

"Obviously," he said, feigning irritation. Mary and Jefferson laughed. "There's too much distraction here," William said. "I'm taking him out for a while."

"I'll come with," said Rupert.

"I'll take Anna and Maurice on a pony ride," Violet said.

Mary and Jefferson found themselves alone, again.

"Have you ever tried saltwater taffy?" He asked.

"Why, of course!"

"I saw some a few tables down." Mary was rather enjoying petting the horses, so she said she'd wait there for him.

The stables were quiet but for the occasional stomping of a horse's hoof, snorting, and swishing of tails. Everyone had moved on to the next event. She stroked Ajax on the forehead as she fed him the last carrot.

The smell of the stables reminded her of her father, but she didn't feel sad. She thought of her past life with happy reminiscence. She could think of the life she left behind and feel a sense of quiet joy.

Only because I am so happy here, she thought. She heard a heavy footstep behind her and turned expecting to see Jefferson returned.

It was Kit.

The sight of him, unexpected as it was, sent a jolt of fear through her veins.

"You look surprised, Darling," he said, with a snicker in his voice.

Mary stood dumbfounded. Moments before, she had been in such a state of peaceful tranquility that this sudden appearance sent her into a few moments of disillusionment.

Fear and anger began to stir, then bubble up inside her.

"What are you doing here?" She asked.

"I've come for you, of course," he responded jovially. Mary hated his mocking friendliness.

"I'm married,"

"So I've heard."

"My husband will be returning any minute."

"Not to worry. He won't be your husband for long. You are rightfully mine, and I have everything I need to prove it. Your marriage to Jefferson will be annulled before long, so I suggest you keep your distance." He looked at her, perceiving something in her face, and continued in mock sympathy, "Oh, don't tell me you're in love already? Poor, sweet thing. So naïve. So innocent."

"Go on and get out of here, Kit. I am Jefferson's wife now, and there's nothing you can do about it. I suggest you leave."

"You must have forgotten that large sum of money you owe me. I wonder what your precious Jefferson will say when he finds out you owe more than he could possibly be worth. You'll be his ruin. Is that what you want to do to the man you love?"

"We'll find a way."

"That's exactly what you said last time, and you hopped on a train and thought I wouldn't find you just a few states away," he scoffed. "You could have at least tried Mexico. As it is, it was quite easy to describe you to the conductor and find out just exactly where you got off. I knew you'd be here today. You'll have to come up with a smarter plan than that."

Mary was boiling up with anger now. Her face turned red, and her jaw ached from gritting her teeth so hard.

"I'll have what's owed me," he said. "And I'll have you, too." He turned to walk away, and Mary stood frozen in place, unable to unclench her jaw. Moments later, Jefferson returned.

"I have a few flavors," he began, but noticing the look on her face, asked, "Mary, dear, are you alright? You look like you just swallowed a toad." Normally, Mary would have laughed, but she was fighting so hard to choke back the tears.

"I have sudden stomach pains," she lied, unable to think of anything else.

"Lean on me. I'll get you to the carriage and we'll find Rupert. I guess he won't have a day off today after all."

Chapter Sixteen

Everything in Mary had wanted to run into Jefferson's arms when he asked her what was wrong. Just two days ago, her heart was soaring with love, and her face glowed with life and hope. Now, in a single instant, it seemed her chances of happiness were dashed to pieces before she even had a chance to relish in them.

She'd fallen quite in love with Jefferson, though she had never told him. Well, not in words at least, but she thought they had slowly come to understand one another and share a mutual respect and affection.

Before Kit showed up at the festival, it had been some time since Mary had even thought about him. In her mind, Kit was gone. Once in a great while, his threatening voice would resurface in her memory, but she had little difficulty in writing off his threats as empty words. When she saw him at the fair, she was as shocked as she could have been. She had not been looking over her shoulder—not at all. She had convinced herself that she had given him the slip.

She realized now that she had mistakenly assumed that he was a dimwitted fool, that she would easily be able to outsmart him. When she tricked him into believing he was winning her heart and then skipped town, she thought that was the end of it. She could be anywhere, after all. Only Susan and John had known where she had gone, and she trusted them with her life.

She had not been prepared for Kit to have eyes and ears all over her hometown of Rosewood, so that people who spotted her at the train station would report back to him. Kit had proved smarter and more powerful than she had imagined.

His appearance at the festival had been such a shock to her that it took her some time to accept that she had actually seen him, and it wasn't just a nightmare. At times, it was hard to believe it, but it was true. He had come, found out that she was married to Jefferson, threatened her, and left.

Then...nothing...for days. When she left Texas, she knew he was a greedy man, but she never imagined to what lengths he would go to find her. Now, she realized this was nothing more than wishful thinking.

How could I have been so foolish? She wondered. *Now I've led him right to them and put them all in harm's way.*

She had always had a way of believing whatever it was that she wanted to be true. Normally, this habit served her well, but now it was coming back to haunt her. She had wanted to be rid of Kit, and so she'd believed she was. Reality, though, had found her, and she had to face the fact that Kit was not giving up so easily.

But what am I to do now? She thought, the words forming in a whisper on her lips.

She could almost hear her mother's soft voice saying, *Be reasonable, darling.* She would attempt to heed that advice now.

But what would a reasonable person do? She wondered. *Oh, how could I be so foolish?*

Kit had scoffed at her for thinking he would never find her. Now, it seemed obvious that she could not hide from a wealthy, powerful man by simply skipping over a few state lines. She wished desperately that she had been more reasonable then; she had put an entire family in danger by her very presence.

Hearts were entangled now, too. It would have been one thing if she had stayed a night and moved along. Now, she had a husband and children whom she loved dearly, and she knew they loved her. There seemed to be no easy way out.

You must be reasonable now, she commanded herself. *You can't do a thing about the past, but you can be reasonable now. Oh, what would mother do?* She thought hard, trying to remember any situation which she could draw from. She cursed herself for having spurned her mother's advice so often, and wracked her brains trying to remember anything that could be of use to her right now.

She just kept hearing, *Be reasonable.* But what did that mean?

She wanted to believe that Jefferson would protect her. She knew he *could.* But what would he think when he found out that she had kept this from him? Was it reasonable to believe that he would simply overlook the fact that she hadn't told him? Was it reasonable to hope that he might take care of the debt?

She thought about the way she had accused Violet of lying. She grimaced as she remembered the way she treated Jefferson when she first arrived. Now, she needed his protection. She had believed that she could just put the past behind her, never speak of it again, never think of it again, and move on.

She could talk to Jefferson now and explain to him what had happened and how she had kept the whole truth of her story from him. But what would happen then?

She wanted nothing more than to confide in Violet and confess to Jefferson, but what if they wouldn't forgive her? What if they couldn't? The rejection would be too much to bear, she was sure.

Maybe I can find my own way out of this, she thought. She had done it before, and she believed she could do it again.

Last night, he tried to ask. He tried...and oh, how I wanted to run into his arms and tell him all. What will he do, though? What will happen to me? The debt my father owed is too much for him to absorb, even if he wanted to. What will become of me? Will he hand me over to Kit? Does he love me? Does it even matter anymore?

Tears welled up in her eyes as her thoughts swirled endlessly in her head. There seemed no beginning or end to them.

She'd fallen asleep crying after forcing herself to hold her composure through dinner and until the children were in bed. She did not know whether to be relieved or upset that Jefferson had left her alone. Part of her wanted him to try harder— to demand that she tell him all and to comfort and reassure her. Yet, she feared that once she *did* tell, he would reject her. Fear flooded her heart, and so she kept her mouth shut while she tried to figure out what she would do.

Kit would be back for her; she was certain of that. She just didn't know when. It wouldn't take him long to find Redwood Ranch.

Every possible scenario played on repeat in her head until she drifted out of consciousness.

She dreamed of him in the night. She was running. She knew she was running from him but dared not turn around to see him. Suddenly, her legs were as heavy as lead. She couldn't move them. She dropped to the ground and found she could only use her arms. She tried to drag herself along the ground, but moved slowly, as if through molasses. She tried to scream, but she had no voice.

She saw a silhouette in the distance and knew it was Jefferson. She tried to scream his name, but she opened her mouth and nothing but silence was there. She wanted him to turn and look at her, to see her, but he did not. He was busy looking at something else. What was he looking at?

The sun was rising. She could see. He was standing with his back to her, looking at a headstone. She dared to turn around, knowing Kit was upon her, his eyes black as night. She tried again to shout Jefferson's name, but it was too late.

She woke up, heart pounding, Kit's terrifying face still clear in her mind.

I need to leave before Kit comes, she thought. She looked out her bedroom window across the green and brown fields, and her heart felt like it was being squeezed inside her chest. She'd had trouble leaving her Texas home where she had lived her entire life, but now she felt that leaving Parkville would be even more painful.

She'd grown to love this place. Violet was her best friend, and her affection for Jefferson was growing by the day. She already felt that the children were her own, and she could not imagine abandoning them. She thought of their little faces and wondered what it would do to them to lose their mother first and then to be abandoned by her. She couldn't bear the thought, and yet...and yet...Kit was coming. She remembered the dream. It felt more real than the day.

Oh, why did I ever come here? She asked herself, burying her head in her hands. Her presence here was only going to cause more pain when she disappeared again without a word. They would never understand. How could they?

She would leave. She decided on that, but she needed one more day with them. Surely, Kit wouldn't come after her that very day. She could stay for the day, and in the morning she would pack her things and be gone before anyone woke up.

Be reasonable, she heard her mother's voice again.

"Oh, but I don't know what's reasonable," she said aloud to herself.

Perhaps I should tell Jefferson everything. Maybe that's the reasonable thing, after all, she thought. She imagined what it might be like to tell Jefferson, to admit that she had misled him, and to tell him of the debt she carried. She couldn't picture his face or imagine what he would say. It seemed impossible that she could say such things and expect anything to ever be the same again.

She would miss them dearly, but in the desperation and heartache, escape seemed her only option.

I'll start again, she thought. *I've done it once before, and I'll do it again. And this time, not a soul will see me leave. I'll give a fake name at the station, and I'll go under cover of night. I'll go in disguise if I have to.*

She sat down to write to Susan and Georgia.

Dear Susan,

Allow me to first express my deep regret that I have not written sooner. I kept thinking I would have more time once I settled in. As it happened, life has never settled down. Kit has found me—hunted me down and found me at a festival. I made the biggest mistake of my life. I tried to forget about Kit. I failed to disclose my whole story to Jefferson, whom I have come to love.

Oh, Susan, I wish you could meet this man. I judged him ill at first. Now, I see that he is as kindhearted as his sister proclaimed him to be. Indeed, I believe he would have loved me had I not been proven to be so dishonest.

I wish I could say that I hope to see you soon, but if I do see you soon, it will be because Kit has dragged me back to Rosewood. I would rather die than go with that man. So, I hope to write to you again, having escaped. I will miss everyone here dearly.

Yours Truly,

Mary

Then she wrote to Georgia.

Dear Georgia,

I promised to write to you and tell if I found my happy ending. I regret to report that I have not. I could have, but I have managed only to break hearts. I know this seems an odd request, but I am looking for a place to stay for a while. I am trying to escape the man who ran me out of my hometown in the first place. I told you about him on the train. He has managed to track me down. I have lost the love of my life, and I no longer belong anywhere. I hope to find honest work where you are, as I have no other friend to speak of. I hope I will be seeing you soon.

Sincerely,

Mary

She placed the letters in envelopes, addressed and sealed them, and stood up. Then, she paused, and sat back down. She picked up her pen and a fresh sheet of paper and wrote,

My Dearest Jefferson,

I don't expect your forgiveness for what I have done. I have married you under false pretenses, and that is unforgivable. I

do, however, wish for you to know that my heart has been yours for some time. You are the love of my life, and I doubt I shall ever find another I love as I do you.

You are kind, generous, and honest. I never deserved you. I have been dishonest, arrogant, and conceited. You have been patient with me, but I understand that, having married you under false pretenses, you cannot see me the same way again. I wish, more than anything, that I could go back in time and tell you the truth. Maybe you would have turned me out that night. It would have been better than this. I am sorry I have broken your heart, and I am sorrier still that I have broken the hearts of three innocent children, whom I cherish. If you can believe that, tell them. I hope they will come to understand.

Love,

Mary

She left this one out on the desk where she'd written it. He would find it there, she was certain.

As she descended the stairs and rounded the corner, her heart lurched as she saw the two of them standing together: the man she feared and the man she had come to love. Her hopes for one last day with the Just family were dashed to pieces. Her heart sunk as the shock of seeing him wore off.

Rusty came bounding around the corner, barking furiously, the hair standing up on his back, his teeth barred.

William rounded the corner after him, calling out, "Calm, boy! Down!" He tried to catch him, but Rusty was too fast. He stood in the doorway, snarling at Kit for a split second before his entire body lurched forward. Jefferson had to put himself between Kit and Rusty before any damage was done.

"Rusty! Down!" Jefferson Bellowed. The dog looked up at Jefferson with trusting eyes, calmed for moment, and then turned back to face Kit, snarling and baring his teeth.

"William, take him out of here."

"I'm trying. I've never seen him like this."

Why, God? Why couldn't you give me one day to say goodbye? That's all I asked. She immediately felt a twinge of guilt as she realized she was demanding something of God when she had not even had the courage to tell the truth to the people she had come to love.

I suppose I am only getting what I deserve, she thought.

Mary had been standing, paralyzed by fear and lost in thought, at the top of the stairs, out of Kit's sight. She watched William struggling to pull Rusty out of the way, Rusty snarling and snapping in Kit's direction all the while.

As soon as William and Rusty were around the corner, Mary descended the stairs and quickly slipped into the kitchen, hoping Kit hadn't seen her. She slipped out the kitchen door and met William.

"I've never seen him do anything like *that*," he said, panting.

"That's a bad man. Rusty knows a bad egg when he sees one," Mary answered, eyes wandering. William looked at her pensively.

"Who is he?" He asked.

"He's come for me," said Mary. "A nightmare, come true."

"What do you mean? He can't take you. Pa won't let him," William said, his voice shaking.

"He might not have a choice," Mary said, but what she was really thinking was that Jefferson wouldn't choose to keep her once he knew the truth of her past and debt. She couldn't say so to William, who looked at her with inquisitive eyes.

"What are you going to do?" William asked the question innocently enough, but it made Mary realize she *had* to do *something.* She'd been running and hiding since the day she left Rosewood. It hadn't worked, and now she was hiding in the backyard, hoping this time would be different.

"I don't know," she answered honestly. She studied William's face. He looked ready to fight, and the fire in his eyes seemed to spread to her soul. She suddenly felt a surge of courage. Her plan to escape under cover of night now seemed utterly ridiculous, as she stood there with William, who was but a boy, but seemed to have more sense than she did.

I must fight, she thought. *I have to fight for this family...to stay with them.*

"I guess it's time for me to face it, isn't it?" She said, standing up slowly.

"Well, there's nothing else to do," said William. Mary smiled. She wished she had his heart. He was right, there was nothing else to do. She still didn't know whether Jefferson could forgive her, but she could at least face Kit and give him the chance.

"You stay here with Rusty. Don't let him loose unless I give you the go ahead," said Mary, turning to go.

"Wait...Mary." Mary turned back to look at William, standing there with Rusty, who was finally starting to calm down under William's kind strokes. William looked up at her with pleading eyes and said, "We need you." Mary felt the tears spring to her eyes.

"I need you all, too," she answered. Then she took a breath, gathered her courage, and turned toward the house.

She stepped into the kitchen and could hear the low rumble of voices though she couldn't make out what was being said.

No more hiding. No more eavesdropping. No more running. No more lying, she told herself firmly. *Go right in there and face him.*

She stepped through the kitchen door into the entryway, trying to ignore the fact that her whole body was trembling.

She relaxed a little when she saw Kit standing with Jefferson, who towered over even him. Jefferson's back was to her, just like in the dream, but he was standing between her and Kit. She gathered her courage once more and lifted her face to look directly into Kit's. His black eyes blazed, and a drop of sweat dripped from his long nose. He looked up as soon as she entered the room.

"That there," Kit said, pointing a finger as Mary entered the house, "is my wife."

Chapter Seventeen

Jefferson stood firm, unmoved.

"You're mistaken, Sir. That is *my* wife," he said, staring back into Kit's eyes with a steely, unwavering glare.

"I'm afraid you have been duped, sir," Kit responded, casting a triumphant glance at Mary.

"I'm going to have to ask you to leave," Jefferson responded through gritted teeth.

"Gladly," Kit responded. "I'll take my wife and go."

"Like I said, she is *my* wife," Jefferson responded, growing redder in the face by the moment.

"And like *I* said, you have been duped. Did she tell you that when you married her, you incurred with her thousands of dollars of debt? Did she tell you that her father agreed to give her hand in marriage to *me* as a means of clearing the debt?"

Jefferson's heart pounded and his mind was swimming. *It couldn't be true, could it? Would Mary have lied to me? Would she have kept something like this hidden from me? It isn't possible. Not my Mary. No, it couldn't be.*

As Jefferson stood, not speaking, Kit only grew more triumphant. The moment he realized Jefferson was clueless about the debt, he smiled wickedly, casting glances at Mary, who stood frozen as if paralyzed behind Jefferson.

Jefferson turned around to look at Mary, his eyes searching for an answer. She looked back at him, her eyes pleading. Without an excuse, she hung her head.

His eyes pleaded with her, begged her to lift her head and look him in the eye and tell him this was all nonsense, but she would not lift her eyes off the floor. Jefferson turned back to Kit, who was idly picking something from his decaying teeth.

He flicked it, drew in a sharp breath, and said, "Now, there's an easy solution to all this. You haven't been married all that long, and seeing as how ya'll got married under false pretenses, it shouldn't be too difficult to get the marriage annulled. You can put this all behind you…pretend it never happened…and get back to your life as it should be." He gave a wide smile, showing various shades of yellow and gray teeth. His breath gave off a putrid stench. Jefferson thought he might have been a handsome enough man if not for the decay in his teeth and the malevolence in his eyes.

His voice was smooth like honey. Some might even have thought it soothing, had they not been looking at the face from which the words came. Jefferson felt rage welling up within him every time Kit looked over him toward where Mary was standing. His eyes looked hungry, as if he wanted to devour her.

Whatever has happened, I will not let this man get past me, he thought. A fierce desire to protect Mary swept over him, overpowering his bewilderment and even his sense of betrayal.

Jefferson turned to look at Mary again, wanting to reassure her, somehow, that he would protect her. To his dismay, Mary had retreated out of sight again.

"Now," said Kit, "This can all be made right. I will take Mary as my wife and clear the debt. All will be set right." He must have perceived a look of indignation on Jefferson's face because he quickly added, "Don't worry about Mary. I will take care of her. She will have everything her heart desires."

Jefferson felt the anger rising in him with every word Kit spoke. His face grew red and tiny droplets of sweat gathered on his forehead. He took a step toward Kit, towering over him, and peered down into his face.

"If you think I'm just going to hand over *my* wife to a man like you, you've got another thing coming. Debt or no debt, Mary is *my* wife. I married her, and I love her."

Kit shifted uncomfortably under Jefferson's towering figure and angry glare, but he quickly regained his composure and returned Jefferson's cold stare.

Looking into his black, empty, eyes, Jefferson instantly felt that he was in the presence of true evil.

There's no soul behind those eyes, he thought, but he did not shudder. He was, in fact, immovable.

Just this past Sunday, the preacher had quoted a verse, and it came to Jefferson's mind now.

Perfect love casts out fear.

He loved Mary. He knew that much. In the face of his love for Mary, no fear could stand, so he stared back into the evil, empty eyes, his heart filled with love for Mary and a fierce desire to protect her from this soulless man.

"Be reasonable," Kit answered, breaking the silence. His voice cracked slightly despite the obvious attempt to sound collected. "Mary is no wife to you. If she respected you at all, she would have told you the truth from the beginning."

Jefferson had realized from the moment he laid eyes on Kit, that the man was no idiot. Jefferson knew what he was doing now—spotting weakness and aiming for it. Jefferson had not been able to hide the bewilderment and pain that filled his heart when he found out that Mary had hidden the truth

173

from him. Kit saw that hurt, and he was using it against him now, but Jefferson was not to be caught off guard again. He took a step towards Kit, grabbed ahold of his shirt, and lifted him so that his toes barely brushed the ground.

"Now, let's not jump too quickly on a decision," Kit answered. "Mary is no wife to you. If she respected you at all, she would have told you the truth from the beginning. She came to you out of nowhere, didn't she? Who's to say she wasn't already married? Who's to say she isn't a murderess on the run? Come, now. You're a reasonable man. Send her back home, where she belongs. You know nothing at all about her. She belongs at home, with me, in Texas, where people know and love her."

At this, Jefferson leaned his face in, and whispered, "We love her. We are her family. You know nothing about Mary, and you know nothing about me, so if you value your life, I suggest you go back to where you came from, and never show your face here again."

Kit's eyes glazed over, and he panted as if trying to catch his breath. Jefferson held him there for another moment, then dropped him. Kit turned and tumbled out of the house, quickly mounted his horse, and rode out toward the edge of the front yard. Jefferson stood on the porch, watching him.

"The law is on my side, Mr. Just. You have no idea the mistake you just made. I will get what is owed to me, one way or another! And I'll get my wife."

"Get *off* my land!" Jefferson bellowed back at him from the doorway as he reached for his rifle which hung above the door.

Kit galloped off into the distance, and Jefferson could feel his heart beating.

Now that Kit was gone, Jefferson could allow his thoughts to surface. He turned toward the stairs, wanting to find Mary, but still confused.

Did she intentionally hide the truth from me? He would forgive her, in time, he knew. Still, he felt the sting of having trusted and had that trust broken.

If only she had told me the truth, he thought. He wondered why she had not trusted him enough to tell him. Did she think he would abandon her? Did she not trust him?

I thought she was growing to trust—and love—me, he thought, his heart sinking into his stomach. His chest felt heavy, like a boulder weighing down on him.

Whenever he felt like this, he went to Rose's grave to speak with her. She had known grief, and she had always known what to say. Part of him wanted to go upstairs and find Mary and demand an explanation, but a stronger part of him needed to be near Rose until his thoughts cleared and his heart settled. Anger and disappointment wrestled for center stage within his heart, and he thought anger might win out if he did not visit Rose. When he went to her grave and spoke to her, anger usually gave way to sadness, and deep down, Jefferson knew that was what he was really feeling.

With these two feelings competing within him, he went to Rose.

Chapter Eighteen

Tears streamed down Mary's cheeks and blurred her vision as she pulled her suitcase out from under her bed. She hadn't used it since the day she arrived in Parkville. In fact, she had only ever used it one other time—when she'd been running from her home in Rosewood. Here she was, running again… The sight of it made her stomach lurch, and she bent over the railing of the bed, hanging on until she could regain her composure.

Jefferson's sad, bewildered eyes refused to leave her mind. She knew what he was thinking the instant she looked into those eyes. She had planned to stay and fight, to face her demons. She had hoped against hope that Jefferson could forgive her, but one look into his eyes, which showed the shock of her betrayal, dashed her hopes.

How could he ever forgive me? She wondered. Then she whispered it. Then she said it aloud.

He can't, she thought, answering her own question. She had seen that look when he turned her way, a look of pained astonishment, and had known at once that it was all over.

She felt dazed. She had gone back and forth so many times. She thought she would flee. She thought she would stay. Now, she knew she *must* flee. Not only had she put them all in danger, but she had done irreparable damage. Jefferson would never think of her the same.

She knew she should be angry at Kit, but somehow, it was Jefferson's face in her mind as she seethed and cried. She could barely see as she scrambled to pack her things and shove them into her suitcase. She hadn't folded anything, and so the suitcase wouldn't close. She slammed down on it with all her weight, but still it popped open.

"Stupid thing!" She shouted, hitting the suitcase again and again, then falling into a heap on the floor. She buried her head in her arms and sobbed.

She heard a faint tap on the door. She lifted her head. Violet stood there, looking confused, but compassionate. Mary began to miss Susan, as Violet stood there looking just the way Susan had looked when Mary had to go through her parents' room after they died.

"Mary...can I come in?" she asked softly. Mary heard the concern in her voice and nodded. "Mary, what's going on?" Violet said through the door.

"He found me," Mary sobbed, unable to keep it in anymore. "Kit found me. I thought I'd given him the slip, but he tracked me down and now I've ruined your lives. I'm so sorry, Violet."

The door creaked, and Violet slipped in and sat down on the floor next to Mary.

"It can't be as bad as you are imagining, Mary. Nothing is ever as bad as it seems."

"I wish that were true," said Mary. "Things are often worse than they seem."

"Mary, please. Tell me what's going on. I bet it's not as bad as you think. Who is Kit? What do you mean he has found you?"

"Can you ever forgive me my hypocrisy? I was furious with you when I found out what you had done in writing on your brother's behalf. All the while, it never even crossed my mind that *I* was lying to *you*."

"What do you mean you were lying to me?" Violet asked, coming to sit near Mary on the floor by her own. They felt

177

warm and comforting, holding Mary's own cold, shivering hands. Mary buried her head again.

"I thought I could escape."

"What? I can't hear you." Violet couldn't hear Mary's words as she had covered her head and was trying to speak through tears and sobs. Mary took a breath and lifted a tearful face toward Violet.

"I lied to you," she said. "Or, at least, I did not tell the whole truth, which is as good as lying."

"Well," said Violet, "You can tell me the truth now."

"It's too late."

"It's never too late."

"What a silly thing to say. Of course it can sometimes be too late, and this is one of those times. Jefferson has agreed to annul our marriage and hand me over to that...that *man*."

"Oh, Mary, now you're the one being silly. How could you think such a thing?" Violet sounded incredulous, certain that Mary was wrong. Mary knew otherwise.

"I saw the look in his eyes, Violet. There was no mistaking it." She buried her head again. Violet put a gentle hand on her back, rubbing lightly.

"Why don't you start from the beginning," she said. "Tell me the truth. Tell me everything."

Mary breathed in and out, a few shaky, sharp breaths and tried to settle herself.

"It all began when my parents died. Kit came to see me."

"Who is Kit?"

"The man who was downstairs talking with Jefferson just now."

"Okay."

"Kit came to see me. He seemed gentlemanly at first. He said he was sorry for my loss and that he was a friend of my father's. But then he made known to me that my father owed him a large sum. He said that my father had agreed that I should marry Kit to clear any debt, in the case that my father should not be able to pay off the debts."

"So, he came to collect the money...or marry you?"

"He knew I wouldn't be able to pay. The house was mortgaged. The farm was mortgaged. Kit knew all of that. He was offering to marry me to clear the debts. I would pay them off with myself."

"Oh, that's awful!"

"He thought he was doing me a favor. So, I strung him along. I knew it was the only way. I made him believe that I just needed time to process. I pretended to let him woo me. It was all until I could find a way out. We responded to your ad. When I heard back from you, we began making plans to get me out of Rosewood."

"Who is 'we'?"

"Susan, who was our maid and my dear friend, and her fiancé, John. They did everything to help me. They even paid my train fare. I didn't have enough money to even get myself out of there. I left the only home I had ever known. I left the graves of my parents and my baby brother who died in infancy. I left it all to come here, where I hoped to find a kind man to take me in."

"Oh, Mary. I can see why you were so shook up that first night."

"I had nowhere else to go." Violet wrapped an arm tightly around her. "And I came to love Jefferson. He did seem rough to me at first, but now I see his kindness. I was beginning to love him, and I thought that he loved me."

"Oh, I think he *does*, Mary."

"No. If he was beginning to, that is all lost now. He feels betrayed."

"Did he tell you as much?"

"No. He didn't need to. You should have seen the way he looked at me, Violet. It nearly broke my heart."

"But you haven't talked to him?"

"No. I can't. I have been a wretched hypocrite, Violet. I accused you of lying. I judged Jefferson for being rough and crude. All the while, it was me who was the wicked one. It was me who lied and cheated and obstructed the truth."

"Now, Mary...don't you think you're being a bit hard on yourself? In your mind, Kit was behind you. You had left your home. You were starting over. Why should you think to bring him up? He was in your past. This was going to be your new life."

"All the same...I should have been honest."

"That may be true," said Violet. "But the past is the past, Mary. All you can do now is to go downstairs and tell Jefferson the truth and see what he says. It isn't fair of you to assume that you can read his mind and pack up your things like this without so much as a word to him."

"You didn't see his face, Violet."

"Maybe not, but I've known my brother my whole life, and you have not. You think you know what he's thinking, but you're not all-knowing. Let him say what he thinks with his own mouth. You owe him at least that."

"Perhaps you are right."

"I know I am."

"But what if he calls me a liar and sends me out?"

"I do not think he will, but even so.... if you run away without a word, you are a coward."

That was more than Mary could handle. She did not come all this way to bow out a coward.

She is right, Mary thought. Even *if he's going to call me a liar and turn me out, I need to have the courage to let him say it to my face.* Mary hoped that Violet was right, and that Jefferson would not annul the marriage and turn her out. She knew what Violet said was true, though; she would be a coward to sneak out without a word.

"Mommy," she heard a little voice and turned to see Anna standing in the doorway. She limped over to Mary, still favoring her ankle a bit.

Mary clasped a hand over her mouth. Had Anna just spoken, and had she just called her 'Mommy'? Mary's heart leaped, and all thoughts of escape vanished at the sound of Anna's first words, spoken in a raspy little voice. Tears formed in Mary's eyes as she reached her arms out to the little girl, and she stumbled across the floor and into Mary's arms. Mary patted her dark head of hair, and Anna squeezed her.

"She's speaking," said Violet, astonished. "I've been wondering when she would speak. I can hardly believe it."

How could I leave her? Mary wondered. *I can't. How could I be so selfish? I can't leave the children.* She resolved that she would find the courage to confront Jefferson, to tell him the truth from start to finish, and to throw herself upon his mercy. Perhaps he would find it in his heart to forgive her and trust her once again.

As for Kit, they would have to face him together, but for right now, she had to find Jefferson and tell him the good news about Anna.

Chapter Nineteen

Jefferson stood silently, holding his hat over his heart. He could feel it beating hard in his chest. He sat down by Rose's grave and ran a rough hand softly over the grass under which she lay.

"Oh, Rose. Rose, what should I do? I can't hand Mary over to that man. I can't...but the money. Where will I come up with that kind of money? It will ruin us. But if she leaves, it will ruin us just the same, and there is no way I would let that evil man have her. No, I have to protect her. I just wish she would have told me the truth."

Jefferson heard a high-pitched whining sound and looked around to find Rusty still tied up. He walked over and untied his leash. Rusty licked at his hands and cuddled up against his legs.

"Good, boy, Rusty. You know a bad man when you see one, don't you? That's a boy." He patted Rusty's head and scratched behind his ears. Rusty seemed to know the words "good boy" and he wiggled around happily at Jefferson's feet, pushing against his legs for more ear scratching. That's when Jefferson heard Mary approaching. He turned. It was obvious she had been crying. Her eyes were dry, but red and puffy, and her face looked pained. He wanted to hug her but held back.

"Why didn't you tell me the truth?" He asked.

"Jefferson. I'm sorry. I understand if you want nothing to do with me. Just, please...give me some time to get away from Kit."

"Nonsense. You're not going anywhere." Mary let out a little surprised gasp and put her hand on her heart. Jefferson continued, "That man is as wicked as they come. I sensed it the moment he stepped foot through the door. Rusty here knew it, too. A good dog knows a bad man when he sees one. There's no way I'm letting you go with him. No way. You're *my* wife, Mary. You think I'd just let you go like that?"

"When Kit suggested annulling the marriage...you...you didn't say anything. Then, when you turned to look at me, the look on your face...I thought...I thought you'd want nothing to do with me after today."

"You thought wrong. I couldn't speak because I was angry. I couldn't spit the words out. I looked at you like that because I wanted you to tell me the truth...to tell me it was all a lie."

"But it wasn't all a lie."

"I know that now. Still, you're my wife. We will stand and fight this together, come what may. When I said, 'for better or worse,' I meant it."

At these words, Mary ran to him and, wrapping her arms tightly around his waist, buried her head in his chest and sobbed.

He patted her head and said, "Mary, I love you. I can finally see that now. I wish you would have told me the truth from the beginning. Then, I could have been on guard, and I could have protected you. I never would have left you alone at the festival if I'd known. I just wish you would have been honest with me. I need that from you, Mary. I need honesty if we are going to be as happy together as I know we can be."

Mary nodded her head. She tried to speak, but the words got choked up in her throat.

"It's okay," Jefferson said soothingly. "It's all going to be okay. Now, when you can calm yourself enough to speak, I want you to tell me everything."

Mary recounted her story, just as she had told Violet, trying hard to remember the details, not to omit or exaggerate. She had promised to be truthful.

After listening intently, Jefferson thought for a while. He still held Mary's head to his chest. She seemed to want to stay there, and he certainly did not want to let her go.

"Mary," he said tenderly. "You've been through a lot of loss. Losing your parents, your home, your farm, and your financial security was both tragic and terrifying, and I am sorry. I am so sorry that you went through all of that and then had to face Kit. You could have taken the easy way out and married him, but I don't think that would have been the easy thing in the long run. I think we both know it would have made for a miserable life."

"Yes," Mary choked out. "It has been more than I thought I could bear. But leaving here...to leave you and the children...that would have been more than I could bear."

"You won't have to bear it, and you won't have to bear Kit alone anymore, either. I know how to handle men like that. They just need to be humbled a bit. I know you've been through a lot, Mary. Let me be there for you. If you're honest with me in this marriage, I can be there for you. We can be there for each other, but only if we're honest." Mary nodded and tightened her grasp on him.

"You've been through a lot, too," she said, looking down toward Rose's grave.

"I have, but I know what Rose would want. She would want me to care for you the same way I cared for her. I hope to provide you with a good life, the best I can give. You don't have to worry about Kit by yourself anymore. You're mine, and I take care of my own. We take this on together."

Mary lifted her face, eyes still filled with tears, and peered up at him. Jefferson saw the desperation in her face, and an overpowering feeling came over him. He knew in that moment that he would protect her at all costs, come what may. He would take on Kit, and anyone else who might try to hurt her. She was *his* wife, and he realized in that moment how much he loved her.

"Jefferson," she said meekly. "I came out here to tell you some news."

"I don't know if I can handle more news," he said softly.

"No...good news. It's Anna. She spoke." Jefferson pulled back to look at Mary in disbelief. He'd long been wondering when Anna would speak. Sometimes, he wondered whether she would ever speak at all. Of course, in those moments when the worry surfaced, he'd told himself that it was nothing to worry about and that all would be alright. Yet, when he heard that she had spoken words, his heart leapt, and he realized how worried he had been.

"Oh, I wish I'd have heard!" He exclaimed.

"I'm sorry you didn't..."

"No, it's okay. I'm just so happy. What did she say?"

Mary hesitated.

"Mommy," said Mary. "She called me Mommy." Jefferson mulled this over in his mind for a moment. Anna had called Mary Mommy. Anna, who had never spoken a word, had called Mary Mommy. Anna, who had only heard stories and memories of her own mother had looked at Mary and spoken her very first word.

"Mary," Jefferson breathed out. "That's wonderful."

186

He hugged Mary tightly, holding on to her as if he'd never let go. He felt her return the squeeze, and his heart soared. With trembling words, he asked. "Mary?" She pulled away just enough to look up at him, her face inviting the question. "Would it be okay...I mean...we're husband and wife and we still have separate bedrooms." Mary smiled sheepishly. He continued. "I thought you could join me tonight." Mary nodded.

That night, he led Mary to his—no, their—room.

Chapter Twenty

Several days had passed, and Kit had not shown up. Mary was beginning to feel at ease again; perhaps Jefferson intimidated him enough to scare him off. The day was warm and breezy, and Mary shooed the flies away from her face as she sweated over her garden, which had become overrun by weeds in the two days she hadn't tended to it.

Gardening was harder work than she had anticipated, and her arms and back grew sore as she pulled the weeds out by the roots, trying to clear them away from the carrots, which were coming up in straight rows now.

Her hands ached, but her heart was full. She kept on pulling. Anna was having her afternoon nap, and William and Maurice were untangling fishing lines yet again, getting ready to head out to the pond to catch trout for dinner. Rusty was running in circles by the front door, waiting eagerly for the boys to be ready to head down the lane.

Mary turned her face up toward the warm sun, closing her eyes and feeling the breeze run over her face and tumble through her hair.

Could this be real? She wondered. Everything had fallen together so perfectly. Kit had disappeared. Jefferson had adamantly affirmed his love and desire for her. She had received him with open arms, and an open heart. Anna, in some of her first words ever spoken, had called her "Mommy". Maurice adored her and hung on her every word. Even William had accepted her into the family.

It seemed to Mary that everything had fallen into place so perfectly—too perfectly. She had a looming suspicion that things felt *too* right.

Maybe that's just because I've never had it so good, she thought. *Not even when mother and father were alive. I didn't know life could be like this.*

Her face was beginning to sweat now, so she turned her eyes back toward the ground, and kept pulling up the weeds. Violet came up behind her.

"Rupert asked if I could help him on some rounds today, but I told him I should stay with you since...well since what happened."

"You should go," Mary said. "Kit would have come back by now if he was going to at all. I've a hunch Jefferson scared him off."

"Even so. You shouldn't be alone. Not yet, anyway. I know you try to be strong, Mary, but he was here just last week. The boys are about to head down to the pond, and Jefferson's way out in the far field with the workers. I just can't stand the thought of his coming here with no one to protect you."

Jefferson had stayed near the house for several days, but he needed to get back out into the fields with his men, and Mary had urged him to go.

"I suppose you think you'll protect me?" Mary joked.

"Two are better than one. Anyway, I could run for help if nothing else," said Violet, with a smile.

"I think he's gone for good, Violet. Jefferson only needed to stand his ground."

"I hope you're right. Maybe I'll join Rupert next week," said Violet. "But for now, I'll stick around here. Anyway, your garden is pathetic. You clearly need some help."

Mary laughed. She couldn't deny that. She'd put up a small wire fence for the beans, but the weeds had choked out the vines and the fence was tipping and most of the leaves were dead.

"You have to stay on top of the weeds to get a good crop," said Violet. "You shouldn't have to do it alone. Send the boys when they've finished their lessons. They don't need to fish every day."

"You're right. I think I'll have to recruit their help. I simply can't keep up with them. Seems like there are more weeds sprouted up every morning."

"Exactly."

"Oh, well, there were too many peas anyway."

Violet cast a condescending look at her. "Don't be ridiculous. There's no such thing as too much harvest. See my raspberry bushes over there?" She pointed to the edge of the yard just before the golden rows of corn began. Mary nodded.

"Every year now, there are far more raspberries than I can pick, and you know we picked enough to make a cellar full of jam. It's never too many, though. You know why? It's because the ones that don't get picked and eaten fall to the ground between the bushes and seep into the soil, making it fertile. The raspberries that come back the following year are bigger and sweeter. Nothing goes to waste."

"Nothing goes to waste," Mary repeated. She liked the sound of that. *Nothing goes to waste*, she thought, as she pulled on the roots of yet another stubborn weed.

***

Mary was still on her knees in the garden pulling weeds when the shots rang out. She sat stunned for a moment but jolted upwards and scrambled to the front yard when she heard Maurice's terrified voice screaming for her.

He ran to her and wrapped his arms around her waist, but Mary, taking in the scene before her, rushed him into the house. More shots rang out, as Mary shouted for William.

He came stumbling up the lane, holding Rusty in his arms.

"William!" Mary shouted frantically as he ran to her, panting for breath.

"They've shot Rusty! I can't believe it. They've shot him!"

Mary shifted some of Rusty's weight into her own arms and said, "We need to get into the house, now." They moved as quickly as they could, carrying Rusty awkwardly between them. More shots. Mary's ears were ringing and her head pounding.

Finally, they got to the door and shut it behind them. They laid Rusty on the floor. Anna was screaming in Violet's arms. Violet had been in the house when the shots rang out and had scooped Anna up in her arms hurriedly in a vain attempt to calm her.

Mary picked up the skirt of her dress and went to her as quickly as she could move.

"Come here, baby, come here." She took Anna in her arms, but the poor child only continued to scream.

"He's hurt," said William, his voice cracking.

Mary rushed to his side and knelt beside him, Anna on her lap. Violet and Maurice came over and knelt by Rusty, too.

"It looks like he's just been grazed," said Violet. "I think he'll be okay. Maurice, will you go up to the bathroom and grab some gauze? William, go to the kitchen and get that bottle of gin off the top shelf." Then, turning to Mary, she said, "I suppose my time helping Rupert is coming in handy."

"Thank you," Mary mouthed over the screams of Anna, who still hadn't settled down. Mary patted her head and spoke soothingly to her, but she couldn't seem to stop wailing.

The boys had returned with the supplies. William sat by Rusty's head and said, "It's okay boy. Good boy. You'll be okay." He pet him gently behind the ears. Violet poured the gin over the wound on Rusty's back. Rusty winced and pink liquid tricked off his back and onto the floor.

"Missed his spine, but it was close," said Violet. "Maurice, be a good boy and get an old towel to wipe up this mess? Thank you."

Violet then proceeded to wrap the gauze around Rusty's back and middle. "Don't you worry, William," she said. "He'll be good as new in a few days. He's just a bit shocked."

Anna's wailing had finally subsided into small whimpers, and Mary was able to think clearly enough to ask, "Did anyone see what happened?"

"It was *him*," said William. "It was that man who was here last week." Mary felt her heart jump into her throat. *Kit.*

"He shot right at Rusty. It was no accident. He was aiming for him. I'd have knocked him right off his horse if he'd a killed him. I would have. I would have...."

"Calm yourself," said Violet. "No use in thinking what you *would* have done. As it is, Rusty looks like he will be okay. It sounds as if they've left."

Just as Mary went to look out the window, more shots rang out, sending Anna back into a fit of panic. A man came bursting through the door and both Mary and Violet screamed.

"It's just me," said Greg, one of the ranch's farm hands.

"Please, go get Jefferson," Violet said.

"I will. Just wanted to see if everyone in here was okay. They've shot several of the cattle."

"Who is *they*?"

"One of them is Pudge," Greg answered. "I know him. He's got a bad reputation, but I never thought he'd do something like this. There's a big, mean looking man with them."

Greg went to the window and looked out.

"They're setting fire to the fence. I ought to stay here and protect you,"

"No, please, get Jefferson for us," Mary pleaded. Greg hesitated.

"Alright, but you all get on down to the cellar. I'll get Jefferson here just as fast as I can."

"Take Ajax," said Violet.

"Yes Ma'am." Greg slipped out the door silently as Violet scooped up Anna, who was still wailing, and handed her to Maurice.

"Carry her down to the cellar," she said.

"You and William get Rusty," said Mary. "I'm going outside to talk to Kit."

"You'll do no such thing!" Violet shouted.

"I have to, and I will," Mary said firmly.

"You're not going out there, Mary," said William.

"I have to," said Mary. "This is all happening because of me. Maybe I can reason with him. He won't shoot me. I know he won't."

"Maybe he won't shoot you, but he might just take you and ride off," said Violet, her voice trembling.

"That's a chance I'm going to have to take," said Mary. "I can't just let him kill our cattle and destroy our property. Don't you see what he's doing? He wants to make sure Jefferson can't afford to pay him off. We needed to sell those cattle before the drive this year, and Kit knows that. He's trying to cripple us. I must reason with him."

"Mary, no!"

"Go with the children." Mary ran to the door before Violet could say another word and swung it open. Kit was riding around the front yard wildly, shooting into the air.

"Kit!" Mary shouted at the top of her lungs. "Stop this! This has to stop! You're not accomplishing anything except scaring the children!"

"Oh, this?" Kit shouted back. Even from a distance, Mary could see that familiar evil gleam in his eye. "This is nothing! A few scared children will be the least of your worries by the time I'm done. This is just a little fun. I'm just getting started," and with that, he swung his horse around and shot directly at the house.

Pudge, having finished setting fire to the fence, mounted his horse and the two galloped off together, yelling gleefully like a pair of demons.

Mary let out the breath she'd been holding and turned to go back into the house. She saw Violet standing by the window, holding a cloth over her arm.

"What happened?" Mary asked, her voice shaking.

"It's nothing. It's just a little cut from the broken glass."

"I thought you were in the cellar."

"I got the kids down there safely, and I was coming to get you when the shot shattered the window, and I was hit with a piece of glass. It's nothing, really. Just a small cut."

"Let me see," said Mary. Violet lifted the blood-stained cloth.

"That's no small cut," said Mary. "That looks deep. Is all the glass out?"

"Yes. It was just one piece."

"Good. Now, let me bandage you up."

"Mary, the fence is burning, we have to—"

"It's already beginning to die out, though some damage is done. Greg should have gotten to Jefferson by now." Mary took the bottle of gin and poured it over Violet's arm. Violet gritted her teeth and winced. Mary took the gauze and wrapped it around her arm.

"This is all my fault," said Mary. "How could I be so foolish as to think Kit was gone for good? It's the same foolish mistake I made when I first got here—thinking he could just forget."

"This is not your fault," said Violet. "This is one hundred percent Kit's fault. Don't start thinking anything otherwise. You may owe him money, but destroying someone's property is against the law, even so, and scaring innocent children is just low down. He's a no good, evil son of a gun, that man. The man who was with him has a pretty bad reputation in these parts too. We thought he'd left and gone farther west where there's less law enforcement, but I guess he's back. Those two make quite the awful pair, don't they?"

Mary nodded, but only because she couldn't speak. The words felt all choked up in her throat again. Just this morning, life had been perfect. Just this morning, she thought she had everything. How is it possible that everything got turned on its head in just a few minutes of chaos?

They both heard Anna screaming from the cellar.

"Oh, we had better tell the children they can come up now," said Violet. "That's plenty of gauze, Mary. I've got it from here." She tied off the gauze and headed toward the cellar door.

Just then, the front door swung open. Mary gave a start, but it was only Jefferson, who rushed to her side and took her in his strong arms.

Chapter Twenty-One

Jefferson held Mary tightly, silently berating himself for leaving the house that day.

"What happened? How bad is the fence?" Mary asked.

"Half of it burned, but the fire died out before it got too close to the house," said Jefferson.

"I should have gone to the well to put it out, but Violet's arm..."

"Shhhh...you did just what you should have. You got the children to safety and took care of Violet. Thank God you were here." Mary looked up at him, bewilderment on her face.

"Thank God I was here? Don't you see? All of this is happening *because* I am here! Violet is only slightly hurt, and Rusty was grazed, but don't you see? They shot at the *house* indiscriminately! Anything could have happened. One of your children could have *died* today."

"I know," said Jefferson. "Kit is an evil man. He couldn't have cared less who he killed today, so long as he gets his money. Well, we're going to fight fire with fire."

He looked down into her face with a stern expression and said, "I forbid you to blame yourself. This is not your fault."

Mary dropped her chin. She couldn't look him in the eye. Jefferson held her firmly by the arms with both hands. He lowered his face to hers and said, "Mary, look at me."

Slowly, she lifted her eyes to meet his. He saw pain, fear, and love in those beautiful green eyes. A fierce need to protect her swept over him like an all-consuming fire.

They looked into each other's eyes. Jefferson's were firm and demanding while Mary's were full of remorse and guilt. They went on looking at each other like that, Jefferson willing her not to fault herself, and Mary unable to let go of the shame she felt in her heart.

"I'm sorry," Violet interrupted. "It's just...I can't stop the bleeding." Mary turned to see the rag Violet held over her arm dripping with blood. The gauze was soaked through. "I'm applying pressure, but I think I need stitches. I should probably get to Rupert, but I don't know if I can drive myself.".

"I'll drive you," said Jefferson. "We'll alert the Sheriff to the situation while we're in town."

Mary nodded but felt her heart sink at the idea of being left alone with the children. She looked at Violet's bleeding arm and knew there was no other choice.

"Okay," she said. "Hurry back, if you can."

"Just as quickly as we can. Mary, you stay with the children. Do not leave the house. Greg and John are standing guard at the edges of the north and east fields. Tom and Jack are butchering the downed cattle so that doesn't all go to waste. They'll be needing to use the smokehouse and the cellar in the next few hours."

Then he looked her in the eye, and said, "Mary...this is *not* your fault." He turned and guided Violet to the door, saying "You'll have to ride Ajax with me. There's no time to hitch the team." Violet nodded.

"Don't leave the house," Jefferson repeated before he and Violet shut the door behind them.

***

The home seemed to be calming down, though Mary's heart still raced, and her head felt like it was buzzing. She pressed her fingers against her temples to stop it, but it was no use.

"Me too," said William, noticing Mary. "Only I can't tell if it's from the gunshots or Anna's screaming."

"Probably both," said Maurice. "My head is killing me, too."

Anna, however, acted as though nothing had ever happened. Maurice picked up a book to read and buried his head in it. William paced the floor, looking out the window, and vowing to be the man of the house should anyone come back.

"You must be starved," Mary said. "I'll start dinner."

"I'll get the chicken," said William.

"That's okay. I'm heading out to the garden for carrots, anyway."

"No, you stay in," said William, clearly seeing himself as the man of the house since his father was out. Mary smiled, trying not to look too patronizing.

"Alright," she said. "I'll stay with the kids. You get the chicken. Maurice, you can help with the plucking, right?"

"As long as I don't have to do the first part!" Maurice shouted, his head still buried in a book.

"I can handle the rest," said William, looking ever more proud and standing taller by the minute. Something about the attack had awakened something in William, Mary noticed. He was strutting around the house, conjuring up courage and muttering to himself about what he would do if they came back.

Rusty had bounced back rather quickly after the shock wore off. He was already right at William's heels. William had trouble getting him to keep the gauze wrapped around his back. Rusty turned around and bit at it whenever he got the chance.

Mary walked over to the window and gazed out. She looked over at the damaged fence, and the dead cattle still lying in the grass.

It is my fault, she thought. *Whatever Jefferson says, it certainly is my fault. No one can deny that. If it's my fault, then it's my responsibility. I must do something. I can't let this happen again.*

She knew Jefferson would talk to the Sheriff and Kit was likely to be arrested, but she was not convinced that could happen quickly enough to keep Kit and this thug from doing more harm. This morning's tirade had shown her the extent of Kit's rage, and she did not trust that he would be tried, convicted, and incarcerated before he had the chance to do irreparable damage. She knew she needed to step in and do *something.*

She was pondering all these things while staring idly out the window when she noticed a man on a horse coming into view over the horizon. She strained her eyes to see. It was not Kit. The man was shorter and fatter than Kit. He came a little closer.

I think it's that man who was with him. What was his name? Greg said his name...Pudge, I think.

Mary moved toward the door, determined to go reason with him. If Kit could not be reasoned with, perhaps Pudge could be. Maybe he could then reason with Kit.

I have to at least try, she thought.

She knew Jefferson had placed field hands near the house. She had to get to Pudge before the field hands did. More violence would not stop this, she knew.

"Maurice?" she asked. "Can you keep a close eye on Anna for a few moments?" He looked up from his book and nodded, moving down to the floor to play with her. "When William comes back in, tell him he must not come after me. He has to stay with you. He's right out back by the chicken coop. Just call to him if you need him. I'll be back as soon as I can."

"What are you going to do?" Maurice asked.

"I'm going to go reason with someone," she answered. Maurice seemed to understand. He was the reasoning type.

"Don't worry. I'll take care of Anna and keep William distracted when he comes back in. You know he'll be after you. Better hurry." Mary smiled. Maurice was growing up, too.

She opened the front door and saw that Pudge was still making his way up the lane. She would have to hurry if she was going to get to him before the field hands. They probably saw him already. She would have to make sure no one saw her.

She remembered a pistol Jefferson kept in the drawer of the bedside table. She mounted the stairs, three at a time, opened the drawer and shoved the pistol into her waistband, taking care that it was not cocked.

When she came back down the stairs, she peeked out the kitchen window and saw that William was still digging up carrots.

She turned to remind Maurice, but he beat her to it saying, "I won't go anywhere. I've got Anna."

"Thank you," she said, and slipped out the door.

She crept along the side of the house, keeping one eye on Pudge. He had stopped, and stood still on his horse at the edge of the lane.

She mapped her route.

I must get there, she thought. She made her way to the stables. She could see them from her hiding place between the corn rows. It was about ten yards away from the edge of the field. She'd be out in the open for a while.

I'll have to take the chance and hope no one sees me, she thought, remembering that Greg was likely somewhere standing guard. He would not have eyes everywhere, though, and Mary figured she'd just have to take her chance.

Crouching down in the rows of corn, she steadied herself, taking deep breaths. She steadied her gaze on Pudge. He picked at his teeth and spat on the ground. Mary couldn't help but notice the empty look in his eyes, even from a distance.

He does not exactly have the look of an intelligent man with whom one might reason, she thought. *And yet, I must try. If anyone can get him to see reason, surely I can.*

The sun was setting behind him, bleeding pink and orange into the sky, a beautiful backdrop that seemed to clash with the rat-faced, foul man.

I have to do this, she thought. She felt certain that if she could only gain his attention for a few moments, she could talk some sense into him.

After all, it's a very dangerous and senseless thing they've done. Anyone could see that, if only it was presented to them adequately.

She stood up straight and squared her shoulders. Pudge did not see her. She took a step forward and noticed that her knees were quavering. She took another step, felt in her waistband for the pistol, and called out, "Pudge, may I have a word?"

Pudge whipped his horse around with a look of shock in his squinty eyes. Then he laughed, a loud, echoing, empty sounding laugh that sent a shiver up Mary's spine.

She had never seen Pudge up close, and she was taken aback when she did. He had a large, round face with slits for eyes and a curved, pointed nose. He reminded her of a fat rat.

When he stopped laughing and squinted at Mary with his squinty black eyes, Mary had to gather her courage once again, for every fiber of her being wanted to turn and run. It was too late for that, though.

She gathered herself and said, "Pudge. Hear me out, please. I am the one Kit is after. I'm the one he wants. I owe him a tremendous amount of money. I admit that. There is a better way for him to get what he wants. We can handle this legally. I've already been talking to Jefferson about how we can repay this debt. Please, tell Kit we have every intention of paying what he's owed. We just need time to get it together." She was panting hard, spitting out words between gasps.

She had intended to sound more cool and persuasive. Instead, when the words came out, she sounded desperate and petrified.

Pudge gave a rotten smile, his teeth shades of yellow, brown, and black. One front tooth was completely missing, and the other had a gleaming gold crown covering its entirety. Mary tried not to focus on his smile, instead looking directly into the slits he had for eyes, trying to scan them for any sign of feeling. She saw none.

"You think he cares about the debt, anymore?" Pudge asked, his voice deep and gruff as though he had smoked for his entire life.

"Well, that's why he's here terrorizing this innocent family, isn't it?"

"Oh, no, my dear. You owe him money, certainly. But you've done more damage than that. You've damaged his pride, you have. You let him think he was winning your heart, didn't you? And then you gave him the slip."

"I did," Mary admitted, readily. "But we *will* pay what we owe." She was secretly hoping to find a legal loophole for getting out of it, but Pudge didn't need to know *that*.

"That was your mortal sin, little lady," Pudge sneered.

"What does it matter so long as he gets what is owed to him?"

"You don't seem to understand. I'm just doing my job," Pudge said, leaning forward and smiling and revealing yellow, rotting teeth. Mary stood silent for a moment, unsure of how to respond.

When Mary was silent, Pudge laughed loudly and mockingly. Mary shuddered at the sound of it but refused to give up. She had come to reason with him, and she wasn't about to give up that easily.

"Pudge, you're a reasonable man. Come now, you must see that what you are doing will land you in jail. You can't tell me you're so loyal to Kit that you would go to jail for him."

"Loyal! Bah!" Pudge scoffed. "I'm loyal to none but myself. Kit has paid me enough to let me retire in peace. That's all I want. I'll do whatever he asks. It has nothing to do with *him*. I want what he can pay me."

She had been so sure that she could convince this man, but all he seemed to care about was getting paid.

"Surely, money is not worth tarnishing your soul. A child could have died today. Could you live with the blood of a child on your hands? What good would all the riches be if you had to live out your life knowing you had taken the life of one of God's precious children?" As Mary made this little speech, tears formed in the corners of her eyes, and she realized that she believed every word of what she was saying.

Pudge, however, looked unmoved. "And just what makes you think I care about children?" he snarled.

"Pudge, I'm begging you. Leave this family alone! They've done nothing to deserve this."

"No, they haven't," he said, an evil grin crossing his face. "But you have. And now it's clear that the best way to get at you is by coming after *them*, so thanks for making that clear."

"Coward!" She shouted, and Pudge lunged toward her. In an instant, Mary pulled the pistol out of her waistband, cocked it, and pointed it directly at Pudge's face. He moved again to grab her, but she put her finger on the trigger and said, "Don't move a muscle."

Pudge froze.

"Give me one good reason why I shouldn't put a bullet through your head right now," said Mary. She was surprised that her voice was cool and her arm steady.

"Because unlike me, you actually care about your integrity," Pudge answered, equally cool. He seemed certain she would not pull the trigger, and Mary began to doubt she would. "I can live with myself if I kill you," he said. "You on the other hand..."

"I'm going to go back to the house now. You will leave this land this minute. I tried to reason with you. You have forced our hand. You'll regret this."

"On the contrary, Miss Mary, *you* are the one who will live to regret this." He pulled on the reins, turned his horse, clicked his spurs, and rode off into the horizon.

Now her hand was shaking. She removed her finger from the trigger and lowered the pistol. She watched until Pudge disappeared into the distance. The sun was just beginning to set, and it would have been a peaceful and beautiful sight, had it not been for the thudding in her heart.

She only noticed that her legs were shaking when she turned on her heel and started walking back toward the house. Greg met her along the way.

"Mary! You shouldn't have. Once I saw you talking, I stayed hidden. I thought showing up might make things worse."

"You made the right choice, Greg. Thank you. He can't be reasoned with."

"I was ready to jump out to your rescue when I saw him lunge at you, but I saw the pistol just as quickly and hid again."

"You're wise and thoughtful, Greg. We're lucky to have you around."

"Oh, thank you, Miss Mary," Greg said, turning pink.

"Just do me a favor? Don't mention this to Jefferson. I have to tell him myself. I promised him I'd tell him the truth from now on."

"Upon my honor," Greg said, placing a hand over his heart and bowing slightly. Then he said, "Jefferson is the best man I've ever worked for. I hope I'll always have a place here."

Mary's heart leapt within her. What greater accolades could a man receive than that of his loyal workers?

Mary watched as Greg went back to his post and wondered what she could possibly do now that her plan to reason with Pudge had failed.

There must be a way out of this, she thought. *There's just no way they can get away with this.*

"Where were you?" William demanded, running out into the yard as she was coming back from the stables.

"Trying to reason with that thug," Mary answered.

"What were you thinking?" William asked, clearly trying to sound superior. Mary heard the worry in his voice and decided to let it go. After all, she had put them through enough.

"William, I'm sorry for all that I have put you and your siblings through. I need you to understand that I am going to do everything within my power to protect you."

"I'll do everything I can to protect them too," said William. "But you shouldn't have gone out there alone."

"I put you all in this situation, and I was trying to get you out of it. I thought he would listen to reason."

"But he didn't, did he?" William snapped. "And if you'd bothered to ask anyone who knows anything around here, they would have told you not to try to reason with Pudge."

"William..."

"You could have died!" he shouted, his voice breaking.

In that moment, Mary realized that she meant more to William than he had ever let on. She also realized that he was right. Her brazen decision to go out on foot, sneak around the guards Jefferson had set up, and go out to talk to Pudge alone was not courageous, but foolish. She'd risked her own life, and if something had happened to her, the children would have been left alone.

In the moment, she had been so convinced that she could get Pudge to see things clearly that it seemed like the courageous thing to do. She realized now that had only been wishful thinking.

"You're right, William," she said softly. "Bravery is commendable, but not without wisdom. I did a foolish thing tonight, and I'm sorry."

William seemed taken aback by her tender apology, and he turned his face. Mary thought it was to hide his tears.

***

That evening, Jefferson arrived home. Rupert and Violet arrived shortly after.

I have to tell him, Mary thought. She remembered the way he had said *Do not leave the house,* and she knew she should have listened to him.

I was so foolish to think I could reason with him, she thought, knowing she had risked herself on a mission that proved futile. What was more, Jefferson had specifically asked her to stay with the children and not to leave the house. She had gone against his order, and she dared not betray his trust by trying to hide it from him.

"Jefferson, I need a word with you," she said nearly as soon as he walked in the door. The children were fascinated by Violet's stitches, and Rupert was happy to give them the details on just how he put them in.

Jefferson and Mary stepped into the kitchen. Mary tried to speak, but the words wouldn't come.

"What is it, Mary?" She looked down at the floor and ran her fingers along a seam in her dress. He took a step closer, running his fingers softly down the side of her face, stopping under her chin, and softly lifting her face toward his.

"You've been through a lot, Mary, but you'll come through just as you have before. Now, where's that fiery spirit?" Tears began to form in her eyes. "Come, here," he said, trying to pull her into her arms. She resisted. She couldn't accept his comfort until she'd confessed. "Mary, don't push me away. I'm here for you." His voice was so unwavering, his eyes so kind.

"I did something today...something you directly asked me *not* to do." Jefferson peered down into her eyes, his hand still resting gently under her chin. Mary dared to look up at him, straight into his eyes. She saw concern and kindness, which gave her the courage to go on.

"I left the house. I know you said not to, but I did. I got it into my head that I could reason with that man...that man, Pudge."

"No one reasons with Pudge, Mary," he said. His voice was stern, but his eyes were still kind.

"I know that now."

"What happened?"

"I thought I could get him to see reason, but he attacked me."

"*Mary*," he said. His voice was desperate and sincere, and Mary immediately felt her regret deepen within her heart.

"Jefferson, I'm sorry. I'm *so* sorry."

"I told you we would face this together. You went and tried to face it alone," he said. His voice was stern and sad.

Mary's eyes fell to the floor again. She couldn't look him in the eye.

"Mary, I need you to trust me. You put yourself in harm's way..."

"I put all of *you* in harm's way!" Mary cried. "Don't you see that? None of this would be happening if it weren't for *me*."

"Mary, I told you before we left that none of this is your fault."

"But it is, Jefferson! Can't you see that? Of course it's my fault! I put your children in danger. How can you be okay with that?"

"Now listen here," he said firmly. "I am *not* okay with what happened today. I'm simply placing the blame on Christopher Edwards and Pudge, where it belongs. Now, I've heard enough of you blaming yourself for their actions. The only thing you need to take responsibility for is what you did this evening. You went against my wishes and put yourself in danger. You went out there *alone*, Mary! You could have been killed! And then who would have been here to watch the children?"

"I know. I thought I could convince him..."

"You thought wrong," he barked. "Do you understand the danger you put yourself in? Mary...I know you think you know better than anyone, but there was a *reason* I asked you to stay in the house. For God's sake, Mary, I had field hands standing guard to *protect* you."

"I can see that now, but I was just trying..."

"I know what you were trying to do. That's not the problem. The problem is you think you're smarter than everyone else. You thought you'd be able to reason with Pudge with your sheer intelligence, didn't you?"

Mary's face flushed red. When she'd decided to defy Jefferson, she was thinking of herself as heroic and self-sacrificing. Jefferson was pointing out that it was nothing but stupid and arrogant. Even William had been able to see that.

"Jefferson..."

By this time, the tears were falling fast from her eyes. He looked down at her, and as he watched her tears fall, the fire went out from his eyes, and the anger melted from his face.

"Mary," he said tenderly. "I just don't want you hurt. I didn't want to leave at all. I left Greg and the other field hands to guard the house. I specifically told you to stay inside. I did that to protect you. I *hated* leaving you. Then you went and took everything into your own hands, without asking anyone...as if you knew better than anyone."

Mary hung her head to hide her flushed face. His kind eyes and soft voice cut to her soul.

He's right, she thought. *And so was William. I thought I knew better than Jefferson, and he was just trying to protect me.*

She struggled to speak over the lump in her throat, but managed to choke out the words, "I'm so sorry."

"I forgive you, but I have to know you're not going to go and do anything so foolish again. I told you that we will fight this *together*. I need to know that you aren't going to try to take this into your own hands again. Promise me."

"I promise," she whispered.

"Now, come here," Jefferson said, holding his arms out to her. She fell into them and wept.

Chapter Twenty-Two

Jefferson woke up feeling hopeful that morning. Rupert had been visiting with his friend when he and Violet had arrived the previous day, one Mr. James Humphrey, who happened to be a lawyer. There had been no time to discuss the details of that meeting with Mary, not after discovering what she'd done. He worried that perhaps he had come down too hard on Mary.

After all, she was trying to end this peacefully, he thought. He could not, however, overlook her arrogance in having made such a decision on her own, with no input from anyone else, and directly against what he asked of her.

He was moved by her genuine repentance. Today, he felt they had the chance for a new start, and he was determined to protect her, whatever came their way.

He sat up in bed and turned to look at her, still sleeping soundly, the sun from the window shining softly on her golden hair.

She looks like an angel, he thought. He thought about waking her to tell her what the lawyer had said but decided against it. The fact that she could sleep peacefully at all after what had happened was a miracle, and he dared not interfere with it.

He got out of the bed slowly, trying not to let it creak under him. He got dressed quietly and descended the stairs. Violet and the children were already awake, and they were eating bread and cheese in the kitchen.

"Sorry, it's all I could manage," she said as Jefferson appeared in the doorway.

"How's your arm?"

"Oh, it's okay. It's pretty sore today. Rupert said he'll stop by and make sure it isn't getting infected."

"Good, what time will that be?"

"This afternoon, I think."

"I'd like to talk with him about Mr. Humphrey."

"Yes, he sounded certain, didn't he? Did you tell Mary?"

"No. Not yet."

"What? Why not? She will be so relieved!"

"We had more pressing things to talk about last night."

"Well, I can't think of anything more pressing, but anyway, you should tell her first thing when she wakes up."

"I will, and I was planning on taking her into town to see Mr. Humphrey. He told us to come see him this afternoon."

"Good! Rupert will stay and help me look after the children while you meet with Mr. Humphrey."

"Is that Emma Humphrey's dad?" William asked, looking interested.

"Yes, I think so," said Jefferson, "why?"

"No reason, just wondering," William answered.

"He's wondering because he thinks Emma's the prettiest girl in school," Maurice said in a sing-song voice with a smirk on his face.

"Shut up!" William retorted, swinging an arm as Maurice ducked out of the way.

"Oh, leave him alone," said Violet, playfully tapping Maurice on the head. "It's perfectly natural that he should be interested in a girl at school." Then, turning to William, who was already blushing a deep shade of red, said, "So, Emma Humphrey. What's she like?"

"Oh, Gawd Aunt Violet, please!" He moaned.

"You're the one who should leave him alone," Jefferson joked. Then he said, "Son, bide your time. If you were a few years older, I'd wish you luck. The Humphreys are a good family. Just bide your time, son."

"I can't handle this," William said, "I'm going fishing."

"I'm coming!" said Maurice.

"No, you are not," William replied.

"Dad!" Maurice whined.

"Not this time, son. He needs some space," Jefferson said to Maurice, who hung his head in disappointment.

"It's not my fault he's in love with Emma Humphrey," Maurice grumbled as he trudged out of the kitchen.

"I'm not ready for this," Jefferson said.

"I'm afraid you'll have to get ready fast," said Violet, laughing. "He's nearly thirteen."

"How did that happen?"

"He seems to be growing into a decent young man," said Violet.

"I hope he is."

"He most certainly is," said Mary. Neither Jefferson nor Violet had heard her approach.

"Good morning, darling," Jefferson said, standing to kiss her lightly on the cheek.

"Tell her the good news, Jefferson!" said Violet eagerly.

"Good news?" questioned Mary.

"Very good news we never quite got to talk about last night. Sit down." He pulled out a kitchen chair for Mary to sit on.

"Yesterday, when we went to find Rupert, he happened to be with a friend. James Humphrey. Mr. Humphrey is a lawyer. We told Rupert what happened here last night and how I'd been injured," Violet said.

"And he said," continued Jefferson, "that he didn't think Kit has a leg to stand on. He told me to come back into town with you tomorrow, and that he'd go over the particulars with us once he has a little more information from you. In the meantime, he said he'd send post to the banker in Rosewood Texas, asking for any details that might be necessary. In short, he doesn't think there's any way Kit could have a legal right to your hand in marriage, not unless it had already been agreed upon..."

"But it has been..."

"In writing. He said it would take a legally binding document for Kit to have a right to anything, including the money. When a person dies, their debts die with him—in most cases, anyway. Mr. Humphrey believes we have a good chance of winning this whole thing legally. Then, we can come after Kit with charges of property vandalism and assault."

Mary leaned back in her chair and let out a sigh.

"Nothing's for sure, yet. He told us to come see him this afternoon. He has some questions for you. He said he would take up our case as a favor to Rupert. He said he owed him one, anyway."

"I can hardly wait to get there," said Mary. "We have to move fast. Case or no case, we're not safe until Kit is tried and convicted."

***

The hours of the evening seemed to crawl. Jefferson had gone out into the fields to prepare them for the winter and to plant a few fall crops along the edges of the biggest field. Tilling was hard work, and even with his team of horses and plow, the work was long and laborious. Jefferson always prayed for rain whenever he worked the ground.

So much depends on what I can't control, he thought, even as he moved his lips in prayer, asking for rain even though it was months before he would plant. All rain was welcome, any time it came. Jefferson had learned to be grateful for the rain, and he had learned to recognize that his own prosperity was due to the rainfall as much as his hard work and mind for business.

My own efforts and good luck. One would do no good without the other, he thought. For Jefferson, working with every fiber of his being went hand in hand with praying for rain. One was entirely within his control, and one was completely outside of his control. Yet, both parts needed to come together to produce what he needed to survive.

Then, his thoughts turned to Kit.

What is within my control, and what isn't? He wondered. With farming, it was easy to figure out. He knew exactly what his job was and what was God's. He sensed that the same principle would apply to other parts of his life, but the specifics were not as clear, so he tended to keep his mind on his farming. With farming, he could understand his role, and

God's, so he kept his eyes in front of him and tried to keep his mind on what he knew best—his fields and crops.

There was no shortage of work to keep his mind occupied. The sun seemed to rise more slowly than usual, creeping upward into the sky inch by inch.

The fields had become a place of solitude for Jefferson. He stood in them, and he somehow felt small and powerful all at once. He felt small because they stretched as far as the eye could see and sometimes grew to tower above him, and he felt powerful because he had been the one to till, plant, water, and weed them. In the fields, he felt thankful.

God's red dirt was something magical. You had only to place tiny seeds into it at just the right time and with just the right care, and they would spring up into something life-giving and sustaining. Jefferson had always loved the earth.

When he was a young boy, he would watch his mother plant tiny seeds in long, even rows in the ground. Every morning, he would wake up and run out to the garden to see if anything had sprouted. Finally, the little sprouts would emerge, and Jefferson remembered thinking it was just like magic. Every day, as the sprouts grew larger and larger, Jefferson would be mesmerized by the miracle happening before his eyes.

Once, he had said to his mother, "Dirt is magical, isn't it?" His mother, being of the Puritan sort, had responded, "There's no such thing as magic, dear," but she had smiled at him, and Jefferson remembered that smile. When he worked in his fields, he felt connected to his mother. He'd often felt the pain from the loss of his mother and father when he was only sixteen, and had lamented that history had repeated itself in taking Rosie from his children when they were young.

218

Today, he didn't think of loss, though. Today, he thought of all the possibilities before him. He loved Mary, and every day he grew to love her more. He loved her despite her flaws, and yet, she seemed to be growing out of arrogance and into humility.

He felt himself growing, too. Just like the harvest must die and fall to the ground to fertilize it for the next crop, so he'd grieved his losses and felt his soul grow fertile enough to love again.

He was watching his sons and daughter grow before his eyes. If ever he had thought the sprouting of plants magical, the maturing of his children was far more miraculous. They were growing and changing every day, and Jefferson felt full and alive when he thought of his family.

It was with these thoughts filling his mind that he had vowed to himself, to his dead parents and late wife, and to God, that he would do all that was in his power to protect his family. He would go through the means of the law, first, but if that failed him, he would not be afraid to take the law into his own hands.

On this warm, fall morning, however, he was growing more confident that he would not have to resort to lawlessness after all, and he was counting the seconds until his meeting with Mr. Humphrey.

Chapter Twenty-Three

The sun was warm, and the clouds shielded them from its rays as they got into the carriage to go into town. They'd hitched up Bessie and Bella and left Violet with the children.

"Greg, Jack, and Tom are on alert," Jefferson said. "They know what to do if anyone comes around."

"We'll be fine," Violet said. She and the children waved, and Jefferson whipped the reins.

The carriage lurched, and Mary grabbed on to her bonnet to keep it from flying off her head. Jefferson looked at her, and she smiled back with that radiant, full of life, hopeful smile of hers.

Jefferson managed a small, half smile back. He'd been feeling hopeful just this morning, but as the day wore on, he began to think about all the possible ways this could go wrong. What if Mr. Humphrey was wrong? What if things did not go their way? He felt a knot growing in the pit of his stomach and tried hard not to let on. It was no use. Mary always knew when something was wrong.

"What is it?" She asked.

"Nothing," he said. She gave him a skeptical look.

"It's not nothing. I know you well enough by now. Come on." He smiled placidly. Sometimes he loved that she could read him like a book. Other times it was aggravating.

"Okay," he relented. "My mind is swimming with everything that could go wrong."

"You're afraid to lose me?" He nodded. Mary moved closer to him on the carriage bench and laid her head on his shoulder.

"I'm right here," she whispered. Jefferson kissed the top of her head, then rested his chin on her soft hair, keeping his eyes on the gravel road.

"We get through this together, right?" She nodded, placed her hand above his knee and squeezed gently.

Together.

***

The long drive felt short to Jefferson. With Mary's head on his shoulder, he felt he could have driven all day and night. The day was warm, but a breeze coming off the gulf cooled his face as the team picked up speed down a winding hill toward main street. Mary still sat with her head on his shoulder and her hand on his knee.

Jefferson breathed in a long, deep breath. The closer they got to town, the more the knot in his stomach dissolved. He had Mary by his side. That is what mattered. He knew he had her heart, and she had his. He let out his breath, slow and long, readying himself for the meeting with Mr. Humphrey. He hoped against hope that this lawyer was right. He was not typically trusting of lawyers, but this was Rupert's friend, and Jefferson trusted Rupert with his life.

They parked the carriage in front of a building. *Humphrey and Humphrey Law* was printed in neat, gold letters across the top of the doorway. It was sandwiched between the bank and the Sheriff's office.

Mary adjusted her skirt, took off her bonnet, and smoothed out her hair. Jefferson helped her down from the carriage. They stood there a moment.

"Well, this is it," said Mary. They held hands and crossed the threshold.

The offices looked much bigger from the inside. A brown-haired woman in a navy blue dress sat at a desk near the entrance, absorbed in papers. Mary recognized her from church services. Finally, she looked up and noticed them.

"How can I help you?" she said, her voice sweet and welcoming.

"We're here to see Mr. Humphrey," Mary responded.

"Mr. James or Mr. John?"

"James," said Jefferson.

"Right this way."

They followed her to the back of the building, which seemed to go on forever. In the far back corner, Mr. James Humphrey sat in a tiny office behind a mahogany desk that was littered with documents, which he peered over.

"Mr. James. Your appointment is here," said the woman. He looked up and smiled. Jefferson was taken aback by how young he looked. When he'd met him the night before, it was after dark, and he saw him by candlelight. This afternoon, seeing him in the light of day, Jefferson realized that he had to be in his early twenties. His dress, spectacles, and pocket watch looked suited to an older man, but failed to mask his youth. He smiled at them.

"Ahhh, Mr. and Mrs. Just! Have a seat!" He said, pulling up a chair.

"Rita, would you be a dear and bring another chair?" He asked.

Jefferson meant to say he was fine standing, but Rita disappeared before he could say so. He gestured for Mary to take a seat.

"So, you're having problems with Pudge."

"Well, it's mostly Kit," said Mary. "Pudge is just in it for the money."

"As he always is. Someone has to catch that rascal red-handed. He always seemed to get off scot-free even when everyone knows he's a good for nothing scoundrel."

Rita returned with the chair, and Jefferson sat down next to Mary.

Jefferson knew he had talked like this with him and Rupert the other night, but he was beginning to lose faith that this young, inexperienced man could help them.

"You're younger than I thought you were, Mr. Humphrey," said Jefferson.

"Please, call me James, and yes, I'm young, I know, but so is Rupert, and he's an excellent physician. I may be young, but I'm good at what I do. Anyway, I've been talking about your case with my brother. He's got a few years on me. Now, I just need a little more information from you," he said, turning his eye on Mary. "Tell me your story, the best you can remember it, in your own words."

He took out a clean sheet of paper, dipped his quill, and looked at Mary in earnest. Mary shifted and looked up at Jefferson.

"Since when have you been shy?" Jefferson joked, trying to lighten the mood. "Go on. Tell him."

"I'm sorry," she said. "It's just the last couple days have been awful, and before what happened, I was trying so hard to forget him. I think I was doing quite well, and now I have to try to remember someone I never want to think about again for as long as I live." Tears formed in the corners of her eyes.

Jefferson put a heavy hand on her knee, bent his face down to her level, and looked into her eyes.

"Mary, there will be a time to forget. That time is not now. When Kit and Pudge are out of our lives, then you can forget. Right now, we need you to remember so that we can all forget and move on." He gave her knee a gentle squeeze. She closed her eyes, took a breath, and began to tell her story. James scribbled furiously all the while.

Then, when she had finished telling all she could remember, James asked, "So there were no vows?"

"Vows? Goodness, no. I never married him, if that's what you mean."

"Good. Not even in the privacy of your home?"

"No! Like I said, the first I heard of it was after my parents died."

"Just crossing my t's and dotting my I's, dear. I'm not questioning your integrity."

"I understand. No, I did not vow anything to him."

"During that time when you were leading him to believe he was winning your heart, did you say anything that could have been misconstrued as a promise?"

"I was careful not to."

"Good. A verbal promise wouldn't bind you to him anyway but I do like to know what we're up against. It looks to me as though you have absolutely no obligation to Kit, whatsoever when it comes to his claim on marriage to you. You are legally married to Jefferson, and that marriage cannot be annulled on the basis of someone else having been promised you. That would never hold up before a jury. Now, as for the debts...what do you know about that?"

"My father owed him thousands. He got into some pretty bad debt, as it turns out. I think he kept it so secret because he was the mayor. It wouldn't have been a good look for the mayor to have personal debts. Kit and Mr. Whalen, the banker back in Rosewood, were the only two that knew how much Dad owed. He kept it even from my own mother."

James shook his head sadly.

"I'm sorry for you, dear, that you had to discover such a mess in the wake of their untimely deaths."

"Thank you," said Mary, her voice shaking.

"Now, when a person dies, certain debts die with him," James said, attempting to get back to business. "I'm sending a telegram to Mr. Whalen asking him to release your father's statements to me. I'll need your signature, Mary. You said this Mr. Whalen was a family friend?"

"Yes, and he despises Kit."

"Good. He will likely give us whatever information we need to help convict him, then. I have high hopes that your debts will be cleared, and your marriage to Mr. Jefferson secure." He gave them both a warm, friendly smile. "Even if there are some debts to be repaid by Mary, the banks can help out in such circumstances. Jefferson, you have a reputation for honesty and being true to your word, so if you need a loan to pay back whatever is owed, I've no doubt you will receive it."

"This is all very helpful, James. I'm grateful to you, but I'm still worried about what Kit and Pudge might do in the meantime. They've already shot at the house, killed several cattle, and injured my sister. It could have been one of the children, and it could have been worse."

Mary shivered visibly. James shook his head.

"What kind of a man shoots at a house full of children?" He asked. "That alone should put him behind bars."

"It *should*," Jefferson responded.

"You have to file charges," said James. "You can do that today. Describe exactly what happened. I'll need to take down Violet's statement, too, and talk to the kids."

"You can come out for dinner next week," Mary suggested.

"Thank you, I think I will! I'll take down your statements, and we'll file the charges against both. I'd be surprised if any jury finds them innocent."

Jefferson was beginning to feel relieved, but the knot in his stomach had not disappeared. All of this would take time— time they might not have.

"I'm grateful to you, James, but I want to know what to do in the meantime. You know what could have happened the other day. This all seems like a long process, and they could come back and do more damage while it's in the works."

"Very true," said James. "My expertise is the law. I don't know that I have great advice outside of the realm, but I do believe he's less likely to attack if there are witnesses."

"I have the field hands."

"That's a start. Are they migrant workers or residents?"

"Mostly migrant workers."

"Can you get some of the townspeople to hang around?"

"I could invite some of the women to afternoon tea," suggested Mary.

"Unfortunately, a woman's word in court isn't taken as seriously. If it's his word against yours, it may not go our way."

"I don't see why that should be," Mary spat out. "We have eyes and ears just like you, do we not?"

James held up his arms as if in surrender.

"I'm not saying it's right," he said. "It's just how it is. Can you bring any men around?"

"I'll ask some friends," Jefferson said, though he couldn't think of any who could leave their fields or work all day, and who knew when Kit would show up again? Rupert was there as often as he could be, but even he couldn't abandon his patients, even for Violet.

"Good," said James. "You gather some witnesses. I'll get all I need from Mr. Whalen. I've got your statements. I'll come by in the next few days to talk to Violet and the children."

He stood and stuck out a hand. Jefferson and Mary stood, shook hands with him, thanked him, and stepped back out into the sunlight where Bessie and Bella stomped their hooves and swished flies away with their tails.

"Well, overall, good news," said Jefferson, smiling. He did feel lighter. He still worried about keeping his family safe in the meantime, but now there was an end in sight. They had filed charges, and Jefferson felt certain Kit would not get away with what he had done. All he needed to do now was to keep his family safe until Kit was safely behind bars.

"Yes!" said Mary, smiling. "Good news! And a relief to be done with that. We'll get back to living our lives soon enough."

She smiled up at him, and her face beamed with joy. The sun seemed to reflect off her golden hair, and her sea-green eyes looked up at him, full of hope and trust. He cupped a hand around the back of her neck and gently pulled her to himself.

"I can't lose you," he said, and bent to kiss her.

Chapter Twenty-Four

Mary melted into the feeling of Jefferson's strong hands around her, and his soft lips on hers. She didn't mind the feeling of his beard as it tickled her face. She felt safe with his arms around her.

She felt lighter already. James was young, but smart and competent, and Jefferson would keep them safe until Mr. Humphrey's work was complete.

"Let's grab a bite to eat," said Jefferson. "We should celebrate, and you don't get much time out of the house. The outdoor market should be open."

They walked hand in hand, Mary bounced a bit with every step, feling like she was young and class had just let out for the summer. She tossed her bonnet aside to let the breeze run through her hair and to feel the sun's rays on her face.

"I can almost feel the freckles popping out on my face, but I don't even care," she said.

"I love your freckles, anyway," said Jefferson, running a finger lightly down the bridge of her nose.

"I've always considered them an annoying flaw in my complexion," she admitted. Then she laughed and said, "I used to rub lemons on my face every night. Someone told me once that would get rid of the freckles."

Jefferson laughed. "Violet used to rub charcoal on her teeth every morning. She swore it cured bad breath and whitened her teeth. Don't tell her I told you that."

They laughed as they walked down into the valley where dozens of booths were set up for the outdoor market. The smell of peaches lingered thickly in the air, as they approached a booth with baskets full to the brim of perfectly ripe, red-orange peaches.

"Oh, we can't resist that smell, now, can we?" Then, turning to the pale-faced, blond woman behind the counter, he asked for two peaches and handed her a two-cent piece.

"Thank you," she said in a heavy Swedish accent.

The peach was soft and fit perfectly into the palm of her hand. Mary bit into it, and the bright yellow juice filled her mouth with the sweet flavor.

"Oh, I don't think I've ever had a peach this good," said Jefferson.

"Nor I," Mary agreed. Jefferson bought a dozen to bring home to Violet and the kids.

"More? Yes?" said the Swede, grinning from ear to ear as she placed several peaches into a brown paper bag. "Delicious, yes?"

"The best peach I've ever tasted," Mary said, happy to indulge this woman, who was clearly taking pride in her crop of peaches. Jefferson readily agreed.

They were just moving on to the next booth filled with delicious-smelling bread and pastries when James came galloping up behind them.

"We need you back at the office," he said, panting for breath. The horse snorted and stomped. "Kit's lawyer showed up at our office shortly after the two of you left. He left a document."

"What document?" Mary asked, alarmed.

"You're going to want to come back to the office and look it over. It could be forged. It likely is. In that case, it won't take much to prove it was a forged signature. Mary, do you think you'd recognize your father's signature if you saw it?"

"Yes, I'll know," she answered. She knew she would. She'd seen it a hundred times and had even tried to forge it herself for a school assignment she had missed.

"Meet me back at my office," James said, turning his horse around and galloping away.

Disillusionment set in. Mary had felt light as a feather just a moment earlier. It took a few moments for the truth to settle in, and she felt her heart growing heavier. The sweet peach seemed to turn bitter in her mouth.

Jefferson took her face in his cupped hands and tilted it upward toward him.

"Don't fret," he said. "James said it's likely forged. This is just a minor setback. We'll get through this. Come on, let's get to the carriage."

The road from the market in the valley to Main Street on the hill seemed longer than it had when they'd left the Humphrey offices. Mary felt her stomach turning, as if something bad were about to happen.

Jefferson pulled her next to him and rested his chin on her head.

Once inside the office, James slammed the document down in front of Mary.

It was dated October of 1878.

This document hereby states that Mr. Walter Baker agrees to repay Mr. Christopher Edwards in the amount of $7,566 calculated with a seven percent interest. Mr. Baker agrees to repay this sum within three years. In the event that Mr. Baker is unable to repay the debt, or in the event of his death, Mr.

Baker and his daughter, Mary Baker, agree that Mr. Edwards will take Mary as his wife, thereby clearing the debts owed.

Signed,

Walter Baker

Mary stared at the paper. She read it over once, twice, three times.

"Well," James asked impatiently. "It's not his signature, is it? It should be easy to prove, if not. Mr. Whalen has already agreed to send over statements. We'll have plenty of authentic signatures to compare."

Mary went on staring, dumbfounded, for it *was* in fact, his signature. It had his signature flowing curve coming off the W in Walter, and his unique way of writing a capital B in Baker. Mary knew instantly that his was a genuine signature, but she couldn't speak, for her eyes kept running over the part of the document that said, "Mr. Baker and his daughter, Mary Baker…"

And his daughter, she thought. *I never agreed to any such thing.* She felt so deeply betrayed by this man whom she had loved. She simply couldn't believe he would sign something like this, but there it was staring her in the face—his signature.

Tears pricked behind her eyes, and a lump formed in her throat.

"Is it…" she choked out the words but couldn't finish the sentence.

"Is it…is it legal?" She finally choked out.

"I'm not sure. It may be. There's still a 1769 law in place in the state of Texas that might make it tricky to prove that you are not already Christopher Edwards' legal wife, thereby nullifying your marriage to Mr. Just."

"What does that mean?" Jefferson asked. His voice was tense, and Mary knew the anger was boiling up in him, about to spill over.

James must have sensed it too. In a soothing voice, he said, "It may not mean anything. In Texas, if a woman has agreed to marry a man, and it's been over a year, they could be considered married legally."

"But we never said any vows!" Mary protested. "There must be a way to prove that!"

"Vows or no vows. If a young woman agrees to marry and is found to have had relations with the man, she is considered married under the law, no matter if she has said vows or not."

"But I've done no such thing!" She said, growing red in the face. Every fiber of her being burned with anger and embarrassment. Mother would have fainted on the spot to even hear that a man had spoken of her supposed "relations" in front of her.

"Well, I'm afraid that is your word against his," said James. "Look, I believe you, but that may not be enough. We'll have to convince a jury. This document says you knew. Your father put his signature on it, saying you were aware of this arrangement. The fact that there is evidence that you were aware and that it was several years ago might make it easy for Kit's lawyer to argue that you're a runaway wife."

"But I never married him! This isn't right! Check the church records in Rosewood. Talk to the reverends. You will see. No one performed a ceremony. We are *not* married and never were!"

Jefferson placed a hand on her knee to calm her down, but Mary noticed that he was shaking as well.

Oh, I hope he believes me, she thought desperately, knowing she had lied to him before and probably did not deserve his trust, but it was God's honest truth. She had never married Kit. She had never said vows. She had certainly never *had relations*, and she had no knowledge of the agreement between Kit and her father.

Chapter Twenty-Five

James looked from Mary to Jefferson and back again before politely asking Mary if he might have a word alone with Jefferson.

Jefferson felt as though his heart might pound right out of his chest. He stood to open the door for Mary, who stood to leave the room, looking confused.

"Don't fret, Mary. We will fight this." He took her by the hand, not wanting to let her out of his sight.

"Jefferson, please, you must believe me when I say that I have never had vows or...." She blushed and lowered her voice and said, "or...relations..."

Jefferson studied her green eyes. They did not shift under his gaze. She looked directly into his eyes, pleading with him. He knew she had lied to him before, but when he looked into her eyes now, he believed her with all his heart.

"I believe you," he said, squeezing her hand. She stepped out of the office, and Jefferson shut the door behind her.

"I wanted to talk off the record," James said, gesturing for Jefferson to sit back down. He did.

"I've only been a lawyer for a short while," he began. "But I've seen a lot of liars." Jefferson felt a muscle twitch in his jaw. "Your wife is not one of them," James continued. "I just wanted to tell you, man to man, not to let her go over this. When she saw that signature, I was studying her face. I saw genuine shock and dismay. I believe she loves you, Jefferson."

Jefferson breathed out slowly and spoke. "Thank you for that, James, but I could tell by looking into her eyes that she was telling me the truth. We've had our run-ins with dishonesty, and I believe we've both given it up for good. I trust her."

"I'm relieved to hear you say that," said James. "I've seen many a man abandon his wife at the mere accusation of infidelity, but when I saw that look on Mary's face, I knew I had to tell you. I believe her, and I'm pretty good at spotting a liar."

"You and I might believe her," Jefferson said. "But can we convince a court?"

"That's my job," said James. "For now, you worry about your job. If you and Mary can trust each other, you can get through this. You worry about protecting your family. I'll worry about convincing a jury. First, we have to get our day in court."

"Are the charges filed?"

"John is working on that end of things as we speak."

Both men stood and shook hands firmly.

"Thank you, James," Jefferson said, feeling relieved to have the case in such capable hands.

He rounded the corner and saw Mary sitting on a bench wringing her hands and tapping her foot. She looked up at him when she heard him approach, and Jefferson saw the desperation in her eyes.

"What did he say that I couldn't hear?" She asked.

"He wanted to make sure I knew that he thought you were telling the truth."

"Oh, I am!"

"I know, dear. I didn't need him to tell me. I knew it by the look in your eyes."

"Oh, Jefferson," she said, wrapping her arms around his waist and putting her head on his chest. "I never meant to put you through all of this. Honestly, I didn't."

He patted her on the head and said, "I know, darling. I know. Let's go home."

They were silent as they mounted the carriage. The sun was setting, spreading a warm glow across the town. They sat in silence. Mary was perched like a bird upon the carriage bench, hands folded in her lap, eyes looking straight ahead, lost in thought.

The only sound was the steady, rhythmic clip-clopping of the horses' hooves, the jingling of their reins, and the crunching of the gravel under the wheels. The sun sank lower, and the dusky gray engulfed them. An owl hooted from the silhouette of a tree as they passed.

"We'd better pick up the pace," said Jefferson, clicking the reins. "It's getting dark."

Chapter Twenty-Six

It had been two days since their visit to the Humphrey office, and Mary had spent every minute of it riddled with fear, not for herself, but for the family. Anna jumped and screamed at every loud noise, from a dropped pan to a slammed door, and Mary winced in pain every time. Poor, dear Anna; she was so shy and timid already.

Mary could hardly bear it, and the thought of Kit and Pudge coming back for another round made her seethe with anger and shake with fear for the safety of the children. She was not comfortable with the way William talked, as if he were just waiting for the chance to be a hero, should Kit and Pudge come back.

"Don't be a fool," she had snapped at him once when he talked about fighting Pudge with his bare hands.

William had looked resolved, though, and it frightened Mary to her core. Maurice clung to her, always wanting her to read to him or tell him a story. He stayed by her side and helped her when she tended the garden or the chickens, and Mary knew he was keeping her close. He, too, was afraid. Mary could hardly bear the thought that she had brought all of this on them.

She loved them too much to let them live like this, and as the days wore on, she was beginning to lose hope that anything could be done to keep everyone safe until Kit was arrested and put away.

She knew he could come back at any time, and that reality stayed with her every hour of every day. She knew it stayed with the children, too.

Violet alone seemed confident that everything would be okay, and she made sure to remind Mary of this throughout the day.

Still, Mary couldn't shake the thought that her very presence was putting the people she loved at risk.

She went to bed early, longing for a little rest from the ceaseless thoughts, but she simply couldn't quiet them, still as she lay. She tried to feel reassured by the lawyer, the promise of a day in court, and the presence of Jefferson, but fear crept up in her heart and grabbed ahold, squeezing the life out of her.

Jefferson lay next to her in bed. They were in his bedroom, where Mary had taken to sleeping on most nights. Her room across the hall was still just as she had arranged it when she'd first decided to stay. Jefferson slept soundly next to her, and she wondered at how he could fall asleep so quickly. Even the night of the attack, he'd been asleep within seconds. No matter what happened, he seemed to be able to empty his mind and fall asleep as if he were still a child without a care in the world. She envied him that, for she seemed to toss and turn for hours before sweet, oblivious sleep would envelope her.

She turned over on her side, closed her eyes, and tried to not to think of all the horrible things that could happen. After some time, she did manage to drift in and out of consciousness, in and out of dreams.

She dreamed she was back at home, in Rosewood, in the old house. She came down the stairs, just as she always had. Her father was sitting there, reading the newspaper. Her mother was sizzling bacon in a frying pan. Everything seemed as it should be, until Kit appeared, sitting in the drawing room as if he belonged there. She screamed at him to get out, but he smiled and said it was his house, now.

Mary turned to plead with her father, but he refused to look up from his newspaper. She looked at her mother, but she was facing the stove, with her back to Mary. Mary screamed, but her father kept the newspaper over his face, and her mother would not turn around. She looked at Kit, who flashed his white teeth in a wicked smile.

Next, she dreamed she was in Parkville, and Kit and Pudge came riding up to the house and began shooting. The shots she heard in her sleep jolted her awake, and she ran to the window. All was silent. Her fitful sleep had not left her any more rested than when she laid down the night before; she was only more afraid. She did not know how close to dawn it was, but the night was black, and the house was still.

Oh, I can't keep my mind off Kit, even in my sleep! She thought angrily. *I just have to keep busy.*

She had been growing bored since she was asked to stay put in the house for her own safety, and on top of the boredom, she was growing more and more anxious each day. The combination of boredom and anxiety threatened to send her into hysteria. She wasn't accustomed to staying put, and she grew more and more restless by the hour. She had a tendency to play out in her head every possible bad thing that could happen. It was driving her mad.

I have got to keep my mind off it, she told herself. She decided that now was as good a time as any to start writing a children's book for Anna. She'd been thinking on it and jotting down notes here and there, and she thought she could write it all out to keep her mind occupied. She didn't know if it would be a good story, but at any rate, it would keep her mind off Kit.

She got out of bed and tiptoed back into the room which had been her own when she first arrived. She still had a desk and writing materials and a lantern. She felt around in her drawer for a box of matches, lit one, and lit the lantern. She shook the match out and sat down to write, running her hands softly over the white paper.

Once upon a time, in a faraway land, there lived a little girl with beautiful curly, dark brown hair and eyes as blue as sapphires.

The thoughts flowed faster than Mary could keep her quill inked. She wrote on, all about a little girl with a special gift of communicating to animals and how she brought a whole town together when she decided to speak to humans, too, and speak on behalf of the animals.

She knew she was not the most accomplished artist, but she'd had some lessons. She began to illustrate pictures on each page to go along with the story. She sketched a picture of a fuzzy little rabbit, sitting on a girl's lap.

She held it out and looked at it approvingly, thinking Anna might like this story very much, if Maurice would read it to her.

Thinking about the children sent her mind reeling yet again. She loved them so, and she was living under the constant fear that Kit would return any day, and something terrible would happen to the children. *They aren't safe...because of me.* she thought. She thought of her home in Rosewood, her home here in Parkville. *Where is home?* She wondered.

She laid the story she'd written to the side, so the ink could dry. That's when she caught sight of the letters she had written when she had planned to run away. Suddenly, all her reasons for wanting to run away in the first place came flooding back to her mind. She was paralyzed by them, for all her former reasoning still stood.

She read over the letter she had written to Jefferson and ripped it up. An ache pounded in her heart. Jefferson had forgiven her, and what was he getting in return? He and his entire family were in danger.

There's a good chance we will lose in court, she thought. *Even if we were to win the case, what would happen to Kit. Would he really be jailed for having attacked us? Could he get himself out of it? What could he do in the meantime?*

Every creak, every sound, every horse or carriage they heard coming up the lane would send everyone into a panic. No one had been the same since the attack, and this was not lost on Mary.

This is all because of me, she thought. Jefferson had pleaded with her not to blame herself, and she had tried to put these thoughts out of her head, but it simply wasn't working.

It's because it truly is my fault, she thought. *That's the truth.*

The truth. She had promised to tell the truth from now on.

She got out a new sheet of paper, and wrote:

Dear Jefferson,

I've promised not to lie to you anymore. What's more, I've promised not to lie to myself. Well, I have been lying to myself. I've been trying to believe that this is not my fault. I can't tell that lie anymore. Not to myself, and not to you. I'm telling you the truth now, Jefferson, as hard as it is to hear.

I am sorry for being such a coward that I cannot tell you to your face. I am afraid if I do, you will convince me to stay. And if you convince me to stay, you will all be in danger. I cannot tell myself the truth and stay. I cannot stay, knowing that m very presence is putting you all in danger. The only way I could stay is if I told myself that the danger you are all in was not my fault. But it is. And I cannot go on lying. I promised to tell the truth, remember?

I'm leaving, Jefferson. Please don't come after me. Know that I love you with all my heart. Know that I have been immeasurably happy here with you. Tell the children that I love them, and if they ask questions, tell them the truth.

Yours Forever,

Mary

On a new sheet, she wrote,

Dear Violet,

My best friend and sister. You of all people will understand why I left. You knew I had meant to before. I thought I was leaving because I had betrayed you all with my secrets. You all forgave me. I shall never forget your forgiveness and compassion. Now, having been forgiven and embraced, I realize that I still must go, and it breaks my heart.

I want to be with you all. You are my family. You are the people I love most in the world, and I don't know how I will go on without you. To stay would be the most selfish thing in the world. I know the danger you are all in because of me. I have stayed for days, knowing in the deepest part of my heart that I am selfish for it. If I leave, you will all be safe. How can I claim to love you if I keep you all in danger?

Please, understand. Please don't believe I have abandoned you. Please know that I love you. Oh, how I love you all! I pray that one day, you will come to see this as an act of love. You have been through loss and grief before, and you have come out strong. You will do it again.

Your loving sister,

Mary

She dressed as quietly as possible, packing her suitcase silently. She left all of Maurice's favorite books on the desk and scribbled a quick note that said.

Maurice,

These are for you. I will never forget you.

Mary

Then, she wrote another note.

William,

You're the man of the house, now. Look after your little siblings, especially when your Auntie gets married. I have left Rusty. He's yours now. Please remind Anna how much I love her. You're growing up into a decent young man. I hope one day to come back and see the life you have made for yourself.

Mary

She ran her hand softly across the stack of letters. A tear trickled from her eye. Quickly, silently, she packed her bags.

Chapter Twenty-Seven

Ever since the meeting with James Humphrey, Jefferson had been wracking his brains about how to pay off Mary's debts. Even if Kit could not prove that Mary was his legal wife, there was still the debt to grapple with. Perhaps, the crimes Kit had committed in killing their cattle and threatening their home would have some impact in nullifying the debt. *Can a prisoner collect debts?* That was a question he had forgotten to ask Mr. Humphrey.

What if the debt remained to be paid in full? What would he do then? He had to do *something*. Mary was his wife. The two were one. Her debt was his debt... but how could he manage it?

I could mortgage the farm, he thought. *But then, what if there's a drought or a year of poor crop? I won't be able to pay back the lender. I could sell Ajax, but that wouldn't even cover half of what is owed.*

Jefferson thought about how much money his ranch made each year raising crops and selling cattle. He owned a lot of land and cattle and was technically a wealthy man. Most of the money he made on his ranch went right back into the place to keep it producing. He couldn't even begin to imagine having thousands of dollars to spare. He would have to mortgage the ranch and the house and sell all his cattle to even come close to touching the amount he needed.

There must be some other way, he thought. He turned to look at Mary, who tossed and turned next to him.

I won't think of these things now, he told himself, finally. *I can't do anything about this now.*

He heard the door open and Rusty bounding up the stairs.

Good, William's home, he thought. He hadn't wanted to fall asleep until he heard William and Rusty come in the door. Normally, he wasn't quite so overbearing with William, but the recent events had made him more apt to want to know where his family members were. That day, Jefferson had second thoughts about letting him go fishing on his own, but in the end had decided to let him go. He wanted to maintain some normalcy for the kids, and for William that meant fishing.

He fell asleep, ready to face the next day.

He was awakened by Rusty, who came into his room and turned in anxious circles and whined by his feet.

"Oh, not yet, boy," Jefferson said, groggily, as he turned over in bed to lay his arm over Mary. He realized she wasn't there and thought she was up earlier than usual. He tried to lay back down and fall asleep, but Rusty bounded to the side of his bed and placed his nose right up by his head and proceeded to lick his face.

"Alright, alright, boy, I'm up!" He said, dragging himself out of bed. Rusty kept turning circles and jumping back and forth from the door to Jefferson. "What's going on, boy? Hungry?" Rusty only whined and kept circling. Jefferson followed him out of the room and Rusty bounded down the hallway to the guest room. Jefferson followed.

He stepped into the room and noticed it looked empty. The closet was open, and he could see only an empty hanger. His eyes scanned the room. Something was off. The bed was made, the books were left on the desk, but the framed picture of her parents was gone.

Then, he noticed the stack of letters neatly written in Mary's delicate cursive. He walked over to them and noticed his name on the top letter. He picked it up.

Chapter Twenty-Eight

William

Usually, when William came down to the pond to fish, he could clear his mind and let it sit, empty and still as he cast his line and reeled repeatedly. Cast and reel, cast and reel. No sound but the swish and plop of his line and the click, click, clicking of his slow and rhythmic reeling.

Tonight, however, he was lost in thought. He replayed that evening in his mind over and over and thought of everything he could have done differently. He could have grabbed dad's rifle and shot at the men before they got anywhere near Rusty.

Maybe they won't listen to reason, but I should have shot at them before they got anywhere near Rusty or the house, he thought, kicking a stone. He thought about Mary, and how even *she* had gone out to face the men, stupid as it was to think she could reason with the lunatic. In truth, he had been surprised at his own fear for Mary, and his feeling of shame that she had gone out to face them and he had not.

Well thank God they're all okay. No thanks to me, he thought, listlessly casting his line again. He looked down at the scabbed over wound healing on Rusty's back, and anger began to well up inside him. He reeled faster. Nothing. He cast again, this time sending his hook and line almost as far as he could see.

"I should have protected you, boy," he said, looking down at Rusty. He ran a hand down his back and grimaced when he felt the rough scabs.

His mother's pale, deathly face flashed in his mind, and he tried to will himself to remember her in the good times. The memory of her sickly face was persistent, though, and eventually he gave way. He thought about how he had felt, standing next to her bed, looking at her sallow, white face.

That same feeling came rushing back to him now, and he suddenly felt small and helpless. He remembered how weak and cold her hand had felt in his, and the way he had looked up at his father, searching his eyes for some sign of reassurance that everything would be okay, but finding only the reflection of his own fear and bewilderment.

He remembered the way his eyes had rested on her soft, brown hair that fell in tumbles around her pale face. He had kept his gaze steadily on her hair, because it was the only part of her that looked like his mother.

Hot tears welled up behind his eyes and blurred his vision.

He felt a tug on his line, jerked his pole, and reeled, but lost it. He cursed when he saw that it had taken his worm.

"I don't think your Pa would much like to hear you cursing like that," said a voice behind him. William whirled around to see Emma Humphrey, standing there with a pail in one hand and Maurice's pole in the other. Rusty jumped up and ran to her, licking her hands and doing circles in front of her. William tried to wipe tears from his eyes discreetly while Emma was distracted with Rusty.

"Funny dog," she said.

"Oh, the circles? That's just his way of asking you to scratch behind his ears."

"Like this?"

"Yeah, see? He's settling down now."

"Well, if that's all he wanted."

"What are you doing here?" William asked briskly.

"My Pa and Uncle are here...said they had a few questions they needed answered and thought they'd stop by. Maurice said you were down here, and I could join you. Pa went to put up a fuss about the bad men, and what if they show up. But Uncle John said, 'Don't be ridiculous, they'd have to come up past the house before they got to the trail to the pond.' Anyway, so Pa let me come and Maurice lent his pole."

William only nodded. He could sense the tears forcing their way back, though he did his best to will them away. He turned away from her and stared out over the pond in case a tear fell.

Don't you dare cry in front of Emma, he ordered himself.

"Something the matter?" She asked as she fidgeted in her pail and pulled out a long, curling worm.

Why do girls always have to ask just the wrong question, he wondered, blinking back tears.

"You only need about half that worm," he said, ignoring her question. Emma cringed slightly. "Here, I'll put it on for you," William said, setting down his pole.

"Are you okay, though?" Emma asked again.

"I'm fine," William said as he worked the worm onto her hook.

"It's just like a boy to always say you're fine when you're not," she said, and William thought she was trying too hard to sound grown up. "Anyone who got his dog shot and his house shot at and his fence burned down would be a little rattled. You don't have to pretend."

"I said I'm fine," he responded irritably. "Cast it that way. Don't cross my line." He sounded more curt than he'd intended, but he was afraid if Emma kept talking like that, he really would cry, and he had to avoid crying in front of Emma at all costs.

"I know how to cast. I have been fishing before, you know," said Emma in a sassy voice.

"Didn't much look like it by the way you went to hook that worm," William teased, but his tone was lighter, and he gave her a wry half-smile. She tossed her head.

"Anything biting today?" She asked.

"Not too good," William said, reeling in his hook. "At least my worm wasn't stolen this time."

Emma cast her line, and it went clear across the pond before plunking into the water near the far bank.

"Not bad," said William, smiling.

"I told you I've been fishing before," she said. "I just don't like putting the worms on the hook."

"It doesn't matter."

"Anyway, like I was saying, I heard what happened," she repeated. "I wasn't *supposed* to hear. Confidentiality and all that. Dad and Uncle are always such sticklers about *that*, but I didn't hear from them. Maurice told my little brother, who told me. Then I heard Dad and Uncle talking about it when they thought I couldn't hear."

She sure talks fast, William thought, but it amused him.

"Well, I suppose everyone'll know sooner or later," he responded.

"Maurice said he wasn't scared because he had you to protect him," Emma said. Her voice had suddenly grown more serious, and she looked up at him with a fixed gaze.

William grunted, thinking about how much braver he should have been in the face of Kit and Pudge.

"Well?" Emma said, jerking her head forward. She fixed her big, brown eyes on him, demanding an answer.

"Well, what?" asked William, turning his attention back to his fishing.

"Are you going to?"

"Going to what?"

"Protect them, you nitwit."

"Well, yes, of course. Of course I'll protect them if it comes to that. Just wish I could've stopped Rusty from getting shot."

Emma was still scratching Rusty's ears, and she ran her fingers tenderly over the wound.

"I'm glad he's alright," she said softly.

"Me, too."

They fished in silence for a few moments before Emma said, "Well, I think you're brave."

William felt his face go hot, and he hoped she didn't notice.

Not as brave as I should have been, he thought, but he dared not say that. Then, he promised himself that if Kit or Pudge ever showed their faces again, he would be brave. What had Mary said about that? Something about courage without wisdom?

Well, I won't be stupid, but I will be brave, he promised himself. *I won't be a coward. I'll be as brave as Emma thinks I am.* This resolve renewed his spirits, and he stood a little straighter.

"Where'd you get the worm?" William asked.

"Stopped and dug up a few on my way down the path," she answered. William looked at her hands and noticed they were in fact very dirty, and all her fingernails were black with dirt. He smiled.

"I didn't know you had it in you. You always seem so prim and proper. Anyway, I thought you didn't like worms?"

"I never said that," she retorted. "I only said I don't like sticking them with the hook. They're living things, too, you know."

"I'm not trying to tease. Just didn't figure you for the worm-digging type. That's all."

"Well, my uncle has taken me fishing with him ever since I was a little girl, and I've always dug up my own worms. He still puts it on the line for me, so I guess I'm too prim and proper for that, but I don't much care," and she flicked her hair and tossed her head in that way that William always found so amusing and charming.

"So, you're a good fisherman...er fisherwoman, then?"

"I like it," she said. "It's...peaceful. When you're out fishing it's like you're doing something worthwhile...like you might get to bring home a meal...but you're also not really doing anything. I like that."

"Yeah, I like that, too," William agreed. Emma reeled in her line and cast again, letting it plop down on the far side of the pond.

"I've got one!" she shouted. Her pole began to bend as she reeled with all her strength. William wedged his pole between two rocks and grabbed his net.

"Keep reeling! I'll use the net once I see it."

He watched her reel with everything she had, jerking and reeling at just the right times.

"You've got it! A bit more!" William waded down into the pond until he was wet up to his knees. "I see it!" He took the net and scooped the fish into it while Emma dropped her pole, clasped her hands together, and cheered.

"What is it! Is it a trout?"

"No, but it's a good sized bass. Looks like a small mouth."

Emma grabbed the pale and quickly filled it up with water. Then she came over to look at the fish. She grabbed ahold of it by the mouth with her finger and thumb and held it up to her forearm to measure it.

"Not bad," she concluded and dropped it into the pail. The bass flopped violently, splashing them both in the face. They laughed as they sat down on a rock.

"Well," said William, "You're not bad. Not bad at all." Emma smiled and wiped water from her forehead, pushing her thick, auburn hair back off her head.

"Well, Uncle said not to be long, so I guess I better be getting back," she said.

"Already?" he asked.

"Yes, they said not to be too long," she answered.

"I'll walk with you," William said, reeling in his line.

They walked in awkward silence for a few yards before Emma said, "You know, your mom was my favorite Sunday School teacher."

William smiled at her. He was grateful to hear someone speak of his mother and to look into that person's eyes and see happiness, not pity. Ever since his mother died, he felt like people avoided talking about her, as if he wasn't already thinking about her anyway. If they did speak of her, they looked at him with pity, like he was a hurt puppy. No one talked about her in a normal way, like Emma just did now. William liked it.

"Do you like Mary very much?" Emma asked. William chuckled.

"You know what? I think I do," he answered.

"What's she like?"

"Oh, I don't know. She's a lady. She talks a little too proper. It used to drive me nuts. Once you get to know her, though, she's alright."

"She sure seems to like you guys."

"Yeah," William nodded. "I think she does."

They were coming around the bend when the Humphrey carriage came into view, coming toward them.

"Well, I guess I'll see you Sunday," Emma said, handing the pail and pole to William and giving Rusty one last scratch behind the ears.

The carriage came to a halt and Emma swung herself swiftly onto the seat.

"Good fishing, today, William?" John Humphrey asked.

"Not today, sir," William answered. Both men tipped their hats at him and urged the horses on. William stood and watched the carriage. Emma turned around and smiled at William. He smiled back, waving at her, watching her auburn hair blowing in the breeze. Even from a distance, he could see her big, brown eyes. They reminded him of a doe.

Rusty, having caught sight of the house, ran on ahead of him. William came to the front steps, where Rusty was whining to be let in. He opened the door and watched him disappear into the house. The night was cool and breezy, and William was far from tired, so he sat out on the bench swing.

He thought of Emma, and the way she'd smiled when she brought up a memory of Ma. *Ma...*

He walked around the house, back to her gravesite, and lay down on the soft, green grass, his hands folded behind his head.

"It's been a tough time, Ma. I wanted to be brave...to save them, but I couldn't. I couldn't save you, either. I'll be brave Ma. I will."

Now, finally, sweet memories of his mother flooded his mind—memories from when she was healthy and strong, and vibrant. He smiled as images of her face flashed before him for this is how he wanted to remember her.

William knew his father thought he was home, and probably wouldn't have approved of him being out at night alone, but he felt he needed to be near his mother for just a few more minutes.

William had intended to lay there by Ma for a few more minutes before going to bed, but the grass beneath him was plush and soft, and thoughts of happy days with his mother swept him away, and he drifted into a deep sleep.

He was awakened by the sound of the back door creaking. He bolted upright and strained his eyes to see. Someone's figure was coming down the back steps, dragging something. He held his breath. It was Mary. He almost called out to her, but something stopped him. She was crying softly. He could tell by the way her shoulders moved up and down, and the way she wiped her eyes with her forearm. He watched her as she took off down the lane.

In that moment, he decided to follow her.

I could go back and tell Pa she's left, he thought. *But perhaps I can convince her to stay.* He wondered where she was going. He thought about going and waking Pa, but then he might not know which direction she was heading.

He followed her discreetly, wondering when he should reveal himself.

He was able to hide himself among the corn for several yards, and wondered where he would hide when the fields ended and the roads toward town were more exposed. He didn't have to wonder for long. In the distance, a stagecoach appeared, drawn by a single horse.

I wonder if she's found someone to come and pick her up, he wondered, thinking hard about who it could be. It wasn't Rupert's horse, and Violet was home.

The stagecoach pulled to a stop, and in the light of the moon, William could make out the shape of the short, fat, Pudge, eyes gleaming in the moonlight.

He heard him say, "Well, well, well. What do we have here?" William recognized Pudge's voice instantly, and as the carriage jolted forward, the glint of the moon shone on Kit's face.

"Leave me alone and leave *them* alone. I'm leaving, and I won't be coming back so there's no use in bothering them again." William watched as she tried to keep walking, but Pudge grabbed her by the hair just as Kit jumped out of the stagecoach and put a hand roughly over her mouth, dragging her inside with him.

William knew he had to think fast. He'd promised himself he wouldn't be a coward, but he couldn't be stupid, either. He'd made a move to jump out of hiding and grab ahold of Pudge, but he thought better of it at the last moment.

Right now, they don't know I've seen them, he thought. *If attack and try to rescue her, I'll be exposed. It's two to one, and I'm no match for either. No, the bravest thing might be the stupidest thing I could do, too,* he thought.

After a brief moment, he decided the smartest thing to do was to stay hidden long enough to see where they went, and then run silently back to Pa and tell him where he could find them.

He crept silently along the corn fields until they came to an end, and then he crouched down into the ditch. He tried to move fast enough to keep up, but silently enough to remain hidden. The full moon gave enough light to keep the stagecoach in view, but he knew that it also gave enough light to give him away if he wasn't careful.

He ran, crouched, for what felt like miles. His legs were beginning to feel weak, and he held on to his side to keep it from aching. Finally, the coach slowed and then stopped. Kit and Pudge pulled Mary out of the stagecoach and up toward a hill. William could see a dilapidated barn sitting on top of the hill and gathered that Pudge and Kit were making their way toward the hill, with Mary.

When they disappeared into the barn doors, he stood and ran as fast as his legs would carry him back toward home.

He'd thought he might collapse when he was trying to keep up with the stagecoach, but suddenly, he couldn't feel anything, and he thought he could run forever.

His legs moved faster and faster, and he breathed deeply in and out. He felt strong and powerful as he raced up the lane and toward the house.

He didn't stop at the front steps. He jumped them, swung open the door in one motion, and ascended the stairs three and a time.

He burst into his father's room, but it was empty.

He raced down the hall to Mary's room and flung open the door. His father was standing there, holding letters in his hands, with tears streaming down his face. For a brief moment, William was taken aback. He had rarely ever seen his father cry—only when his mother had died.

"Pa," he said, softly.

"She's gone," Pa replied.

"Kit and Pudge have taken her. I saw them! It was Kit and Pudge. They were both in there. I heard Pudge's voice and caught a glimpse of Kit's face. I can't explain everything now, but I know where they've taken her. We have to go, now."

"Get Rusty," said Pa, after a split second of bewilderment. "Take me to her." William shot out of the room to get Rusty, and Jefferson went quickly to Violet's room.

"Violet," he said, shaking her awake. "It's Mary. Kit's taken her. We're going after her."

"I'm coming," she said.

"Someone needs to stay with the children."

"We'll ask Greg. He's standing guard anyway. I'm coming." Not wanting to waste any time arguing, Jefferson agreed.

Soon, they were racing down the lane, Violet and William on Bessie and Jefferson on Ajax.

"Are you sure you can take us right there, son?" Jefferson asked.

"Yeah, it's the old barn on the Potter property. You know, the one that's almost falling over? Jack knows the one, and he's already heading into town to get the Sheriff."

"Well done, William. Now, there's no time to lose." They all mounted and kicked their horses until they were galloping at full speed.

The night was still, and the full moon shown on their scared faces as they galloped along silently.

Chapter Twenty-Nine

Jefferson's heart was beating so hard he could feel it in his head, and William looked every bit as scared. Rage welled up within Jefferson. He wouldn't allow himself to wonder what they might have done to Mary by this time. All he could do was get to her as quickly as possible and thank God William had seen where they had gone. Thank *God* he'd had the sense to follow her long enough to see where they had taken her and to come back to get him.

Jefferson looked at his son and saw him in an entirely different light. He was no longer the same stubborn boy he'd been when Mary showed up, who had held unfounded resentment toward her and wanted her gone. He was a young man, who had kept his wits about him in a crisis and had the courage to do the right thing.

If it weren't for William, God knows what would have happened, Jefferson thought.

He knew it would take some quick thinking and strategy to get Mary safely back into his arms. If Kit and Pudge caught wind of them coming, they could possibly get away. *We'll have to be quick, and approach quietly.* He knew they'd have to arrive on foot, leaving the horses so that their thundering hooves would not be heard from the barn.

He patted Ajax on the neck and said, "We'll tie them up about a half mile before we get to the barn. There's no telling what they'll do if they hear us coming up on them."

The ride from the house to the entrance of the Potter property felt like it took hours to Jefferson. Time seemed to stand still as he wondered what Kit and Pudge would do. He wished, desperately, that he could have protected Mary. He wondered why she had decided to run. The words of her letters were running through his head, but he couldn't think about that now. Now, he had to get to Mary.

Just get to Mary, he told himself over and over until the words in his mind fell into the rhythm of the horse's hooves.

He rode Ajax alone. Next to him, Bessie carried William and Violet. He felt his pistol rubbing against his leg in the saddlebag, and his rifle jostling about on his back. The horses rode swiftly, neck and neck, as if racing. A glint of the moon reflected off Violet's face, and Jefferson thought he saw a tear glisten on her white cheek. He turned his face forward so as not to see. He couldn't think about what he or anyone else was feeling. Not now. He could only think about his next move, and getting to Mary.

"Slow down, we should be coming up on it soon," he said, pulling his horse off the gravel onto a beaten path. Violet followed behind.

"This looks familiar," said William.

"Let's hook the horses up on the fence post here," said Jefferson. "We'll have to walk the rest of the way."

They all dismounted and quickly tied up the horses. Jefferson noticed that Violet's hands were shaking as she did.

They ran down the path, until Violet was panting and needed to slow down. They came up over a hill and saw the dilapidated barn in the distance. Jefferson motioned for them to crouch down.

"We don't know who they have standing guard, if anyone and we don't know what part of the barn they're in," he whispered. "William, you've got light feet. Think you can keep quiet enough to figure out where they are?" William nodded and took off in a silent glide toward the barn while Violet and Jefferson followed at a distance.

They watched William disappear around one side of the barn. When William appeared from around the other side, Jefferson realized he'd been holding his breath. They crept along in the tall weeds until they met up with William, who was already gliding back toward them.

"They're in the right corner, far back, lower level," he reported. "I caught a glimpse of Mary. She's alive." Jefferson heard himself gasp. Until William said it, he hadn't allowed himself to even think the thought that had been threatening to force itself into his mind... *What if it was too late already?* But it wasn't. William had seen Mary, and Jefferson felt a wave of relief.

They crouched down in the tall grasses and Jefferson handed Violet the pistol. He tried not to notice how her hand shook when she took it from him. She'd need a steady hand to shoot it. He handed William the rifle, knowing he'd been practicing to take down a deer. Jefferson wondered if it was a mistake not to keep any weapon for himself, but he was stronger than the others, and he figured William was a better shot.

"How sure is your shot?"

"Pretty consistent at twenty yards," William answered, without hesitation.

"Good. I want you to climb up the far side over there. You see that window?" William nodded. "Get up there and take aim at Kit. Do not fire unless I tell you to. Got it?" He nodded with a look of severity. "Violet, you'll follow me."

Jefferson looked forward toward the abandoned barn. He took two deep breaths. He knew he didn't have time to waste, but he also knew he had to be smart. He couldn't make a mistake. He crept forward, Violet following closely behind.

They crept silently through the brush until they came to the back corner of the barn, where William had said Kit Pudge, and Mary were. Slowly, Jefferson stood until he could peek into the window.

The sight of Mary made his heart lurch. It took every ounce of willpower he had to keep himself from jumping through the window to her rescue, but he controlled his impulses long enough to realize that she had suffered no bodily injury as of this moment. Her pale blue dress was dirty and torn, though, and it looked as though she had cried, smeared dirt across her face, and cried some more. Her blond hair was disheveled and out of place, stray strands sticking to her sweaty, dirty face. Her eyes were glassy and red. She was sitting on her knees on the barn floor, with her hands tied behind her back.

There's three of us and only two of them, Jefferson thought *If we're smart, we can surround them.* Getting Mary out safely was the main goal. Detaining Kit until the Sheriff arrived was secondary.

"Violet," he whispered. "She looks safe for now. I can see a door on the far side. I want you to go around the back to that door," he pointed, "and wait. The wood by this window is nearly falling apart. I can knock it down easily." He demonstrated, gently scuffing at the wood, and they both watched as it sloughed away. "Come in, pistol pointed at Pudge, as soon as you see me." Violet nodded and disappeared silently into the brush. Jefferson waited until he was certain Violet had enough time to get to the far side of the barn.

Kit's voice, smooth as honey, spoke what were obviously supposed to be soothing words to Mary, and Jefferson felt anger rising within him as he listened.

"Mary, my dear, you must be brought to see reason. You know your father only meant for you to have the best. He always wanted that for you. You can't deny that, now, can you? All his life, he did everything within his power to give you all that your heart desires. Didn't he?" Mary didn't answer, but kept her eyes steadily trained on the floor.

Kit took two steps toward her, stopping only inches from her face. Jefferson flinched. Kit grabbed Mary's chin between his thumb and forefinger, forcing her face upward toward him, though she kept her eyes averted.

"Answer me," he commanded. "Your father always gave you the best, didn't he?" Mary nodded slightly. "Good girl," Kit said, letting go of her chin. "Now, it stands to reason that your father was setting you up for a lifetime of having all your heart desires. After all, you'd grown accustomed to such luxury throughout your lavish childhood. In order to ensure that you would always have everything you could ever want, your father agreed to your marriage to me. How is it that you would dare refuse to carry out your father's dying wish?"

Mary remained silent.

"Answer me!" He thundered.

Mary lifted her head, looked him dead in the eyes, and said, "If my father knew what a brute you are, he would never have consigned me to a life with you. I know my father, and he would have wanted me to stand up for myself. I wanted a life with Jefferson…"

"Then why were you running away from him when we caught you?" he asked, and he sounded sinister. Jefferson felt like he'd been punched in the gut.

"Because you have put them all in danger," Mary answered. "And I can't do that to them."

"Then marry me," he said.

"Not if you were the last man on earth," she said, her eyes still fixed on him. Jefferson watched as Kit raised a hand. He tore through the rotting wood in a clamor of broken glass.

At just the same time, Violet busted through the door pointing her gun directly at Pudge, who threw his hands in the air and ran for his life.

Violet ran to Mary and quickly untied her hands, tossing the rope to Jefferson.

Kit was stunned, and in that moment of shock, Jefferson had enough time to grab Kit by the throat and slam him up against the barn wall, knocking down more pieces of rotting wood and breaking another window. Kit reached for his pistol and lifted it, pointing it not at Jefferson, but at Mary, just as Rusty came running through the barn door, growling with the hair on his back standing on end.

"You see that rifle up there?" Jefferson said, pointing to the upper window of the barn. "My son's a dead shot, and you're well within range." Between William's rifle trained on him and Rusty's vicious growling, Kit lowered his pistol to the ground with one hand raised in surrender, and Jefferson loosened his grip. Jefferson slid Kit's pistol across the floor to Mary, who grabbed it and pointed it directly at Kit. Jefferson took the rope and began fastening it around Kit's arms.

"The Sheriff has already been alerted and should be here any minute. You'll be charged with kidnapping and vandalism. Any document stating that Mary is your legal wife will be null and void when we all testify, and you will be behind bars where you belong."

Violet ran to Mary, whose arms were shaking as she kept the pistol aimed at Kit.

"Mary, are you okay? Did they hurt you?" She asked, panting. Mary shook her head but couldn't choke out any words.

The steady clip clopping of horses' hooves could be heard faintly in the distance, and it grew louder every moment. They heard voices calling,

"Jefferson? Mary?"

"We're here!" Jefferson shouted. "In the back!"

Sheriff Allen came into view with several of the townsmen at his heels. James and John Humphrey held Pudge by the arms between them.

"Ran into this rapscallion on the way over," said Sheriff Allen, gesturing toward Pudge. "We'll take it from here." Sheriff Allen grabbed Kit roughly by his arms, releasing him from Jefferson's grip.

William came running in just then, out of breath but looking very solemn, carrying the rifle across his chest.

"Well done, Son," Jefferson said, as William approached.

"I didn't know what it would feel like to have my sights on a man," he said, his eyes big and wondering. "I'm glad I didn't have to pull the trigger."

Jefferson nodded and took his son into his arms.

He turned then and saw Mary, her blond hair hanging in dirty, sweaty strands and sticking to her smeared face. Her dress was muddied up to the knee and torn. He thought she was the most beautiful creature he had ever seen, and he went to her, scooped her up into his strong arms, and held her.

Tears formed and streamed down her dirt-smeared face. He gently wiped them away, saying, "You're safe now. It's all over. I'm taking you home."

By the time they all stepped out of the barn, the darkness was beginning to lift, though the sun hadn't yet appeared. Even Rusty seemed to understand the somber mood. He trotted along beside them, not even wagging his tail, as he normally would on a walk.

The morning felt still and cool. The dew wet Jefferson's ankles as he carried Mary in his arms, with Violet and William trotting at his heels, trying to keep up with his long strides.

They walked in the silence of the morning, with only the occasional songs of the birds and breaking the silence. As they arrived at the posts where they'd tied up the horses, the sun began to peek over the tops of the golden fields in the distance, and the warmth spread across the dark earth and warmed their faces.

Jefferson hoisted Mary up onto Ajax first, then swung himself up behind her as Violet and William mounted Bessie. Rusty trotted along faithfully at the horse's heels.

Jefferson moved with Ajax, the familiar feel of the stallion's movement comforting him. The steady clapping of horse hooves, also a familiar sound, steadied his mind. He thought *I love her*, and it seemed to him in that moment that nothing else in the world mattered so much.

"I'll take care of the horses," William said as they approached the house. He took them by the reins and led them away after the others dismounted. Rusty followed William to the barn.

Violet opened the door as Jefferson carried Mary, who clung to him as if she might never let him go.

Upon entering, they found Rupert asleep on the couch and Anna delicately attempting to fasten Mary's blue silk hair bow into his hair. Violet couldn't contain herself and let out a roaring laugh which startled Rupert awake.

"Oh! Oh, good morning," he said in his usual jovial way, as if nothing out of the ordinary had happened at all. "One of your field hands sent for me, so I thought I'd come right over and wait for you all to get home."

They all laughed then, and when Rupert sat upright, they could see that Anna had been at work for quite a while, fastening all of Violet and Mary's hair bows into his hair. Even Mary laughed this time.

"What?" Asked Rupert, trying to figure out just what was so funny.

"Hair pretty," said Anna, pointing at his head. He felt his hair and let out a guffawing laugh too.

As their laughter died down, Rupert grew serious again. He stood and strode over to Jefferson, who was still holding Mary.

"Lay her on the sofa," he said to Jefferson, pulling the hair bows from his head one at a time. "I'll do a quick check up." He turned to Mary. "Then you can get cleaned up," he said, in his most soothing doctor voice.

Jefferson laid her carefully on the couch just as William came back in and Maurice woke up and came trotting down the stairs.

"What happened to her?" Maurice asked, obviously alarmed.

"I'll explain," said William, guiding him out of the room.

Rusty walked slowly up to Mary and gently placed his head on her chest, licking her face.

Chapter Thirty

Mary tried to speak, but her lips felt so dry she could barely open them.

"Can someone bring her some water?" Rupert asked gently. Violet quickly disappeared and reentered with a cup of cool water, which she pressed to Mary's lips. It felt like heaven, her lips and throat a dry desert and the cool water like a blessed rain.

She panted, wiped her lips, and said, "Thank you," weakly.

"Here, lay back," Rupert said. He felt her head, her throat, her abdomen. "Are you cut or bleeding anywhere?" He asked.

Mary shook her head.

"You got off alright, considering," said Rupert. "Of course, you've had quite a scare."

Mary tried to lay back and get some rest, but her head was spinning. *How did Kit and Pudge know I would be leaving? Did they just happen to be on their way to the house? How did Jefferson and William find me? How did they know where to look?*

She replayed it in her mind, and none of it made sense to her. She'd left, planning on getting to town and getting on a train under the cover of night. That, she could remember perfectly. Then, it all seemed a blur. She remembered being pulled into the cab. She could picture Kit's menacing, victorious, face. She remembered him saying, *Your little ruse is up, my dear.* She remembered how cold she'd felt, and how she'd wondered whether or not they would kill her.

When they dragged her out of the cab and into the dilapidated barn, she had thought it was all over. She'd prayed, *God, send me a miracle. God, save me.*

A miracle, she thought. *God sent me a miracle.* She looked up into Jefferson's face, and she saw a tenderness in his eyes that came through his rough exterior. *He's my miracle,* she thought.

When Rupert had declared that she was not injured in any serious way, Violet suggested that she take Mary upstairs and help her wash up and get into clean clothes. Mary, however, wanted to know how they found her.

"I've been wondering myself," Rupert admitted, so Violet and Jefferson recounted the series of events, answering questions until all was finally understood.

"The chances that William would have picked that night to stay up late, and that he would have thought to follow me far enough to see where they had taken me..."

"I know," said Jefferson. "He's quite a kid."

"And the letters..." said Mary, her face going white.

"Don't mention it," said Jefferson. "It's in the past. You were trying to protect my family. I was trying to protect you."

"I knew if I told you, you'd try to stop me, and I couldn't live with myself if something happened to..."

"I said, don't mention it," Jefferson repeated firmly, but with tender love in his voice. Mary knew he meant it, and it was in the past. She felt a weight lift from her heart.

"Is Kit really gone?" She asked.

"He's detained. There'll be a trial, but I don't think you have a thing to worry about as far as that goes. There are enough witnesses to the kidnapping charge alone. Any jury will see that." Mary let out a long sigh of relief, hardly daring to believe it. Just hours earlier, she'd thought her life was at its end. Now, she was home with the people she loved most in the world around her, safe at last.

***

They had to ride over an hour by carriage to arrive at the nearest official courthouse in Savannah. It was a large, white, building with two enormous pillars. Mary felt like a tiny ant walking up the steps. She felt apprehensive about seeing Kit again. She wasn't sure whether she would feel avenged, seeing him sitting there facing the consequences of his own actions, or whether she would feel small and frightened again, as she had felt when she was in his clutches.

She felt her knees shaking as she walked up the white steps. A strong arm reached around her.

"Are you okay?" Jefferson asked. "We don't have to go in there. You know John said he could get a guilty verdict without your witness."

Mary thought for a moment. She could turn around, leave that courthouse, and never set eyes on Kit or Pudge ever again. She hesitated on the courthouse steps. Anna held onto Violet's hand with her chubby little fingers, swishing her new dress back and forth. Maurice wandered a few steps behind, mesmerized by the enormous building. He'd never been to a city of this size. William, Violet, Rupert, and Jefferson all stared at her, waiting in silence to see if she had changed her mind.

"No," she said decisively. "I am going in. This is for me. I need to see the look on his face when they pronounce him guilty."

She said this, but a small part of her wondered whethe there was a chance he would get off the hook. He was a rich powerful man after all. Either way, she decided she needed to be there to see.

So, with shaking knees and a pounding heart, she took Jefferson's arm and walked up the steps. They stood before two large doors, above which a brass plaque displayed the ten commandments. *Thou Shalt not bear false witness against thy neighbor.* She breathed in deeply. *All I need to do is tell the truth, exactly as I remember it*, she thought.

"We have the truth on our side," she said. Violet grabbed ahold of her hand and squeezed.

"Yes, we do," she said. Together, they stepped through the doors. Mary felt renewed confidence, knowing that she had truth and her loved ones on her side.

She could almost hear her mother's comforting, kind voice telling her that everything would be alright. She saw he father's lively eyes and felt certain that he would be proud o her.

James and Emma Humphrey greeted them at the door Emma looked sheepishly at William and sat next to him when James led them to seats in the front row. James wore a pale gray suit with two rows of buttons and a gold chain crossing them. A puffed-up white shirt peeked through his suit coa and a black bow tie balanced above it.

John Humphrey was already at the front of th courthouse, dressed in a similar manner. His top hat rested on the large wooden desk. His thick eyebrows furrowed over papers that lay in front of him. He ran a finger over his thick black mustache.

Mary could see the back of Kit's head. He sat next to a very young-looking lawyer with a handsome face, blond hair, and inquisitive blue eyes. The young lawyer wore a fashion Mary hadn't seen before, and she figured it was the latest from New England. His top hat was shorter than the typical fashion Mary had seen, and his buttons were smaller. His suit pants were cut closer than a typical man's suit, and his hair was slicked back smooth off his forehead. His young face was clean-shaven, showing a defined jawline. He looked young and fashionable, and Mary hoped his skills as a lawyer weren't as smooth as he looked.

The young lawyer leaned over and whispered something to Kit, who nodded his head in return. Mary felt a knot growing in her stomach. *What if they twisted the story?*

Jefferson leaned over and whispered, "We have truth on our side." How did he know what she was thinking? She looked at him, and that strong face and those tender eyes calmed her soul.

"Mary! Mary!" she heard a voice behind her. She turned to see the fiery red hair bouncing down the aisle.

"Georgia! You came!"

"Of course I came! You're in my backyard. I wouldn't have missed this for the world. You have such an exciting life! Tell me everything." Mary laughed. Georgia did have a way of making things seem light-hearted. She'd written to her just after the arrest of Kit, telling her all that had happened.

"How did you know..."

"Oh, I read the news," said Georgia. "I saw the court date. It's an open court, isn't it? So I came, of course."

"Well, have a seat, then. This is my sister-law, Violet, and this is William, Maurice, and Anna."

"Where's Rusty?"

Mary laughed. "We would have brought him, but apparently they aren't allowed in the courtroom."

Georgia laughed.

"Mary!" She turned to see Susan and John making their way up the aisle toward them. Mary felt tears spring to her eyes when she saw sweet, delicate Susan who had walked her through so much pain, and who had thought up the plan of responding to the ad in the first place. Mary had so much to thank her for.

She stood and made her way out of her seat to greet her.

"Susan!" She exclaimed. "You came all this way?"

"Of course I did. Not just for you, either. You think I don't want to see the look on Kit's face when he's found guilty? Anyway, your lawyer contacted me. He said he might call me to the stand to testify about the night Kit first came."

Mary hugged her tightly. She hadn't been privy to much information regarding who would take the stand, but now it made perfect sense that Susan and John should be there. She looked up at John.

"How are you, Mary?" John asked.

"Oh, John!" Mary hugged him, too. He'd been so helpful in getting her out of Rosewood and to Parkville.

"Mary, I've wanted to tell you I'm sorry if I wasn't more careful about getting you away under cover. We went in broad daylight. I should have known Kit...."

"No," said Mary. "There's no room for blaming anyone but Kit. You couldn't have known the lengths to which he would go. I didn't even know. There's no need to apologize, but come, I want you to meet Jefferson and Violet."

The judge in a long, white wig was just taking his seat as Jefferson and Violet shook hands with Susan, John, and Georgia. Mary looked around and felt grateful that so many people she loved were gathered in one place, even if it was under such circumstances as these.

The judge brought the gavel down, commanding the attention of the courtroom. The talking and bustling died down quickly, and silence fell on the room.

John Humphrey called several witnesses to the stand, and questioned them one after another, asking them to clarify times and events over and over, again.

Mary couldn't tell why he was asking so many repetitive questions, until it became apparent that he was revealing to the jury how so many different witnesses' stories all fell into place and lined up with what had happened that night.

John Humphrey did call both Susan and John to the stand. Susan recounted Kit's threatening visits to the Baker home in Rosewood. John recalled helping Mary escape. Both testified that Mary had never been the wife of Kit and had no knowledge of the agreement between Kit and her late father.

Mary studied the faces of the jury members as they listened to these stories.

The young lawyer with the handsome face stood then, and tried to cross examine Susan and John, but even he looked flustered as he said, "no further questions, your honor," and took his seat.

Next, John Humphrey called Georgia, who told about when and where she met Mary on the train and Mary's story as told to her at the time. She also testified about receiving a letter from Mary, detailing the events that had happened since she'd moved to Parkville, and her need to come and stay with her for fear of Kit doing something to harm the family.

"So, you have reason to believe that Mrs. Mary Just was requesting to come to stay with you because she feared for her life?" John Humphrey asked Georgia.

"Yes, and the lives of the children in the home. She said she was trying to make sure they were out of harm's way," Georgia said.

"Did you notice anyone following Mary while you were on your trip?" Georgia thought for a moment, but answered that she had not.

Kit's lawyer had no questions for Georgia. All this time, Mary could only see the back of Kit's head, but she was certain that he was becoming unsettled as he shifted in his seat.

Greg and Jack took the stand, and they talked about the vandalism, the killing of the cattle, the burning of the fence. They recounted, in vivid detail, the way Kit and Pudge had shot at the house and wounded Violet and Rusty. Kit shifted in his seat, and his lawyer leaned over and whispered to him for a long while. He did not request to cross-examine any of the hired field hands.

John tried to call William to the stand, but the judge would not allow a child to testify.

"I'd like to call Mary Just to the stand," John Humphrey said. Mary felt her heart flutter, and Jefferson placed a hand on her knee.

"You know you don't have to," Jefferson said. "He said he can prosecute without your testimony."

"I need to," Mary said. She stood on shaking legs and made her way to the front of the courtroom, placed her hand on the Bible, swore to tell the truth, and took the stand.

She kept her eyes down at first, trying to gather her composure before lifting her eyes and looking into Kit's face.

"Mrs. Just, can you describe the kidnapping…"

"Objection!" shouted the young lawyer.

"Sustained," said the judge.

"Can you describe what happened to you on the night of November fourth?" John Humphrey rephrased the question.

Mary closed her eyes and remembered the night, but what she remembered most was the cool wind, the feel of the grass on her ankles, and the fear and loss that filled her heart. The moment of her abduction was a blur. Still, she tried her best to recount the details she did remember: the cab, the barn, Kit's words.

She told it all to the best of her ability, being careful only to tell it exactly as she remembered. She was aware that her story sounded a bit jumbled, but better that than try to fill in the gaps with her imagination. When she was finished, she lifted her eyes and looked right at Kit's face for the first time since they'd arrived. He gave her a wry, triumphant, smile, and her heart dropped to her stomach.

In the silence that followed, she prayed, desperately, that Kit's lawyers would have no questions for her. Slowly, the young lawyer stood and walked over to be closer to Mary. He looked at her for a moment before he said,

"Now, Mary. You said you didn't know exactly what time it was when Kit and his friend allegedly picked you up on the road, correct?"

"That's right. I was not aware of the time."

"And you don't remember how long it took you to get to this supposed barn, where they questioned you."

"That's right."

"Now, doesn't it seem odd that Kit, if he had kidnapped you, would take you to an abandoned barn near Mr. Just's property?" Mary didn't know how to answer that. Now that she thought about it, it did seem odd that he would stop there with her.

"I don't know if it seems odd," she replied. "All I know is that's where I ended up."

"And that's where your friends found you?"

"Yes."

"No further questions."

The young lawyer did not call anyone to the stand for his own questioning, which seemed odd to Mary. He only requested a recess, which the judge granted.

Jefferson, Mary, Violet, Rupert, the children, John and James and Emma Humphrey and Georgia, Susan, and John gathered in a grassy area outside the courthouse steps.

"We have a few hours break," Jefferson announced. "I say we find an eating house." Everyone readily agreed. Mary was just beginning to notice the pangs of hunger through the twisted knot in her stomach. She didn't know if she was faint from hunger or anxiety, but decided it was probably a little bit of both.

She leaned on Jefferson's arm. He kissed the top of her head and guided her to the carriage.

Mary wished she could enjoy this moment, with her old and new friends around her, delicious food being served to her, and her husband by her side. She could not shake the feeling, however, that something wasn't right. The look on the lawyer's face told her that he had something up his sleeve

She did not like the way he questioned her, as if a few gaps in her story meant that it was all made up.

But there are so many witnesses, she told herself. *It doesn't depend on me, alone. After all, the Humphreys said they could prosecute without my testimony at all.*

She leaned over and asked John Humphrey, "Do you think I did more damage than good, testifying like that? It was all such a blur. I remember how I felt more than I remember the details." John shook his head.

"No," he said. "That's to be expected. No one's memory is perfect. You were under a significant amount of stress. I wouldn't expect you to remember every detail." Mary tried to be reassured by this, but the look on the young lawyer's face was a steady image in her mind and kept her in a state of uncertainty.

The sweet and salty smells of broiled duck and brandied peaches filled Mary's nostrils, but she found that she could only take a few bites before her stomach turned. Everyone else ate heartily, and Mary let William finish her plate of food when he had all but inhaled his own.

Anna climbed onto her lap, and Mary ran her fingers through Anna's thick, black curls, and hugged the toddler for comfort. Anna, completely unaware of the circumstances, offered up a light-hearted giggle and a wide grin that brought Mary comfort.

"We'd better head back," said James, pulling his pocket watch out of his vest pocket. Jefferson paid the bill, and everyone stood to leave. There was a general light-heartedness about the group, as if they were all old friends. Everyone, it seemed, except for Mary, was certain of their victory.

They arrived at the courthouse steps early, and they spread out on the grass beneath a big oak tree. Susan, Violet, and Georgia were chatting like old friends. The Humphreys, Jefferson, and John were talking in a more serious manner. Maurice and Anna ran around the big oak tree, tagging each other and laughing. Emma and William stood off on their own, talking in hushed tones.

Mary sat beneath the tree, picking strands of grass one by one, trying unsuccessfully not to think about her testimony. She couldn't help it. She replayed every word she said, thought of ways she could have said it differently, and wondered whether she'd hurt her own cause.

"Hey, don't overthink it," Jefferson said. He'd noticed Mary sitting alone against the tree and had excused himself from the conversation with the men. Mary wondered how it was that he seemed to know what she was thinking, yet again.

"I'm not sure that I can help it," she replied.

"You told the truth the best you could remember it. That's the best you could do."

"The young lawyer," she said. "I didn't like the look on his face."

"I didn't either," Jefferson admitted. This wasn't comforting to Mary. She was hoping she had been imagining that conniving, triumphant look. "But it doesn't matter," Jefferson continued. "There are so many witnesses, and we're all saying the same thing. Put it out of your mind. Your part is done. The rest is up to the Humphreys...and the jury."

"And God," Mary added, still thinking about her answered prayer when she cried out for God to send someone to help her as she sat in that old barn with her hands tied with ropes, completely at the mercy of those wicked men. The fact that she had come out unscathed still took her breath away.

"It's time," said James, leading the way back into the courtroom, which somehow seemed more packed than it was earlier that morning.

When Mary reached the threshold, she looked up at the ten commandments again, resting her eyes on the command, *Thou shalt not bear false witness,* once again.

Whatever happens, she thought, *I'll know I've been true.*

The session had hardly begun when Violet had to step out with Anna, who was growing increasingly restless. Maurice went along, growing restless himself. William, however, sat on the edge of his seat with bated breath, asking Emma occasional questions about what certain legal terms meant. She answered him obligingly.

The young lawyer called no further witnesses, and John Humphrey stood to make his final address to the jury.

"Ladies and gentlemen of the jury. You have heard the stories of several witnesses, and all their stories tell of the same thing: a rich, and powerful man who thought he had a claim to a young, helpless girl who had just lost her parents. Knowing that her father had left behind a great debt, this man offered to take care of that debt in exchange for this young woman's hand in marriage.

"It's clear that Kit is not a man who is accustomed to being denied what he wants, and when Mary refused him, he vowed his revenge. He threatened her to the point of forcing her to flee her home. And then, when she found safety in another home, he followed her there and threatened the home and the children of Mr. Just. When that didn't work, he kidnapped Mary and threatened her. We don't know what would have become of Mary, had they not been discovered." He paused for a moment, giving the jury a chance to imagine what might have happened, then continued.

"You've heard the account of several people who were there that night, all of whom say the same thing: Christopher Edwards, a rich and powerful man, would not be denied the woman he wished to have as his wife. When she refused him he threatened her. When she escaped, he followed her. When she married someone else, he threatened her family. When that didn't work, he simply took her. This, ladies and gentlemen, is a man who believes he is entitled to this woman, to have her as his wife, despite the fact that she has refused him and is now married to someone else. Christopher Edwards was merely taking revenge because he did not get what he wanted, like a small child, throwing a tantrum when he doesn't get what he wants."

Mary desperately wished she could have seen Kit's face when Humphrey referred to him as a toddler throwing a tantrum. It would have made her laugh, had it not been so serious.

John Humphrey rested his case and took his seat. The jury members seemed to shift in their seats now, and Mary wondered what they were thinking.

The young, blond lawyer stood and walked slowly over to the jury. He took one step up and leaned a foot on the railing. He put an elbow on his knee and his thumb under his chin. He looked pensive and thoughtful for a moment. Then, he stood to his full height and said, "Ladies and gentlemen of the jury. The stories you've heard here tonight are nothing more than a ruse...the imagination of several friends who have banded together to wrongly accuse this man." He gestured toward Kit, then continued.

"This man, whose only crime was to come after his wife and bring her back home. What wouldn't you do, to bring your wife back? These people, as you can clearly see, are all friends. Even the son of Mr. Jefferson and the daughter of Mr. Humphrey are sweet on each other..."

"Objection!" John Humphrey bellowed.

Mary stole a glance at William and Emma, who both blushed crimson and hid their faces as the judge said, "sustained."

That was a low blow, Mary thought, the anger growing within her.

The young lawyer continued, "So you can see that they are all friends, who have worked together to concoct a preposterous story about a threat and an abduction. But that is all it is, ladies and gentlemen. At story. You've heard the story from the alleged abductee yourself. She barely remembers anything about it.

"You can judge for yourselves, then. Does it make more sense that this man came to rescue and redeem his wife, the love of his life? Or does it make more sense that he randomly followed a woman he barely knew out of town, abducted her, took her to a random barn, and all her friends just happened to find her? Something doesn't add up. There are too many gaps, and too many coincidences in their stories. And may I remind you that the law of the land states that you cannot convict unless you believe, beyond a shadow of a doubt, that this man is guilty.

"I stand before you today asking you to look at this man, Christopher Edwards, and acknowledge that he was a man grieving for his wife, who was willing to do anything to bring her back home, and that the accusations brought against him are only a story concocted by those who resent him of for his money and his position. So I ask you, men, what lengths would you go to to bring your own wife back home?"

Mary scanned the jury, and silently cursed the fact that only men could serve. If any women had been allowed on the jury, surely, they'd see through this lie. What woman would run away from a happy marriage, after all? But they were al men, and Mary could only pray that they, too, would see through this false narrative.

While the jury deliberated, many spectators went home for the evening, not waiting to hear the verdict, but Mary and her family and friends made themselves comfortable outside the courthouse. Anna had fallen asleep, and Violet and Ruper discussed whether they should take the children home now In the end, Violet, Rupert, and the children did go home, as Maurice was doing his best to stay cheerful, but was growing increasingly bored and tired, and Anna was falling asleep or Violet's lap.

They'd have to wait to hear the news until tomorrow.

"It'll kill me to wait," said Violet, "but these children need their beds and some dinner. Get home as soon as you car after the verdict," she told them.

Susan and John also had a long ride back to Texas, and i they did not leave now there would be no more trains unti the following day. They each hugged Mary.

"I'm certain he'll be found guilty," said Susan, squeezing her tightly. "And when he is, please come back to Rosewood to visit."

"I promise," said Mary, not wanting to let her go.

"And send a telegram the moment you hear the verdict even though I already know what it will be," she winked.

As Mary released Susan from her embrace, she felt a heaviness come back into her heart. She hoped Susan was right, and she longed for the day she could move freely, fee safe at home and even visit Rosewood without fear. Dare she hope for such a thing?

She thought about some of the arguments Kit's lawyer had made and wondered how they would sound to the jury. They had not seemed impressed or convinced by the production of the contract Mary's father had signed. Anyway, John Humphrey had been able to argue that it was null and void, and Mary thought he argued that point quite effectively. Still, she wondered if the jury had come to the same conclusions when presented with the evidence.

She wanted to hope that there would be enough people in that group that they would see Kit for the man he was—a dangerous man who needed to be behind bars for the safety of society. She certainly saw him that way, but had John Humphrey been able to convince the jury? She would have to wait to find out the answer to that question.

Mary was not the type to let things lie and put them out of her mind. She found herself overcome with worry that her testimony had hurt her cause rather than helped it. She kept telling herself to wait, just to wait and hear the verdict. There was nothing she could do about it now, anyway. But when she caught James Humphrey alone for a moment, she couldn't contain herself.

"Did my testimony devastate your prosecution?" She asked hurriedly, bracing herself for the answer.

"My dear, no," he said assuredly. "What would make you think such a thing?"

"All that Kit's lawyer said about my story not adding up."

"Don't you worry about that. You told the truth as you could remember it, and that will be what matters most in the end. Now, if you had all come in here with the exact same stories with no gaps and no discrepancies, that would have seemed like you'd made it up. When real things happen, people tend to see and remember them just a bit differently

287

from one another. Don't let that comment get under your skin. He's grasping at straws."

With this, Mary felt a slight relief, but she couldn't breathe easy until she was certain the jury had seen it that way.

***

William, Emma, Jefferson, and Mary sat in the near-empty courtroom, awaiting the verdict. The jury had just come out and filed back into their seats. One member stood, and said,

"On one count of harassment, we the jury find the defendant not guilty." Mary drew in a sharp breath.

"It's not time to worry," said Jefferson. "The kidnapping charge will be enough."

The jury member continued.

"On one count of assault, we the jury find the defendant not guilty." Mary drew another sharp breath, and Emma hung her head. Mary kept her eyes on John Humphrey, who did not look defeated.

Kit turned around just enough so that Mary could see a cruel smile forming on his face.

"On one count of kidnapping, we the jury find the defendant guilty."

Mary felt as though her heart would soar. She could have cried out for joy. Jefferson turned and hugged her so tightly she couldn't catch her breath. William and Emma hugged, too, and William's face lit up with joy. Even the stately James Humphrey smiled with one corner of his mouth.

The wave of exhaustion finally swept over Mary as they drove the carriage to the only hotel in Savannah with vacancy.

"Violet told us to come home just as soon as we could," said Mary, sleepily.

"We couldn't have known how long the judge would take on sentencing," Jefferson replied, giving the reins a flick.

"All the same."

"I'll drive through the night if you like,"

"No, it isn't safe. There might be bandits."

Jefferson laughed. "I think they've driven the bandits out of these parts. You won't find any till the west side of Texas. Still, I'd like to get a night's rest."

"Violet will understand. We'll head out first thing in the morning."

Mary thought over the day. The wave of relief which had swept over her when she heard the "guilty" verdict had grown as the judge had given him the maximum sentence for a kidnapping charge. Kit would be an old man by the time he was released, and Mary felt free.

The swaying motion of the carriage lulled Mary to sleep as she rested her head on Jefferson's shoulder.

She woke up in the hotel bed the next morning, still wearing the pale green dress she'd worn to the hearing.

She jumped out of bed when she noticed the sun was already high in the sky.

"We've slept so late!" She said, as she tumbled out of bed.

"I've sent a telegram that will likely arrive before we do," said Jefferson. "So let's get some breakfast and head back when we've had our fill. Anyway, I've never been to Savannah. Let's enjoy it while we're here."

She smiled, appreciating the gesture, but truly anxious to just get back to Redwood Ranch, the place she could finally call home for good.

She obliged Jefferson, however. She fixed up her hair and brushed out her dress, trying her best to make it look fresh.

After breakfast and a quick stroll through town, Mary said, "I'm anxious to go home." Jefferson smiled down at her with that loving, tender look of his.

"Yes, my darling wife. Let's go home."

The two-hour carriage ride seemed to last a lifetime. The sky was a bright blue, streaked with white clouds. The sun shone bright overhead, and Mary pulled her green bonnet up, fastening it under her chin. Jefferson squinted and smiled at her.

"What?" She asked.

"Just thinking how green your eyes look in that bonnet," he said, taking the reins in one hand and placing his other arm around her shoulders.

"Just think...we're going home together, and we'll be left alone. We'll be free."

"Just as it should have been all along," said Jefferson.

"And we can visit Susan and John. I can visit my parent's graves," she said, her tone growing more somber.

"You're not in hiding anymore, Mary. You're free."

A soft breeze blew over them, caressing Mary's face and giving a brief reprieve from the warmth of the sun.

To Mary, nothing had ever felt so right. Her soul finally felt still, as though she could rest and love and exist without a care in the world.

"You saved my life," said Mary.

"If it hadn't been for William..."

"You all saved my life."

He tightened his arm around her.

"You're safe, Mary. You'll always be safe with me."

Epilogue

Six Months Later

The day was crisp and clear. Only a few puffy, white clouds spotted the sky. Mary had curled her blond hair so that it hung in thick ringlets around her face and down her back. She wore a large-brimmed hat of the latest London fashion. Georgia had sent it to her as a congratulatory gift after the trial. It was trimmed with a pink floral pattern.

Mary felt ridiculous in it on regular occasions, but it seemed perfect for a wedding. She wore a pale pink and white dress with white trim, a new dress Violet and Jefferson had conspired to have made for her birthday.

They were on their way to the wedding—the long-awaited day on which Rupert and Violet would finally say their vows.

It was late morning, and the ceremony was to begin at noon at the church.

"Couldn't have asked for a better wedding day," Jefferson noted, as he helped Anna up into the carriage. Anna was all smiles as her dark ringlets bounced up and down on her head, framing her chubby face.

William also had a new Sunday best, as he'd grown several inches over the past few months. He seemed to be taking extra care about how he looked, combing his hair carefully, keeping his teeth clean, and his clothes starched and pressed.

Mary noticed he was especially careful when he knew he would be seeing Emma, and today was one of those days. He came out to the carriage looking like a well-kempt young man. Mary saw that Jefferson was beaming with pride.

Maurice, on the other hand, could not understand William's newfound obsession with his appearance. Mary had needed to ask him several times that morning to wash the smudges off his face. When he did finally come out, his shirt was only half tucked in. He carried a book under one arm, "in case I get bored," he said.

"Go put that back. You will not be reading a book at your aunt's wedding," Mary said, stifling a laugh. Maurice hung his head but obeyed and came trotting back to the carriage where they were all waiting to make the short trek to the church for the festivities.

The children tumbled out of the carriage as they pulled the team to a halt, and Mary doubted they heard her calling after them not to soil their clothes before the ceremony.

Rupert welcomed them. He wore a starched black suit with a collared white undershirt and vest. His normally curly, unruly hair was trimmed down and combed over. He wore his usual light-hearted grin, but his eyes shone with a delight of more intensity than usual. He walked, as always, with a bounce in his step.

"Jefferson, my best man!" He said, slapping him on the back. "The minister will be here in a few hours. Mary, Violet is waiting for you at the back of the church. She says I can't see her yet," Rupert winked and led Jefferson away, saying, " Come, we have a few hours before the ceremony."

"Jefferson, please remind the children not to play in the dirt until after the ceremony!" Mary called out. Jefferson nodded, and Mary headed to the back of the church to find Violet.

When she saw Violet, she gasped at her beauty. Her long raven-black hair was half plaited at the back of her head into an intricate design, while the rest fell in bouncing curls around her face and down the back of her dress, which was a pale, dull white, contrasting with her hair and eyes beautifully. Her deep brown eyes shone with pure joy. Her face radiated excitement and happiness when she smiled.

"Mary! You look marvelous!"

"I was just about to say the same!" said Mary. "Violet, you have to be the most beautiful bride I have ever seen. Just exquisite!"

The two embraced, and Mary felt that sensation of sheer joy that one feels when truly happy for another.

"I can't believe it's almost here," said Violet.

"You've waited so long for this day," Mary said, squeezing her tighter. Violet had shared in Mary's happiness the day they returned home, knowing Kit would be out of their lives for good. Now, Mary had the chance to share in Violet's happiness at finally exchanging vows with the man she'd been engaged to for so long.

Moments of true happiness like this are so precious, Mary thought. *To share in one another's joys must be one of life's greatest gifts.*

"Jefferson will both walk me down the aisle, and be Rupert's best man," Violet said. "He's been the rock of this family. I don't know what I would do without him."

"I'm sorry that your father isn't here to give you away," said Mary, remembering what it felt like to get married when her father had so recently passed. "It's something to be grieved."

"It is," said Violet, looking grave, but not sad. "We've lost some good people. Both of us. But we have each other. We have our husbands."

"We have the children," Mary said, looking out a window to where she could see Anna and William chasing each other around a tree.

"We have the children," Violet repeated, following Mary's gaze out the window and smiling.

"And would you look at Anna!"

"Her ankle is good as new, isn't it?"

"Like it never happened."

"I don't want Rupert to see me until I walk down the aisle," Violet said. "Will you find out who is here?"

"Of course," said Mary.

James and John Humphrey had arrived, as they were both a part of Rupert's wedding party. Emma and her mother emerged, each wearing a shade of emerald green which suited their dark eyes and hair.

Mary welcomed them and thanked them for coming. Maurice and William's job was to guide people to their proper row in the church, and William blushed a little as he took Emma by the arm and led her and her mother to their seats.

The church was slowly beginning to fill. The small town church did not boast its own organ; Mr. Blanchard, however, was an accomplished fiddle player and he stood at the back of the church playing soft music as people trickled in and waited to be seated. The minister was at the front of the church already, his Bible open on a podium.

Mary made her way back to Violet.

"It's filling up fast!" she said.

"I wanted a small wedding, you know," she laughed. "But my dear Rupert knows everyone, and every patient he's ever treated fancies himself the doctor's best friend."

"Well, that's just the kind of man Rupert is though, isn't it? He kind of makes you feel important when he talks to you."

"That's the wonderful thing about him," Violet said, eyes glazing over dreamily. "People matter to him so much. I suppose it's why he went into his profession in the first place. When he asked me to marry him, I about fell over. I knew he made people feel special, but he made everyone feel that way; I didn't know how he felt about me until he asked me to marry him. Jefferson said he could tell it was different with me from the moment he saw us together."

"I bet there was no shortage of young women from town upset to find out he was taken," Mary said.

Violet laughed. "Probably not." Then she smiled a mischievous sort of smile and said, "Too bad for them."

Mary laughed, and they both peeked out the door at the back of the church to see that the seats were full, and people were still coming in and standing at the back.

"Oh, I'm so nervous now," said Violet. "So many people will be looking at me!"

"Don't worry about that. Just look right up to the front at Rupert. He's the one you're here for, anyway." Violet nodded and smiled, hugging Mary.

At the back of the church, Mary met John Humphrey. He took her arm in a gentlemanly way, and they proceeded down the aisle.

"Did I ever tell you how grateful I am for all you've done for us?" she whispered as they walked.

"You didn't have to," he responded in a low whisper, smiling at the crowd of smiling guests. "It was my pleasure to help put that man behind bars, truly."

At the front of the church, they parted ways, and Mary took her place and turned to face the back of the chapel. Violet emerged, with Jefferson on her arm. Mary's heart skipped a beat as she laid eyes on their faces, first Jefferson's and then Violet's.

Jefferson beamed, looking as proud as ever of his little sister. He smiled at Rupert, and Mary could tell that there was no better man Jefferson could have hoped for his sister to wed.

When she looked at Violet, she saw pure joy, and that joy quickly spread to Mary, who couldn't help smiling from ear to ear as she watched Violet walk down the aisle. Her lovely black hair was curled and pinned in some places, and loose in others so that soft, bouncy curls framed her radiant face, which glowed even through her veil. She wore a long, white gown which flowed elegantly behind her, and she walked with excitement, as though she could have sprinted down the aisle but was forcing herself to be poised.

Mary met Violet's gaze as she stepped up to the front of the church, and thought she might tear up for the joy she saw. She knew how long Violet had waited for this day to come, and she shared in her revelry.

When she stood before the clergyman, Violet turned to face Rupert so that Mary now stood behind her, also facing Rupert, who looked absolutely enraptured with Violet. He kept his eyes steady on her. He smiled as if he couldn't stop, and his eyes danced with delight in his new bride.

Mary's heart soared as she turned her gaze upon Jefferson, her beloved husband. He was looking at her, and the love in his eyes could have moved mountains. The way he looked at her made Mary's heart leap. She didn't know whether she was about to laugh or cry, but she didn't know if she could contain herself for the duration of the wedding ceremony. She dared not look at the children, all seated in the front row. If she did, she feared she might just shout out in delight.

After the ceremony, everyone went back to the Just house for food and drink. Guests meandered about the home and yard, chatting happily and eating cold cut meats and cheeses.

Rupert bounced happily from one guest to the next, asking each of them about their own lives, hardships, and triumphs. Violet seemed satisfied to be on his arm, engaging with her guests in her own soft, charming way. Mary and Jefferson having greeted and chatted with their guests, decided to take a stroll about the yard. They walked in silent peacefulness even among the chatter and bustle of the many guests. Mary watched Violet and Rupert.

They suit each other so well, she thought. Rupert's bright eyes and zest for life was somehow tempered and deepened by Violet's soulful eyes and compassionate gaze. They were meant for each other, Mary believed.

And I for Jefferson, she said to herself.

His stoic, hardened exterior was no longer scary to her, for she had seen the fullness of his tender heart, and she felt fully alive when she was with him.

She looked up into his face and thought about how she felt when she was with him.

As Jefferson's wife, she felt secure, protected, loved, and free.

A sense of peacefulness settled into Mary's heart, lulling her into a tranquil state of mind, and she stood quite still and speechless for some time. She stood there, feeling the fence post against her back, the warmth of the sun on her face, and the soft caress of the breeze as it tousled her hair. She felt at ease and peaceful. A stillness settled over her soul, and it was like nothing she had ever felt before. Jefferson must be feeling the same sort of tranquility, Mary thought, for he was neither speaking nor doing anything in particular.

Jefferson and Mary leaned against the newly built fence and watched Maurice and Anna playing and chasing each other around the old oak tree. Emma and William walked along the fence at the far end of the yard. The sky was crystal clear and blue. The warm May sun shone brightly, and a soft breeze rippled through the air.

Mary turned to look at Jefferson, and he turned his face toward her and smiled.

"I love you, Mary, my wife," he said softly, brushing a strand of hair gently away from her upturned face. Mary closed her eyes as she felt his large, rough hand travel gently down the side of face.

"I love you, too, Jefferson."

"I've come to love you as I never imagined I would," he said, in almost a whisper.

"And I, you," she replied softly.

He leaned his face down toward her as his arms wrapped around her waist. He drew her in, and she put her arms around his neck, looking up at him with pure adoration in her eyes.

"Thank you," she said.

NORA J. CALLAWAY

"Thank you?"

"For saving me."

"I think it's you who saved me," he replied, leaning in and kissing her gently on her lips.

Mary returned the kiss with a passion swelling up in her heart.

She thought to herself, *I didn't know life could feel this good.*

"Come on, let's join the others," Jefferson said, taking her by the arm and leading her back toward the house.

***

When the guests had slowly trickled out of the yard and exhausted, climbed into their carriages to ride home Jefferson and Mary took the children back to the house Maurice looked as though a light wind might knock him over he was so tired. Even William seemed exhausted.

Anna, who should in all likelihood have fallen asleep hours earlier, seemed full of wild, childish energy. She had an almost crazed look in her eye as she spun around in her dress, once pristine, and now covered in dirt and grass stains. She didn't seem to mind, though, and she spun around in circles, letting it twirl and swish about at her sides and looking as though she thought she was the most beautiful princess in the world. Indeed, she was, in Mary's mind.

The children ran ahead of Jefferson and Mary, who walked listlessly toward the house. Mary was overwhelmed by fatigue, but she was also unspeakably happy, and she smiled as walked toward the house in a sort of dream-like trance.

"It will be strange not having Violet in the house tonight, won't it?" Mary asked.

"No," Jefferson answered. "We'll miss her, I'm sure, but it won't be strange. It was time for her to branch out and start her own family, and it feels right with you here by my side." He smiled, though he looked every bit as tired as Mary.

They came in the front door, and William and Maurice were already making their way up to their rooms.

"You know they're tired when they don't even have to be told to go to bed," Jefferson laughed.

"But what are we going to do about that one?" Mary asked, giggling and pointing to Anna, who was now upside-down, doing a headstand against the sofa.

"I have just the thing," Jefferson said, disappearing up the stairs. When he returned, he carried in his hands the draft of the children's book Mary had written on the night she'd ran away.

"Oh," said Mary, softly, remembering that night.

"I assume you wrote it for her?" Mary nodded.

"I don't know if it's any good, though."

"I hope you don't mind. I took the liberty of reading it, and I think it's very good."

Mary smiled. "All right," she said, taking it from him and seating herself in the rocking chair. She reached her arms out to Anna and said, "Come here, my little princess. I have a special story for you."

"Mommy!" Anna squealed as she scrambled up into Mary's lap and nestled her head into her bosom.

Mary kissed the top of her head and began reading.

"Once upon a time, in a faraway land, there lived a little girl with beautiful curly, dark brown hair and eyes as blue as sapphires. This little girl had a very special gift that no one knew about except for her. She could speak to animals." Anna reached her chubby hand out to the page and touched the picture.

"This little girl did not like to speak to people. She was very shy and worried someone might laugh at her. One day, when she was playing out in the yard. She saw a little bunny rabbit and decided to chase it. Instead of running away, the bunny said, 'Please don't chase and hurt me.' The little girl looked curiously at the rabbit, wondering if all rabbits could speak. 'I won't hurt you,' she said to the baby bunny. 'I only thought you were very cute, and I wanted to hold and pet you.'

'Well, if that's all,' said the bunny, and he hopped right onto her lap! The little girl patted the bunny softly until she heard her mother calling her for dinner.

When the little girl with the sapphire eyes came home for dinner, she didn't say a word. You see, she was very shy around people, and didn't want to speak. She wanted to tell them that she had spoken with the rabbit, but she couldn't get the words out of her mouth.

The next day, she went down to the stables and thought she would try talking to her favorite horse, Beauty. She patted her softly on the next and said, 'Hello Beauty. I talked to a rabbit yesterday.' The horse perked up his ears, so the little girl continued. 'I was wondering if you could talk to me, too.' To her amazement, the horse snorted and said, 'You can understand me?'

From that day on, the little girl with the sapphire eyes went to the stables to talk with the horses. Whenever she saw a rabbit or a squirrel, she asked it if it was doing well and whether it had collected enough food for the winter. She was very careful only to speak to the animals when no person was around to hear. She was still very afraid to talk to humans.

One day, when she was playing out in the yard while her mother was cooking dinner, she saw the same little bunny she had ever spoken to.

'How are you little one?' the bunny asked, with a gleam in his eye.

'Happy,' the little girl replied.

'Are you happy because you can speak to animals?'

The little girl nodded her head.

'Well, little one, now it is time for you to know. I have given you a very special gift, a gift not many children ever get. I'm a magical bunny, you see, and I am the one who made you able to talk to animals of all kinds.'

'Oh, thank you!' said the little girl. 'I do love to talk to the animals.'

The bunny suddenly looked very serious, and it said, 'I'm afraid your time is now up. I visited you once to give you the power to speak to animals, and I visit you now to take it away.'

'But why?' asked the little girl, tearing up.

'Because I'm going to give you something better,' the bunny replied. 'The confidence to speak to your own kind.'

Then, the little magical rabbit disappeared down a hole. The little girl ran to the stables as fast as her legs could carry her.

'Hi Beauty!' she said, but the horse only snorted and whinnied in return. The little girl felt big tears come into her eyes. She could no longer speak to her very best friends in the world.

Her mother had come looking for her and she entered the stables just at that moment.

'Why darling? Whatever is the matter?' she asked.

'Mama,' the little girl said. Then, her mother hugged her and smiled and laughed. She was so happy to hear her little girl speaking to her.

The little girl with the sapphire eyes decided she was very happy to speak to humans, but she never forgot her little bunny friend and the time when she could speak to animals.

Years later, she saw that same little bunny in the yard, and she was almost sure she saw it wink at her.

The end."

"Well, I think she liked it," Jefferson said, and Mary thought she saw his eyes glistening.

Anna was fast asleep, breathing heavily, her head resting against Mary.

"Oh, we've forgotten to change her into her nightgown," Mary whispered.

"That's okay," Jefferson said. "She'll wake up feeling like a princess for one more day. Come on, lets get her to bed."

Jefferson lifted Anna from Mary's arms and together, they walked up to her room and laid her down in her bed. She looked so peaceful and happy.

They backed quietly out of the room. Once in the hall, Jefferson wrapped his arms around Mary and said, "Come on, let's get to bed."

For the first time since she had moved there, Mary could go to bed feeling safe and at peace. Finally, this place felt like her true home, where she would live with the people she loved for the rest of her days.

She laid awake in bed, tired though she was, smiling at the thought.

THE END

Also by Nora J. Callaway

Thank you for reading **"An Unwelcome Bride to Warm his Mountain Heart"**!

I hope you enjoyed it! If you did, here are some of my other books!

Also, if you liked this book, you can also check out **my full Amazon Book Catalogue at:**
https://go.norajcallaway.com/bc-authorpage

Thank you for allowing me to keep doing what I love! ❤

Made in United States
North Haven, CT
28 September 2023

42106578R00167